Secrets
in the Attic

David Paton

xulon PRESS

Appreciation

To my wonderful wife, Debbie, who has been by my side throughout the writing of this book. She has taken on the job of editing, which is no easy task. Without her, this book would still be in my old, blue notebook with the pages turning yellow.

To Sue Safe, who took a chance and escorted me through her church, so I could do research into the sights, sounds, and feelings of my main character. To Don Wyatt, my high school English teacher and later in life a good friend, who offered his help in so many ways.

Thank you all!

CHAPTER 1

Once Upon A Time

A t the urging of my teenage children, I am writing this story down so they can tell it to their children. I must have told this story many times over the years as each of my children have asked me about their Grandma and Grandpa Wilson. My son has heard it so many times he helps me when I forget some part of the story. I asked him, "Carl, do you get tired of hearing this story time after time after all these years?"

Carl is a chip off the old block. He answered me with a question, "Dad, do you ever get tired of telling the story time after time after all these years?" My son could hear the excitement in my voice and see the sparkle in my eyes each time I told the story.

I remember the first time Carl asked me about where his Grandma and Grandpa Wilson were. Carl was not more than seven years old. His little sister, Kayla, was five years old and followed big brother everywhere.

One day the two of them were sitting by the old willow tree. Carl called it his "think tree." I watched from the house for a while and then went out to do my gardening. Some time had passed, and I had not heard much from the children. As any parent knows, silence is not always golden. It is more like, what are the children up to now? But I wanted to finish weeding the garden before supper. As I was finishing up weeding the carrots, two pair of little, bare feet came into my view. I pretended not to see them and kept picking weeds. I was going to have fun and pull the children's toes as if they were weeds. As I reached for Carl's big toe, something wet hit my hand. First there was one drop, and then there was another that fell on my hand. That was odd because the sun was shining. Then I heard a sniffle.

Kayla spoke with a soft voice, "Don't cry Carl."

I looked up into Carl's face, and it was wet from crying. His eyes were all red and puffy, and his nose was starting to run. I reached for my hanky, but before I could pull it from my pocket, I heard that familiar sound that is made when a child has just wiped his nose on his shirtsleeve. I asked Carl what all the tears were for.

Before Carl could answer, Kayla jumped right in and said, "We don't have any other grandma and grandpa besides Grandma and Grandpa Edwards."

"Quiet Kayla, I'll tell dad myself." Between the tears Carl told me how some of the other children were talking about their grandparents, and they asked him about his. My heart ached as Carl cried harder, harder than I had ever seen him cry before. "I told them I did have grandmas and grandpas but they didn't all live here. I told them there were Grandma and Grandpa Edwards. Don't I have a Grandma and Grandpa Wilson, too, Dad?"

"Yes son, you do have a Grandma and Grandpa Wilson, but they still live back in the city."

"Why?" Carl stared at me and waited for an answer.

"Well, it's a long story."

"Tell me dad. I need to know about Grandma and Grandpa Wilson."

"It would be best if I started back at the beginning when I was just a boy."

"About my age dad?"

"No, son, I was older. I was 16 at the time. I too asked that same question: Where are my grandmother and grandfather? You know, Carl, your Great Grandma and Great Grandpa Wilson that live here in the settlement. I knew where my Grandma and Grandpa Olson were. They were in the same place every day. Their ashes were in an urn on the shelf."

"What is an urn dad?"

"It is like a fancy jar."

"Oh, like mom's pickle jars."

"A little fancier than mom's pickle jars, but you've got the idea. As I was saying, my Grandma and Grandpa Olson were . . ."

"In the pickle jars!"

"Carl!"

"Sorry."

I was trying not to let him see me laughing. You know how children are. They repeat everything they hear. All I needed was for a friend or family member to hear Carl saying that we pickled my Grandma and Grandpa Olson.

"Dad! Dad, are you mad?"

"No, Carl, I'm not mad. I was just going to say that I never knew the Olsons. They died shortly after I was born." I continued with my story. One day when I was home from school sick, I saw my mom walk by my bedroom door, so I called out to her, 'Mother! Mother!'"

She appeared in the doorway in a flash with a dust mop in her hand. "What do you need, Mark?"

"Mother, where are my grandmothers and grandfathers?"

"Well, my mother and father are downstairs on the shelf in those two big urns."

9

"I know that, mother, but where are father's mother and father, the Wilsons?"

I'll never forget the look that came over my mother's face. First it was the look of surprise. She was surprised that I asked that question after all these years. Then came the look of fear. Fear of what I did not know. She said, "I have to finish dusting before your father gets home. Lay back down and get some rest so you can go back to school tomorrow."

"Okay, mother, but can you tell me later? I've been wondering about them. Mother! Mother!"

"What!"

"Did you hear what I was saying?"

"Yes! Did you hear me? Now lay back down and get some rest."

"I know, so I can go back to school tomorrow." Mother waited for me to lie down, and then she pulled the covers up around my chin. As she did, I said to her, "Mother, I'm 16 and not 5 years old."

"I know; I'm your mother, and I remember how I would tuck you in every night when you were just a wee little boy." With a tap on the forehead she said, "Now get some rest and I'll call you when supper is ready."

As my mother was walking away, I still had so many unanswered questions; and with mother giving me the brush off, now even more questions were popping into my mind. I lay there staring up at the ceiling and started to think about why I had never heard dad talk about my Grandmother and Grandfather Wilson, why they had not come for a visit, and why we had never visited them. Why weren't there any pictures of them? Mother had pictures of Grandmother and Grandfather Olson. All this thinking was making me sleepy. Maybe I'd ask father some of those questions after supper tonight.

I settled in and fell asleep; before I knew it, mother was

shaking me. "Mark, wake up. Mark, it is time for supper. Don't be long because your father is waiting."

I got my robe and slippers on to go downstairs for supper. I walked to the head of the stairs where I heard mother and father talking. I don't think they knew I was at the top of the stairs and that the sound of their voices carried very well. I stopped to listen.

Mother said to father, "Mark asked me about your mother and father." What she said must have really surprised father because I heard a dish hitting the floor and breaking. I ran down the stairs and turned the corner to see my mother and father crawling on the floor picking up pieces of the broken dish. They didn't see me, so I stood off to the side of the dining room doorway to listen.

Father said with anger in his voice, "Don't tell him anything. It is for his own good."

"And if he asks again, what do I tell him?" mother questioned.

I walked in just then and said, "Tell me what?" Both mother and father looked at me as if they were two children caught with their hand in the cookie jar.

"Tell him that the bowl of mashed potatoes were . . ."

"Very hot and I was burning my finger, and I just did not make it to the table in time," mother jumped in to help father get out of a jam. They looked somewhat relieved thinking I believed the story of the potato bowl, but I knew father was upset about the question I had asked mother earlier in the day. I went to sit at the table. I could still hear them whispering about something.

"Do you need some help down there?"

Dad's head popped up and he said sharply, "No, we are almost done." There were a few more whispers and then silence. The silence seemed to go on forever. During the silence I decided that today was not a good day to ask father about my Grandmother and Grandfather Wilson.

Then dad sat in his chair and asked me, "Mark, how was school today?" Mother rolled her eyes and took what was left of the broken bowl to the kitchen. She was shaking her head all the way there.

I answered my father, "I was sick today and didn't go to school."

Feeling rather silly, he then asked me, "Are you feeling any better?"

"Yes, I feel well enough to go to school tomorrow."

"That's good."

Supper that night was quiet. I finished supper and asked mother and father if it would be okay to go up to my room and work on my homework.

Mother said, "Yes, that would be fine."

As I was leaving the dining room, the question was still burning in my mind: What happened to my Grandmother and Grandfather Wilson? I turned to face my parents. "Mother, Father?" They both turned and looked at me, afraid I was going to ask questions about father's parents but they were relieved when I said, "Good night. I'll see you in the morning."

I headed up to my room, and mother and father started talking again. "What do you think he knows about your parents?" I heard mother ask in a hushed voice.

I sat on the steps to listen. Maybe I would hear a clue as to what the secret was about Grandmother and Grandfather Wilson. I didn't even know their first names or if they were alive or dead. I sat for a moment but there was silence. What were they doing? I couldn't hear anything. I peaked around the corner, but they were gone.

Then I headed up to my room to finish my homework. As I sat at my desk, I could hear quiet voices. I got up to look down the hall; there was no one there. When I was walking back to my desk, I saw my mother and father talking outside. It was more my father talking angrily at my mother. I went to the window and knelt down so they would not see me there listening. It was hard to hear what they were saying. I tried to open the window, but it was stuck. I pulled and pulled. Finally it came free, but I made so much noise that mother and father turned and looked directly in my window. There I was for them to see. I did the only thing I could think of to do. I waved to them hoping that they would not think I was trying to listen to what they were talking about even though that is what I was doing. Mother and father slowly raised their arms and waved back to me.

Then father took mother's arm and they walked to the end of the driveway. It was too far to hear anything now. I had to find out what was so secretive about my grandmother and grandfather. Why were they so afraid? What happened that would make my father talk so angrily to mother? My father was talking a mile a minute. He was pointing and his arms were flapping like a chicken.

I was thinking as I walked away from the window that there must be some way to find out about my grandparents. What were my mother and father hiding from me? Where should I start the search? As I sat on my bed, I thought, of course, the computer. I could check the hospital records, marriage licenses and death certificates at the city hall. How many Wilsons could have lived in this town?

I turned on the computer and waited for it to boot up. Then I went to the Internet and typed in the City Hall web address so their web site would come up. As I scrolled through the city hall departments, I noticed red stars by some of them. That really got me to wondering what the red stars were all about, so I tried to enter into one of those red star departments. I clicked on the button for the water department and it came up on the screen. The screen said: City Water Department-access password required. Password! Why would you need a password to look at old water bills? Oh well, I gave it a try to see if I could get in. I put the word faucet in and clicked enter. Password incorrect. Access denied. Then I tried the word flush and clicked enter. Password incorrect. Access denied. Okay, one more time. I used the word plunger and clicked enter. Password correct. Access granted. Now that I was in, I decided to see what was on the main menu. They had: Billing, Maps, Projects. I chose to look at the map section just for fun, and since I was in the map section, I looked for my house. I put in my street name, Old Mill Road. Cool! There were all kinds of lines for water, sewer, storm sewer and tunnels. I didn't know we had tunnels under our city. That was so cool! They ran all over the city, right past my house, out to the old mill and beyond. The city planner must have thought that the city would still be growing. Ever since the collapse of the government, not much of anything had grown. All the private companies had been taken over by the state government. I decided to exit this file and see what else I could find. I was looking at the menu scrolling by for other departments to enter.

What was that sound? It sounded like . . . like the state police sirens, and they were coming this way. I craned my neck to see out the window where they were going. They were coming toward our house and slowing down. They turned into our driveway. Oh no! They must have found out I had accessed the city files. Then I heard them pounding on the front door, and my heart was pounding just as hard. I better exit the city files and put in my homework.

I could hear mother and father rushing to the door. "Good evening, officers!" I heard my father say as I stood in my doorway trying to look between the stairway railing to see the officers and to hear what was being said.

With a stern voice the officer said, "Mr. and Mrs. Wilson, our security systems tracked down unauthorized access to the city's classified department files, and it came from somewhere in this section of the city."

Oh no! They knew it was me, and I was going to jail! Maybe I should run away. Wait! Listen to me! If they knew it was me, they would not just be talking; they would be storming up the stairs, kicking in my door and dragging me down to the city jail.

Then I heard my mother ask, "Officer, are you saying that it was someone in this house?"

"No, Mrs. Wilson, the person or persons were not in the file long enough for our system to pinpoint their location. It will be only a matter of time. We will find this person or persons and figure out what they were doing accessing classified files."

I could tell my father was getting a little mad at the officer. "I'll have you know, officers, I work down at the city hall in the information gathering department. I know what the penalty is for unauthorized access, and I would not allow that type of activity to go on in my house. I'm also a member of the Governor's Auxiliary State Police Force, and I'm sworn to turn in people that would access information that they are not cleared to have access to."

You tell them father, I thought to myself.

"I would even turn in my own family if they were to break the smallest law of the state."

Father, are you crazy? You're talking about me, don't you know?

The one officer was not impressed with father's speech; he was determined to search the house. "Save the speech for someone who will listen. I'm going to have a look around anyway. Is there anyone else in the house?"

Mother replied, "Our son is upstairs in his room working on his homework."

"Sergeant!"

"Yes sir!"

"Look around upstairs, and I'll look around down here."

I ran back to my room and pretended like I was doing

some homework. I could hear the sergeant banging around in the other rooms. It seemed to go on forever, and then there was silence. The sergeant must have gone back downstairs. I decided to go back to my listening spot at the top of the stairs.

"Lieutenant Terrell!" the sergeant yelled. There he was standing in the doorway looking at me. I could not move my feet and legs because they felt like lead. How long had he been standing there? What did he see that he needed to have the lieutenant come up here?

I was so scared I did not know what to do, so I said, "Hello Sergeant." There was no reaction from him. I really did say hello to him, didn't I; or did I just think that I said it? Maybe I should say it again. No! He might think I'm nervous and guilty of something.

Now I could hear the lieutenant running up the stairs. I could tell by the heavy footsteps of his boots. Then there were more footsteps coming up the stairs. That must be mother and father following the officer up to my room. Then the sergeant stepped aside as the lieutenant appeared in the doorway. He was a huge man. He didn't look that big when I saw him from the top of the stairs looking through the railing, but now he was a mountain of a man.

The sergeant pointed toward me and said, "Look Sir, at what is on the boy's desk."

The lieutenant walked over to my desk, and he was staring holes through me. "This computer is the oldest pile of junk I have ever seen. I'm surprised it is still working. Most of those models wore out 20 to 30 years ago. They have not made that type of computer for so long I cannot remember when that company went bankrupt. This pile of junk would never be able to access city files. Let's get out of here, Sergeant. There is nothing here for us."

They turned to leave, but suddenly the lieutenant stopped and said to my father, "Remember, Mr. Wilson, the state police will be watching this area of the city, and we will get the person or persons responsible for the computer break-in. We could use your help. Keep your eyes and ears open and report anything strange to me or to the state police right away."

"Yes sir. Oh course, lieutenant."

We all followed the officers out of my room and down the hallway to the stairs as if we were little ducklings following their mother. The lieutenant started down the stairs, and then he stopped quickly and turned around. He came back up to the top of the stairs and looked down the hall and pointed. "Where does that door lead to?" Nobody said a word. The lieutenant repeated the question again with anger in his voice, "Where does that door lead to?"

The lieutenant walked toward the door at the end of the hall. He grabbed the doorknob and tried to open it. Father spoke up and said, "It goes to the attic where we just store old junk."

That answer seemed to satisfy the lieutenant. The two officers and my mother and father headed down the stairs and my mother and father showed them to the door. I was still at the top of the stairs looking down the hall at the locked door to the attic wondering what was behind it. What answers could there be behind the door, or would there just be more questions to add to the already burning question: Where are my grandmother and grandfather?

I found myself walking toward the attic door like I was in an uncontrolled trance. I was reaching for the doorknob and I heard mother yelling from the bottom of the stairs, "Mark? Mark." It woke me out of the trance that took hold over me.

I quickly answered back, "What mother?"

"I think you should go to bed a little earlier to get some sleep before you go to school tomorrow."

"Okay, mother. That sounds like a good idea." There's

something about a mother's voice that can cut through the thickest fog of an uncontrollable trance.

"Do you know what I mean Carl? Carl!" He didn't hear me.

Then out of the blue my wife, Maggie, called for our son, "Carl! Carl!" The look on my son's face said it all. Carl's eyes were glazed over in a stare from listening to my story, and then his mother's voice cut through it all.

Carl shook his head, rubbed his eyes and yelled back to his mom, "I'm out here with dad."

"You need to come in and start your chores."

"Okay, I'll be in in a minute."

He turned to me and replied, "I see what you mean about the power of a mom's voice. When can I hear the rest of the story? Did you ever get into the attic? And what about . . . ?"

I stopped Carl from the flood of questions coming my way. "We'll finish the story after you are done with your chores. Hurry along. The sooner you get started, the sooner I can tell you more of the story."

CHAPTER 2

The Attic

———◆———

"**D**ad, I'm almost done with my chores and then I'll be out to hear the rest of the story," Carl yelled. You could hear in his voice that he was excited to continue with my story about the search for my grandparents.

It wasn't long before Carl came over to the garden with Kayla not far behind him. "Okay dad, I'm ready!" he said as he plopped down in the grass next to the garden where I was still weeding.

Kayla repeated the same thing as her big brother, "Okay dad, I'm ready," as she too plopped her little seat in the grass next to Carl. There they sat with big smiles on their faces and eyes wide open.

Carl couldn't wait. He started with a bombardment of questions. "Did you get up in the attic? What did you find? Did the state police come back?"

"Carl, slow down. I'll get to all those questions in just a little bit. Now I believe I had just finished telling you about the state police and how they had pointed out the attic door. My mother and father told the police officer that there was junk up in the attic, but something told me that there was more. There were more than just old clothes, old suitcases and old furniture behind that door. I did not do anything about the attic that day; but the next day while I was at school, I found myself thinking a lot about what I was possibly going to find beyond the attic door."

The school day seemed to go on forever, but finally the last bell rang. I grabbed my books and headed out the door of the school. I grabbed my bicycle and peddled hard because I knew that my mother and father would still be at work for about another half hour after I got home. I had planned all day how I was going to get into the attic.

I had a big surprise as I turned the corner to go down Old Mill Road, the road that goes by my house. There, sitting in the driveway, were my parents' cars. What were they doing home? They were still supposed to be at work. I didn't peddle as fast now that I knew they were home. I just stared at the attic window as I rolled into the driveway. All my plans were shot to pieces.

What was that? There was a light in the attic window. Somebody was up in the attic. It frightened me at first when I thought I saw a body walk by the window. Well, maybe not. My eyes could just be playing tricks on me. Wait, there it was again! It was my father, and he was carrying something.

I dropped my bicycle by the bushes in the backyard and ran into the house and towards the stairway. I slowly climbed the stairs trying to miss all the steps that creaked. When I reached the top of the stairs, I heard footsteps coming down the attic steps. I made a dash to my room so I could see what was going on and what my parents were doing in the attic after all these years. If I could only hear what they were talking about, maybe I could get some clues as to what happened to my grandfather and grandmother. If I listened, maybe I could hear what father was talking to mother about. "Have you found it yet?" my father asked. "I'm not sure if we even have it yet or if we got rid of it years ago."

My mother seemed unsure about what they were doing in the attic. She said, "Why don't we just tell him the truth and let him make up his own mind?"

Then my father blew a gasket. Boy, was he mad. "We will not tell Mark anything! I repeat, we will not tell Mark anything! My parents told the truth, and look what happened to them."

My heart was racing. I was finally going to hear what happened to my grandparents. There I was, ready to hear the story when my father said, "Grab that stuff, and we will take it outside and burn it in the barbecue pit."

"Is this all of it?" my mother asked my father.

"No, but this is a good start. I should have done this a long time ago. Let's go and get this done before Mark gets home from school."

I could hear them coming down the steps. With every step I could hear a creak or a crack and their voices were getting louder. My father was in the hallway and my mother was still coming down the steps. My father's arms were full of photo albums, books and some old clothes.

Mother had just made it to the bottom of the attic steps and into the hallway. "Russell," she said, "Are you going to shut this door now or later?"

"We can get it later because we need to get the fire going to burn these things before Mark gets home."

I watched them walk by my room and to the head of the stairs carrying the bags and boxes of secrets that could answer so many of my questions. As they walked down the stairs out of sight, I stood there behind my bedroom door wondering what clues and what secrets they had left up in the attic. They would be out by the barbecue pit burning part of the past that I would never know. The door was open, so I took the opportunity to see what had been locked away from my eyes for so many years.

I crept out into the hallway looking to see if my parents were around. I was alone in the house, and I could smell the smoke from the fire pit. I felt somewhat numb knowing that my parents were burning things I would never have a chance to see, touch or read about. I walked towards the attic door; waves of excitement and fear ran through me. I reached for the doorknob to open the attic door wider and entered the stairway up to the attic. The steps were just bare wood. I could hear the boards creak under my feet as I made my way up to the top. Each step I took made my senses come alive with new things never seen, touched or smelled. The smell was somewhat familiar, but it was very strong. The cold, damp, fall air made it a little chilly, but that was all right because my time was short before my parents would be looking for me to be coming home from school.

Where would I even begin to look for clues about my grandparents, and would I even know what a clue would look like if I did find one? The piles of things stored up there were amazing. There were things in bags, things in boxes and things too big for a bag or a box just covered with old sheets and blankets. The one bare light bulb was hanging in the peak of the roof and was not much help. The small window in the front of the house gave only a glow of a fall setting sun. I was seeing things up in the attic for the first time. I saw old combat boots with the toes curled up from not being used. Whose feet had they been on? Surely not my father's feet, but maybe my grandfather's or great-grandfather's. Next to the boots hung a navy seaman's uniform. It was hanging there with cobwebs draped over the shoulders and down the chest where medals of honor were hung. I brushed the other clothes away so I could take in the whole uniform. There was a name pinned to the chest of the uniform. It said Wilson. Was it grandfather? Did I dare take the coat off the hanger that it had hung on for so long?

As I reached for the coat, I felt a tingling in my fingers

and my face. Was it the cold, damp air, or was it the excitement of possibly wearing the same uniform coat of my grandfather? As my arms slid into the sleeves and the coat settled on my shoulders, I felt a strange warmth. The coat felt good, and it even fit. Okay, maybe a little big, but possibly someday I would know or meet the man that wore this uniform with pride and honor.

I continued to look around, still wearing the coat. I saw a big sheet draped over something. As I lifted the corner of the sheet, I could read the words that were painted on it. "Shhh! Baby Asleep!" with a picture of a teddy bear next to the words. It was the crib I had slept in until I was almost two. My father had slept in it when he was a baby. Maybe someday my son or daughter would sleep in it also. I looked around for more clues. I spotted a wooden box next to the edge of the stairs. I must have overlooked it when I walked by it. Maybe there were some clues in there to help me in my search for the truth. When the word truth came out of my mouth, it rang in my ear. That was the word my mother used when she said, "Why don't we just tell him the truth?" Father had said, "We will not tell Mark anything!" What was he so afraid of? Why would the truth be so bad that they had to keep it locked up in the attic? Now they were going to such lengths to burn the past. Why?

It was as I was reaching for the small wooden box that I heard the voices of my mother and father coming back in the house. I had to get down to my room. If they found me up here, who knew what would happen. My father was getting so angry lately; I probably would not make it to my next birthday. I picked up the box. They would never miss it. As I was holding the box in my hand, I noticed that I still had the uniform coat on. I had to hang it up in the exact place I found it. There's a place for everything and everything in its place. Oh man. I was starting to sound like my mother. I hoped I would never say that to my kids.

I put the box on the floor again and rushed to put the coat back in its place. I hoped that I would make it to my room before mother and father came upstairs. There, the coat was in place. I got the box and was going to head downstairs and see what I could find in it to lead me to the Wilson family secret. Oh great, I'd taken too much time putting the coat back. I heard mother's voice as she came down the hallway. Now what should I do?

There was no time to stand around thinking. The door at the bottom of the steps was starting to slowly close. "Russell," my mother said, "Do you want me to lock the door, or are you still going for those missing items?"

NO! I screamed in my head. Don't come up and don't lock the door. I'd be trapped up here. I waited for my father to answer. Finally he replied, "I would like to look one more time before Mark gets home."

I had to hide fast, but where? I know; over there under the window beneath all the old clothes. I quickly worked my way back to the window. I guess I was in so much of a hurry that I bumped into some old dishes in a box. A cup fell out of the box and broke. My mother heard it break and asked, "Russell, did you hear that?"

"Hear what?" my father questioned.

"I'm not sure what but I heard something."

My father was getting anxious to look for more things. While they were discussing about whether or not mother had heard something, I had crawled under a pile of old clothes. I was feeling somewhat safe thinking that they would not find me. I could still watch and listen to them as they poked around. My father was looking around as if there was one thing in particular that he wanted to find and get rid of.

I kept my eye on the wooden box. Mother walked so close to the box I thought she was going to step on it, but her foot landed beside it. She reached down to pick the wooden box up.

My heart jumped, and I must have gasped for air out of fear that I would not be able to look in that box. I even scared my mother because she asked father if he heard a noise.

"Oh no! We're not going through 'did you hear that stuff again?' It's probably a mouse or something," father said.

My mother felt a little silly and reached to pick up an old sweater. As she unfolded it, a mouse dropped out and landed on the floor. It ran under some junk. Mother screamed so loud she could have awakened the dead. Father, on the other hand, was laughing so hard I thought he was going to cry. I had never seen him laugh so hard. Mother was so mad at father for laughing, but when she saw that he was almost in tears, she began to laugh, too. Laughter was something that was missing in our house. It was great to be able to share in this time of laughter even if I was buried underneath some old clothes.

My father was wiping the tears from his eyes when he spotted the wooden box still in mother's hand. The laughter stopped and my old father was back. "There it is! That's the box I've been looking for!"

"Now that you've got it, what are you going to do with it?" mother asked.

"I don't know. Maybe I'll bury it out back. I'll think about it for a while. Let's get out of here before Mark comes home."

"He is a little late. I hope he is all right. It is getting dark so early," mother said. She worried too much about me.

My father, on the other hand, said, "Well, maybe he got himself a girlfriend finally."

Yeah, right, father. The girls in school didn't even know I exist.

Father took the wooden box from mother, put it under his arm and went down the steps. Mother was still holding the same old sweater in her other hand. She was examining the hole the mouse had chewed in it.

Father yelled up the steps, "Are you coming or not, Ramona?"

"Yes, I'm coming." Mother tossed the sweater aside, and it landed across my little peephole; everything went black. Mother walked down the steps, and I reached to pull the sweater off so I could see again. Then I heard it but did not want to believe it.

They locked the door. Now what was I going to do? Well, at least they forgot to turn off the light so I would be able to see well enough to figure a way out.

I crawled out from under the pile of clothes. Brrrr! It was cold out here! Wait, I heard voices! They were coming back! They must have forgotten something. It was my father saying something to my mother. "You must remember to turn off the attic light. We do not need to draw attention to it." I heard my father unlock the door, and then there was a click. The attic went black. As father walked away, I heard him say, "We do not need the neighbors calling the state police because they see the light on in our attic night after night. Speaking of late at night, where is Mark anyway?"

I sat in the dark. I was cold and hungry and didn't have any idea of how to get out. Then a beam of light filled the attic where I was sitting. It was a full moon that had come out from behind the clouds.

That was it! The window! I'd crawl out the window onto the roof. Then I'd crawl over to the cedar tree that mother said was too close to the house. Father kept saying he would cut it someday. I hoped the attic window would open, or I'd be in big trouble. The moon was so bright I could see my way to the window.

I needed to open the window quietly. I pushed and pushed but it would only wiggle a little. I needed to find something to help pry open the window. What could I use? I looked around the attic until I happened to see some old

camping equipment. Maybe, just maybe, there was something in there. I rifled through the camping equipment to see
if I could use anything to help me get out. There was a big,
heavy kettle. That was only good for cooking that mouse
now that I was locked in the attic, or for throwing through
the window. No, too much noise, and besides father would
kill me for breaking the window and denting the kettle. Hey,
wait a minute! Our family didn't camp. Why did we have all
the camping stuff? There was something written on the lid
of the kettle: W.R. I had to get more light on it . . . W.R.
Wilson. That's not father's name. That meant that the camping equipment belonged to my grandfather.

I got so excited I tripped over a box of old framed
pictures. The moonlight was fading in and out of the clouds
as they passed by. It made it hard to see the faces. From
what I could see, the faces on the pictures were faces of
strangers to me. There was one picture of three people
standing in front of this old car. The car must have been
really old. It looked like the car was back from the late
1990's. The two people were holding a baby, but they
looked too old to be the parents. The more I studied the
picture, the more the lady in the picture seemed somewhat
familiar. Maybe it was just the light. I put the pictures away.

I had to find something to pry the window open with. I
found a little shovel that I thought would work. Yes, it
would work just fine. Oh, there was some string tangled up
on it. Cool! It was a compass with a map pouch. Hey, it
had a map in it too! I was going to look at that later. I had
to get out soon. I unfolded the shovel and put the tip of it
between the windowsill and the window. Nothing
happened, so I tried again. It had to work! Then the
window moved with a loud pop. I stopped and listened to
see if my parents had heard the noise. I quickly put the
shovel down, pushed open the window and crawled out
onto the roof. I had to shut the window quietly and then

move quickly towards the cedar tree.

Great! Now the window was stuck open. I had to get it closed or mother and father would know that I'd been in the attic. Maybe if I pressed down on the window, lifted my feet, and used my full body weight, it would be enough to get the window closed. As I placed my hands on what little window there was to press down on, I gave a little jump and lifted my feet up hoping that it would be enough to get the window closed. To my surprise the window came down fast and with a loud crash. My fingers slipped off the window and I fell to my knees. With the heavy dew on the roof, I started to slide down the steep-pitched roof. I was trying to stop myself but the shingles were cutting my hands and tearing my clothes. The edge of the roof was coming closer and closer. If I couldn't stop in time, it would be a long drop to the ground below. My only hope was if I could reach out and get a hold of the big cedar tree. It seemed as if I had been sliding down the roof for a long time, but I'm sure it was only a few seconds. I was approaching he cedar tree. I had to reach for the tree NOW! I got it! I heard a crack. Oh no, the branch broke! I had to grab another branch. The branches were coming so fast and hitting me in the face. All I could see was green.

Suddenly, I stopped with a jerk and I felt a tremendous pain in my leg. I thought I had hit the ground and that my leg was broken. I pushed the tree branches out of my face and there was the real answer. My leg was wedged in a crotch of the tree just about three feet from the ground. I was right in front of the living room window, and I saw mother pacing back and forth. Father was at the computer getting the news from the state-run information web site.

As I was getting my leg unstuck from the crotch of the tree, my mother walked toward the window. I pulled myself closer to the tree so she would not see me. She was staring out the window hoping to see me riding home from school, and worry was written all over her face.

Then my mother left the window. I had to get down from the tree as fast as I could. It was only three feet down, so I decided to jump. I let go of the tree hoping to land on my feet, but that was when a big branch hit me in the face. I landed flat on my back knocking the wind out of me. I lay there for a few minutes gasping for air. I didn't know if my leg, back, or my pride hurt more. This was not the way I planned this to go when I was in the attic. The plan seemed to go so much smoother in my mind than it did in real life. I'd better get up off the ground and come up with a story to tell my parents why I was so late. Wow, I was a mess! I was dirty, bleeding and my clothes were shredded. It had better be a good story, a really good story. I know, I'd tell them that I tripped and fell. Yes, that's what I'd say. Wait a minute! Look at me! I tripped and fell? I looked like I had fallen into the Grand Canyon. I had to come up with a better story, a more believable story like . . . I fell off my bike. That was it; that would work.

"Okay Carl and Kayla; I'll finish the story tomorrow after morning chores are done."

"Dad!" Carl whined, "You stopped in the middle of such an important spot. Did your mom and dad believe your story? Did you get a spanking for shredding your clothes?" Carl just sat there with eager ears to hear the answers to his questions.

"Carl."

"Yes dad?" Carl said with excitement in his voice thinking I was going to answer the questions.

"Carl, I will tell you more of the story tomorrow while we are at the pond fishing."

"Okay dad, but it's just me and you, right? Kayla isn't coming." Carl turned to his little sister and said, "Just me and dad are going fishing."

"Oh no! I hate to break this to you, son, but Kayla is

coming with us. Your mom has a prayer group meeting with the ladies at the Larsons, so we will be taking your sister along. Besides, she would like to hear the rest of the story, too. Isn't that right, Kayla?"

"Yes, dad, I do; and I want to catch a big fish 100 feet long."

"See, dad, she doesn't even know there is no such thing as a 100 foot long fish. She is so . . ."

"Carl, that is about enough. Now get in the house and get ready for supper."

Carl walked away scratching his head wondering where the story would go from there. He was a lot like me, always full of questions and always looking for answers.

It was then that I felt two little arms around my neck and two little lips whispering in my ear, "I love you, dad." It was Kayla. She released her hug she had around my neck from behind me and ran to catch up to her big brother.

I better put my tools away in the shed. There was a place for everything and everything should be in its place. Wow! There was my mother again. I had to quit saying that phrase.

CHAPTER 3

Fishing For Answers

Morning came quickly with a crash and a bang. There was the sound of rushing feet back and forth by my bedroom door. I rubbed the sleep from my eyes, found my clothes and started to get dressed. The door burst open and there, standing in the doorway, were two little fisher persons. Carl was holding the fishing poles and a brown paper bag. Kayla was hugging a bucket of worms.

"Well, dad, are you ready to go fishing? Our chores are done," Carl announced.

"I haven't even had breakfast yet," I replied.

"That's okay, dad. Kayla and I have made your breakfast, and we have it here in this bag."

What could it be, I thought to myself? Maggie walked by the doorway with a smirk on her face. I pleaded for her to help me, "Maggie."

All she said was, "Bon appetite dear!" I could hear her laughing in the kitchen.

"Okay kids, I'll be ready in just a few minutes. I'll meet you out by the garden."

"All right, dad, but hurry; the fish bite best in the early

31

morning," Carl said as he and his sister left through the door. Was I like that when I was his age? "And dad, remember you said you would tell us more of that story," Carl surprised me. I thought he was outside already. That kid of mine just gave me a few more gray hairs, and that was not good since I had so few hairs on top of my head the way it was.

I grabbed my coat and my old fishing hat that I had had since I was a young boy. Then I headed for the door to go outside. I walked by the kitchen to say goodbye to Maggie.

"Maggie dear, have a good time at prayer group. I'll see you when we get home."

"Okay, dear; have a good time with the kids fishing."

I leaned forward to give Maggie a kiss goodbye; the door swung open and Carl urged, "Come on dad. Quit goofing off, and let's go fishing." In the middle of my goodbye kiss to Maggie, Carl grabbed my arm and dragged me out of the door.

"Carl, what is your hurry?" I asked.

"I want to hear more of the story. What happened to you when you went into your house after falling off the roof into the tree?"

"Well, kids, if I remember right, the story went like this. . . I brushed off most of the dirt and the green stuff from the cedar tree. My leg was hurting bad as I walked up the steps to the back door. I walked into the kitchen where I saw my mother sitting at the table wiping tears from her eyes with her tissue."

"Hi, mother, I'm home. I'm sorry I'm so late, but I fell off my bicycle. I'll be all right though." When I spoke, she started to cry again; this time they were tears of joy.

"Russell, he's home. Mark's home and he's all right." Mother was so happy to see me; she ran over to hug me. I thought I was going to die. My back was so sore, but I could not let on that I was in pain. Mother yelled one more time to father, "Russell, Mark is home!"

Father's response was, "That's nice."

Mother's tone of voice changed when she yelled back to father sitting in the living room, "Russell, the least you could do is come in here and show Mark that you care!"

Father said nothing until he got to the kitchen, "What happened to you, Mark?"

"I fell off my bike, father."

"Is the bike all right? I had to work long hours to buy that bike."

"Yes father, the bike is fine." Father seemed more worried about my bicycle than he did about my health, I thought to myself.

"Mark, why don't you go wash up, and I'll get supper ready."

"Okay, mother," I said as I left the kitchen.

I heard mother say to father, "Why? Why do you always have to bring up the cost of everything?"

"Mark has got to learn that you cannot just go out and buy anything you want. It's not like in the olden days when you got a paycheck. Mark will have to learn that the state has controlled our credit system ever since the collapse of the American dollar. He will have to learn that on his 17th birthday he will get his state account number. Then he will have to start earning his own way. It seems that Mark thinks we have an unlimited supply of credit in our account. When the state burns in the invisible tattooed state account number, then he will know what it is all about."

Mother had no reply that I could hear. Father must have thought I was stupid or something, thinking that I didn't understand the credit system. We had learned in history class the United States' ability to borrow was cut off some years before, and the national debt was over $400 quadrillion. Why was I telling myself this? I knew it already. I should tell father I understood about the credit system and about the invisible tattoo on the back of your hand. If you didn't have one, you couldn't buy or do anything.

I found myself hobbling up the stairs to my room to get out of my torn and bloody clothes. Some of my cuts had started to scab over. When I took my shirt off, it ripped them open again. Man, did that hurt! I took my pants off, or at least what was left of them. I threw them over the chair at my desk. When they came to a final rest on the back of the chair, something fell out of my pocket. I had forgotten that I had put the compass, map and pouch in my pocket. I'd better hide them until after supper when I could examine them better. I had to get cleaned up before supper was ready. I was surprised they didn't ask more questions. Maybe they didn't hear all the thumping, crashing and slamming of the attic window.

When I walked into the bathroom, I looked into the mirror and saw the dried blood on my face, arms and legs. It looked like I had been in a dog fight and lost. What were the kids at school going to say when they saw all the cuts and bruises? I would have to tell them the same story I told my parents. If my father ever found out I was in the attic, he would . . . Well, I don't even want to think about that.

With the sink full of hot, soapy water, I washed the dirt and blood off my face and body. Now that I had cleaned up a little, the cuts didn't appear so bad. I'd better get downstairs for supper. On my way back to my room, my eyes happened to glance into my parent's bedroom. There, on top of my father's chest of drawers, was the wooden box. What should I do? Should I go into the room and open the box or wait for a better time? If I waited for a better time, father may burn it like the other things from the attic. I decided to go in now.

I crossed the room to the chest of drawers where the hand-carved wooden box was sitting. As I grasped the hinged cover and opened it slowly, my mother yelled up the stairs, "Mark, are you ready for supper?" She frightened me, so I dropped the lid and ran out of the room. I answered from out in the hallway so she would not know I was in their bedroom.

"Yes I am, mother. I'll be down in a minute."

I was so close to seeing what was in the box. I would have to try again soon before father did something to it. Supper was waiting so I had to get downstairs. I hoped my parents wouldn't ask too many questions about my story of falling off my bicycle.

My father was walking in the back door when I entered the kitchen to sit down at the table. He said, "I put your bike in the garage." My heart jumped. I just knew that my worst fears were going to happen. They were going to pick apart my story. "Your bike doesn't look like it got any damage compared to the damage your body and clothes endured. That seemed a little strange. How would you explain that?"

"Well, I. . . ahhh . . . I found it to be a strange accident. It happened so fast I'm not sure how it all happened. I was just riding along and the next thing I knew, I was on the ground."

It was pretty quiet the rest of the suppertime. I would look up at mother and father. They would be looking at each other making faces, and then they would look at me. I would quickly look down at my food. When supper was done, I asked to be excused to go to my room to do my homework. Father looked like he wanted to ask more questions about my accident, but mother saved me. She spoke up and said, "Yes, Mark, you can be excused. Are you sure you're okay?"

"Yes, mother, I'm fine." I tried to reassure her that I was going to be fine so I could get up from the table. The pains in my back and leg were killing me. I put on a big smile and gritted my teeth to show my mother I was fine. The real reason I gritted my teeth was so I would not scream because of the pain.

When I got out of sight of my mother and father, I had to

stop and lean against the wall to rest. After a short rest stop, I continued on and reached the stairs leading to my room. I grabbed the railing and pulled myself to the top of the stairs. Just a few short steps to my room and I could rest some more. As I got to my door, I felt something pulling me, something trying to turn me around. I glanced around to see if mother had followed me upstairs to ask again if I was going to be all right, but no one was there. I started through the doorway of my room and I felt a strange feeling. I turned around and found myself looking into my parent's bedroom directly at the old wooden box that sat on my father's chest of drawers. It was as if it was calling me to come and open it and find the secrets inside. As much as I was in pain, the urge to know what was in the box drew me to check it out. I hurriedly shuffled across the room to the box. This time I quickly opened the lid. The box was lined with red velvet, and there was an inscription: "To my son with love from William R. Wilson". My grandfather did make this box. I knew it! I just knew it!

You should have seen all the stuff in there: an old pocket knife, compass, baseball cards, a ribbon for a high school track meet (that must have been way back when my father was in school) and there was an old picture of one of father's old girlfriends. There was something written on the back. "Russell, you will always be a special man in my life. Love, Ramona." Hey, that was my mother's picture! They must have been boyfriend and girlfriend back in high school. Oh, what was this? It was just a plain envelope that read: "To our son". It was a letter to my father. It must have been from my grandfather and grandmother. I quickly flipped to the last page to find the signature of the writer. It was from William R. and Frieda R. Wilson. I wanted to read the letter, because I knew it would possibly answer some questions I had.

"Well kids, here we are at the pond. Are you ready to do

some fishing?"

"Dad! How can you do that?" Carl said with disgust in his voice.

"Do what? I thought we came to go fishing."

"Yes I know, dad, but you always stop in such interesting spots."

"I will continue the story after I bait your hooks and get your lines in the water. I'll bait Kayla's first, then yours, and then I'll do mine last."

"Okay, Dad, but hurry!" Carl was eager to hear what was in the letter; just as I was eager to read it the first time I saw it.

CHAPTER 4

The Letter

—————◆————

"Okay, Dad, what about that letter that you found in the old wooden box?"

"Oh yes, the letter."

"What did it say, dad?"

"The envelope read: 'To my son.' There was no address and no stamp. It must have been hand-delivered. The envelope had yellowed from age. No telling how long the envelope was in the box. I wasn't even sure if my father had even read the letter or not. As I held the letter in my hand, a wave of excitement and then fear came over me of what I might read in that letter. I finally decided to read it. It said: 'To my son, Russell F. Wilson

Dear Russell,

Your mother and I are writing you this letter to let you know . . .'"

"Mark, are you sleeping?" Oh no, mother was calling. I took the letter with me to read later. I couldn't let her see me in their room. I hurried out hoping to find a place to hide it. I ran across the bedroom trying to get out into the hallway before mother got to the top of the stairs.

I reached the hallway just a few steps ahead of her. I said, "Were you calling me?"

Mother said, "Yes, I was. I have your clean clothes for you." Mother had a funny look on her face. I couldn't tell if she had seen me come out of their bedroom. She probably wondered why I had that silly "I was not doing anything wrong" look on my face. She handed me the clean clothes and said, "Put these clothes away tonight. I don't want to see them in a pile on your desk." Oh no, here she goes with the dirty clothes speech that I had heard a million times in my life. I was hoping she would give me the short version because I still wanted to read that letter tonight. One nice thing about when mother got rolling on her speeches you had heard before was that you knew when to say, "Yes mother, I understand." Here was one of those times. "I do not wash these clothes for you to leave in a pile on your desk. Mark, do you understand?"

"Yes mother, I understand."

"Okay then, enough said. Good night dear. I'll see you in the morning." Mother turned and left my room. I got by with the short version of the dirty clothes, clean clothes speech. I had no sooner said that to myself than she popped her head into the doorway of my room and said, "Remember what I said about those clothes."

"Yes mother, I'm putting them away now. See, there go the socks."

"All right; I'll see you in the morning, Mark."

"Good night, mother."

Was she really gone, or would she be back in less than ten seconds. All I knew was I better put my clean clothes away. I opened up the big, bottom drawer of my chest and with one sweep of my arm pushed the rest of the clothes into the drawer. There, all done. I hoped mother wouldn't come back for an encore performance. I shut my bedroom door and turned off my ceiling light. I was going to use the small lamp at the desk to read the letter from my grandfather. I quickly prepared my room to look as if I was sleeping if my parents would happen to come by to check on me.

I searched for the envelope. It was gone. Where did it go? I had put it in the front of my shirt. Did I drop it in the hallway, or was it in my room? I searched frantically under furniture, and as I bent over, something poked me in the back. It was the letter. It had shifted from the front of my shirt where I had first tucked it to the back of my shirt during all the running around hoping not to be found in my parent's room.

I opened the envelope once again to read the words my grandfather wrote a long time ago. I paused one more time to hear if my mother was on a return trip to my room to see if I'd put my clothes away. I didn't hear anything outside my door.

I read: "To my son, Russell F. Wilson

Dear Russell,

Your mother and I are writing you this letter to let you know that during these past few months we have prayed for you daily and that we love you very much.

Your mother and I had hoped to make it to Mark's second birthday party, but it was time to go. The persecution by the state was getting too hard on us at our age. Since the state took our jobs away when they closed down the old mill and did not hire us back when the new state-owned mill opened, we had no way to make the last five years of payments on our loan for the house that we had lived in ever since you were a baby.

Friends tried to help us at first, but the local state police started to put pressure on them, and soon they stopped helping. The police hoped that with no help from friends and family, the state would force us to get the state credit system tattoo. We felt that this was what the Bible talked about as 'receiving the mark of the beast'. As it is written in the

Bible in Revelation chapter 13, verses 16 and 17, 'He also forced everyone, small and great, rich and poor, free and slave, to receive a mark on his right hand or on his forehead, so that no one could buy or sell unless he had the mark, which is the name of the beast or the number of his name.'

There was nothing else that your mother and I could do but to try to find a group of believers that we believe had made a new life. To stay in the city, we would surely be put in prison under false arrest like so many of our fellow believers, or we would die a slow death of starvation and loneliness. Our journey was hard, traveling at night to meet up with people that may know something of the new settlement. Many times the state police were just minutes behind us. Time after time we would see the people we had just met with beaten and hauled away.

After weeks of searching for the way to the settlement, we came across an old man sitting in the park. It was late one night. We greeted him, 'Good evening brother.'

He returned the greeting, 'Good evening brother and sister.' He was a believer. We told him our story and that we were looking for someone to take us to the new settlement. He said, 'Yes, I know of a person that can help you. Meet back here two nights from tonight.'

We asked him how we would know the person. He said the person would be standing by the statue of the child with its hands reaching toward heaven. The old man pointed to the statue behind us. We turned to look to make sure we would remember the meeting spot. We had only turned around for what seemed like a few seconds, and when we turned back, the old man was gone into the blackness of the night. A fog was rolling in, and it would make it too hard to find him. But we had many questions to ask him. They would have to wait for two more nights.

When that night arrived, your mother and I came to the park and waited in the shadows made by the moon. It was full, and the shadows of the tall pine trees gave us refuge. The state police were everywhere. They were patrolling the street as if they were looking for someone. How would the person that was to take us to the settlement get through all the patrols? Your mother said to have faith in the Lord. The Lord would get us to the settlement.

Just then we saw a small person appear from behind the statue that the old man told us about two nights ago. We came out of the shadows and walked toward him. I was just about to say hello when the city park was flooded with lights. He grabbed your mother's hand and told us to run. We ran for hours, always hiding from the state police. Everywhere we turned they seemed to be only seconds behind us. We finally ran to an old, boarded-up church. We hid in the back room behind the baptistery. The person we met in the park said we could rest before moving on. Our helper pulled back the hood on the jacket; it was a young girl!

We were surprised and wanted to ask questions, but we had to stay quiet. The state police were still outside. We could hear the sirens and the footsteps running past the windows. We had only been there a short time when the police kicked in the front door. We could hear the commotion of state policemen rushing in. They must have wanted us very badly; it sounded like they were tearing up the church. Then the office door opened, and we heard footsteps coming our way. Then they stopped and we breathed a sigh of relief. Suddenly the door to our hiding place flew open. Our hearts raced with fear, and I'm sure you remember the expression on your mother's face, son, as we looked at the young auxiliary state policeman. You were there. When your captain yelled to you for your status report, you yelled back, 'All clear sir!'

You left as fast as you came. The Bible says in Proverbs 22:6, 'Train up a child in the way he should go, and when he is old he will not turn from it.' We would like to think that we had trained you in the Christian way when you were young.

What you did, son, in the back of the old church tells your mother and me that you still have a good heart. Yes, son, thanks to you, we made it to the new settlement. It is a hard life, but we are free to worship God just like we did when you were young. When the love of God has been rekindled in you heart, we will be waiting to welcome you and your family home to the new settlement.

We have come back, given you clues on how to find us, and left you this letter and your first clue. Start in the center of the city in the park. Find the statue of the child with its hands reaching toward heaven. Place your chin on top of the child's head. Look between the child's hands and you will see the place to find clue number 2. It will ring a bell.

With love,

William R. and Frieda R. Wilson"

I couldn't believe that what I had just read in this letter was true. This could mean my grandparents were still alive and my father and mother believe in a God. Why hadn't they told me and why, if my father was an auxiliary state police, hadn't he turned them in? Had my father ever tried to find his parents by following the clues, and were the clues still in place after all these years? How long ago was this letter written? I had so many questions, and the deeper I dug to find my grandparents, the more questions I ran into. This was too much to think about so late at night. I'd get up early and read the letter again to see what other clues I could gather to help find answers to my questions.

The night went on forever, but finally 5:59 a.m. came. I turned off the alarm before it rang so my mother and father wouldn't know I was up so early. I re-read the letter and jotted down some notes of things to check out. They were things like what was the date of my grandparent's escape, and when was the letter written? I knew according to the letter they missed my second birthday party, and since I was 16, almost 17, that would mean that it happened about this time of the year 14 years ago. Father said that the old city newspaper closed down ten years ago. Maybe I could look in the archives of the old city newspaper to find out about that night. The city museum may have saved the old city newspaper archives, and I could bring them up on my computer. Sitting at my desk, I turned on my computer and waited for it to boot up. I just stared at the letter in my hands. The computer finished booting up, and I checked the city main menu first to see under what heading it might be. They had both city news and city museum. I decided to go with city news. Great! The city newspaper web site link was closed. Then I tried the link under city museum. I got into the museum web site.

I ran through the list of items on the menu. As I watched the list of items roll by, I was thinking it could take forever. I should just go down to the museum and . . . Wait, I needed to back up the list. Bingo! City News Archives, yes! Now all I needed to do was find the paper that reported the police activity the night my grandfather and grandmother were talking about some 14 years ago. I put in the date two weeks before my second birthday. I thought something like that would make the front page. Okay here, the big headline for Monday, September 14, was a robbery at the 1st State Bank. Now that they had the state credit system, that money would be worthless. What about September 15? Nothing there. Okay, the 16th. Nothing there. Now, what about the 17th of September? Yes, there it was! The headlines read, "State Police Search for Two That Are Wanted for Questioning". It said that William Wilson and his wife, Frieda, were wanted for questioning about some recent break-ins and other possible crimes against the state. The state police spokesperson said that an all out search of the city was done with the help of the auxiliary state police. The search was called off after hours of searching. The picture showed Captain Anderson of the state police personally thanking a few of the auxiliary police for helping in the search. Pictured from left to right were: Tom Heber, Alan Langston and Russell Wilson.

It was true what my grandfather said in his letter that my father was there that night and he helped them escape. Why was it that every time I found an answer to one of my questions, so many more questions popped up? Now that I knew what happened that night and that the letter was true, I had questions like: Where was this settlement? How old was the girl that helped them? What happened to the old man in the park?

Oh, I'd better get ready for school! I'd put the letter back in the box after mother and father had left to work. They would never know that I knew anything about it. I hurriedly wrote the first clue down on a piece of paper, and then I placed it under the keyboard of my computer.

"Mark, are you up yet for school?" It was mother. I couldn't let her see what I had been doing.

"Yes mother, I'm up."

"Your father and I are leaving for work now. Your break-fast is on the table. Goodbye."

"Goodbye." Good! They would be gone in just a few minutes, and then I could put the letter back in the box.

As I got dressed for school, I could hear car doors slamming and cars driving away. Now that they were gone, I could put the letter back. I was still wondering if my father had ever read the letter. If he had, did he follow the clues to find his parents? There I go again, thinking of more questions that I may never find answers to.

The box was still in the same place I found it last night. I quickly crossed the room to the box and lifted the lid to place the letter under some of the other items in there. I shut the lid and turned to go back to my room. I was going to finish getting dressed, and then pick up my books before I went downstairs to eat breakfast.

"Mark?"

"Mother!"

"Mark, what are you doing in our room?"

"Well . . . ahh . . . what are you doing back home?"

"Don't avoid the question, Mark."

"What was the question again, Mother?"

"What are you doing in our bedroom?"

"Well, I was looking for a pair of socks."

"Socks!" mother exclaimed. "I just gave you a pile of them last night. I saw you put them in your drawer, or did you forget because you're not accustomed to putting your clothes away?"

"I must have forgotten. Well, I must finish getting ready for school." I squeezed past mother and hurried to my room. "I found my socks, mother. Have a nice day at work!"

I could hear mother muttering all the way down the hall and out to the car. Boy, that was a close call with her coming back home and finding me in their room. I'd better hurry to school or I'd be late.

CHAPTER 5

School Day

———◆———

After I finished getting dressed, I ran to the stairs and threw my leg over the banister and slid down. For something that was so much fun, parents could think of a hundred reasons for you not to slide down the banister.

I went into the kitchen and there on the table was a small plate with two bagel halves with cream cheese, a glass of juice and a vitamin. I drank the glass of juice, took my vitamin, grabbed the two bagel halves and made a sandwich out of them and popped them in my mouth. I grabbed my book bag and headed out the back door to get my bicycle.

As I was bicycling to school, the pain in my body from falling off the roof into the tree was starting to come back. It was good I lived only a mile outside of town. While I was peddling, I tried to figure out why mother came back home. I couldn't figure it out, and it was driving me crazy. I could see the schoolyard as I rounded the last bend. I must not be late because I could still hear the kids playing outside in front of the school.

Oh no! There was the first bell. That meant I had 15 minutes to get to my first hour class. I'd better get moving, or Mrs. Carlstrom would have me doing detention for an hour after school for a week. I peddled hard and fast, not stopping for anything. I had to make it to class on time.

Oooops! I forgot to stop at the stop sign. Oh well, too late now. I had just a block to go and I'd be at the school. I decided to just lean my bicycle up against the tree next to the door. I'd lock it up before next hour because I didn't have time to do it now. I was glad Mrs. Carlstrom's classroom was so close to the door. I thought I was going to make it. I had just a few more steps.

No, oh no! It was the last bell and I was late. I stopped at the door to peek in the window to see where Mrs. Carlstrom was. Good deal! She was in the back of the room working on her bulletin board. I would just slip into the classroom and then over to my desk.

As I opened the door, all eyes were focused on me. Mrs. Carlstrom was still working on the bulletin board. I had just three more desks to go. Bang! Someone dropped a book on the floor. Mrs. Carlstrom turned around just in time to see me half in my desk. "Mark, are you late again?"

All the kids in class were laughing at me as I hung my head and replied, "Yes, Mrs. Carlstrom."

"Stop by my desk at the end of the hour. I would like to talk to you about your tardiness." Boy, did I feel stupid, but I was mad at the same time. I could have gotten into my desk without Mrs. Carlstrom even knowing I was late if it weren't for some joker. Now I had to meet with Mrs. Carlstrom after class. Who would drop a book like that so I would get caught?

None of my classmates would look at me the whole hour until there were about five minutes left of the class. I got a poke in the back, but I ignored it. I was in enough trouble with Mrs. Carlstrom. Then came a second poke in the back followed by a third. I turned around, and Bobby pointed to the back of the room where Kyle Anderson was sitting. Kyle had a big grin on his face and was holding his history book up and mimed that he was sorry for dropping the book. I bet he was sorry. He was still mad because I would not write his research paper a few weeks ago.

"Mark, is there something in the back of the classroom more important than what I am saying up front?"

"No, Mrs. Carlstrom."

"Well, I suggest you turn around in your desk and pay attention."

"Yes, Mrs. Carlstrom." Boy, did I feel silly being caught twice in one day doing something wrong, and the kids in class got to laugh at me again.

The bell rang for the end of class. Now I had to face Mrs. Carlstrom and find out how many hours of detention I'd have to do because I was late. I should thank Kyle for his help in getting me caught coming late. He passed by me with that silly little grin. Boy, I would have liked to knock off the grin on his face, but he was twice my size, and he would squash me like a grape. I'd better get up to Mrs. Carlstrom's desk to get my punishment. I suppose I should have my "have mercy on me" speech ready, but then again she had never shown mercy on any of the kids that she handed out punishment to. I'd just have to take it like a man.

"Mrs. Carlstrom, you said you wanted to talk to me after class."

"Yes I did, Mark. I thought all during the hour on what punishment I would give you." Oh great! She had a whole hour to brew up a terrible punishment. "Mark, are you listening to me?"

"Yes, Mrs. Carlstrom." I hoped she wouldn't ask me to repeat what she said. I hated when teachers did that.

"Mark, what I would like you to do is write a report on the history of the flour mill in town and what affect it had on our town. You have until the first Monday after our two week break to hand it in. No less than 1000 words."

"Is that it, Mrs. Carlstrom?"

"Yes Mark, that is it, and don't be late anymore the rest of the quarter."

"Thank you, Mrs. Carlstrom. I'll try not to be late the rest of the year."

I grabbed my books, ran out of the classroom and down the hall. I still had to lock up my bicycle. As I rushed out the door, there was Kyle with that same silly grin. What had he done to me now?

Great! He stole my bicycle, and he thought it was funny. "What's so funny, Kyle?"

"Did you lose something, Mark?"

"What did you do with my bicycle, Kyle?"

He didn't say a word. He just pointed up in the tree. There it was, 20 feet up in the tree. I didn't have time to get it down, or I would be late for my next class. It would just have to wait. No one would steal it from 20 feet in the tree. I picked up my books and ran back into the school to my next class. (I made it to class just on time.) Kyle seemed unhappy that he didn't get to see me struggle to get my bicycle out of the tree. If I waited until the end of the school day, then there would be hundreds of kids watching. I decided to ask Mr. Wyatt, my last hour teacher, if I could get out of class early to get my bicycle down from the tree. I'd just explain to him what happened. He was a good teacher.

School seemed to drag on forever. The hands of the clock on the wall moved slower and slower each time I glanced at it. As class neared the end, I gathered my books and went up to Mr. Wyatt's desk. I quietly told Mr. Wyatt the situation with my bike up in the tree and that I would like to leave early to get it down before the whole school would be standing around to laugh at me. He said I could have a hall pass to leave early. With a few strokes of his pen, I was on my way out the door and down the hall. It sure was nice of Mr. Wyatt to let me out early to get my bicycle.

Hey! What was Ronnie, the janitor, doing with a bicycle in the school? Hey, wait a minute! That was my bicycle! I ran down the hall to talk with Ronnie. He was a little slow, but he was the nicest janitor in the school. "Hey Ronnie!"

"Hi, Mark, is this your bicycle?"

"Yes it is! It was up in the tree in front of the school. How did you get it down?"

Ronnie got a little smile on his face, "I didn't!"

"If you didn't get it down, then how did it get down?"

"Well, there were two boys trying so hard to put it up higher in the tree. I just told them to bring that bicycle down right now or I'd report them to the principal. Kyle brought it down."

"Kyle got it down? Kyle Anderson?"

"Yes, Kyle Anderson. You better lock up your bike next time, Mark."

"Thank you, Ronnie."

A big smile came across Ronnie's face as he said, "You're welcome."

"Ronnie?"

"Yes, Mark?"

"Where is Kyle now?"

"He had to go to the nurse's office."

"Why?"

"Well, after he got your bicycle down, he fell out of the tree and twisted his knee."

"Thank you again, Ronnie, for making Kyle get my bicycle for me and have a nice day."

As I wheeled my bicycle down the hall and out the doors to the street, I thought to myself how painful that must have been for Kyle to have to get my bicycle out of the tree after he had worked so hard to put it up there. I would like to have been there to watch him get it down and to see him fall out of the tree. That would have been a moment to treasure. Now that I had some extra time, I decided to go over to the park and look for that statue that my grandfather mentioned in his letter. I don't remember ever going to that park with my mother and father. They had taken me to the other parks in town, but not the park in the center of town. I wonder why that was?

The park was up ahead just one more block. I stopped peddling and just coasted to the front gate. Wow, the park was really nice. There were all kinds of statues. How was I going to find the right one? I'd just have to look at them all until I found the right one. There was a statue of Col. Colvill and there was one of a Mr. T. W. Brown, the founder of the first flour mill in our town. I could use that in my report for Mrs. Carlstrom. There was a statue of a child with its hands reaching toward heaven over by the old tree stumps. I ran over to the statue. What did it say on the plaque? "To every child that has ever dreamed they could fly."

The first clue said to start in the center of the city in the park. Find the statue of the child with its hands reaching toward heaven. Place your chin on top of the child's head. Look between the hands and you will see the place to find clue number 2. It would ring a bell.

If I had to put my chin on top of the child's head, then I'd have to climb up on the statue. The only problem was that there were people walking all around the park. I had to follow the instructions of the first clue in order to find the second clue though. I waited until the time was right and nobody was around that part of the park. I took a last quick look around. The statue was tall and the base was up to the top of my head with smooth granite sides. To reach the child's one foot would be my only hope of climbing up on the statue.

As I was about to jump to grab the foot, I heard a voice from behind me say, "Hello young man." I froze in my tracks almost too afraid to turn around to see who said it. "What are you doing? Are you hoping to fly like the child on the statue?"

I turned. There stood a little, old man with a smile on his white, whisker-covered face. "Do not be afraid," said the old man. I <u>was</u> afraid though. Who was this man? Was he going to call the police, or had he called them already and he was stalling me until they came?

"I've got to go." I reached for my bicycle.

"Wait my friend. I just wanted to talk," said the little, old man. I was not waiting around for the police to pick me up and haul me to jail. "I did not call the police as you think I did. I am your friend." For some reason I believed the old guy.

"Do you have a name, mister?"

"Yes, my friends call me Ernie."

"Ernie?" I asked. "What kind of name is Ernie?"

"It is the name my father gave me a long time ago." Ernie hung his head.

Now look what I'd done. I had hurt his feelings. What a jerk I was. "Ernie . . . it's not a bad name. No, not at all. It's just different. I don't think I've known any Ernie's until now. My name is Mark, Mark Wilson." I reached out my hand to shake hands with Ernie. His head was still hanging down. I called his name one more time, "Ernie?" Ernie's head slowly rose up until our eyes met. I smiled the biggest smile I could muster up hoping to get a smile back. It was slow in coming, but a smile started to come until it grew into a full smile.

"Hey, Ernie, do you think we could be friends? I know we just met and, well, the thing is, I really don't have a lot of friends. If it would be okay . . ." Ernie was quiet for a moment, and then he spoke, "That would be great. I could always use a friend, too."

I heard footsteps in the distance headed my way. I turned around to see who was coming but there was no one. I asked Ernie, "Ernie, do you see anybody coming?" Ernie said nothing. I turned back to ask Ernie again, thinking maybe he was hard of hearing. He was gone. I looked all around the park in every direction. It was like he had disappeared into thin air.

I still had to get up on the statue and see what the child was looking at. I had to hurry. Time was moving quickly and the sun would be setting. Then I wouldn't be able to see anything. My parents would also be home soon, and they would be wondering where I was. All I needed to do was jump high enough to grab the foot of the statue and then pull myself up. It was now or never. I got it! Now I had to pull myself up. I was almost up; just a little bit more. Yes, I did it! If the guys in my gym class could have seen this, they would not call me a sissy. The clue said to put my chin on top of the child's head, look between the outstretched hands, and I would see the next clue. I did that. My chin was on the top of the head. I gazed between the hands but all I saw was trees, more trees, a church steeple and more trees.

"Hello, young man. What are you doing? Are you hoping to fly like the child on the statue?"

"Come on, Ernie. You already asked me that a little while ago."

"My name is not Ernie."

"Oooops!"

"My name is Steve Anderson, Captain Steve Anderson, of the state police."

"Oh no!"

"Oh yes!"

I turned around hoping that it was really Ernie playing a joke on his new friend. It wasn't Ernie. It was a state policeman just like he said.

"Why don't you climb down from there so we can talk."

"What would you like to talk about, officer?"

"When you get down on the ground, I'm sure we will have plenty to talk about."

As I was climbing off the back of the statue, a thought came to me, how was I going to get down? I pondered that thought for just a few seconds and then decided to jump because the officer was waiting. I leaped off the base of the statue and hit the ground with a big thud.

The officer laughed and said, "Well, that answers one question."

"What is that, Sir?"

"You can't fly."

"Well, if that is all the questions, officer, I'll be heading home now." I reached for my bicycle.

"Wait just a minute. There are many more questions for you to answer before I'm done with you. Get your bicycle and we'll talk on the way to the squad car."

While I was reaching to get my bicycle, just for a second or two, I thought about what would happen if I just grabbed my bicycle and rode off. The officer was far from his squad car, and I could be long gone by the time he got to the car.

"Don't even think about riding off. I ran track in college. I would be on you so fast," said the officer.

How did he know what I was thinking?

"Do you have a name young man?"

"Yes sir." Great! I was going to get the third degree. "My name is Mark Wilson."

"Where do you live?"

"1425 Old Mill Road, Sir."

"Okay young man. Put your bicycle in the trunk and I'll give you a ride home."

"That's okay, officer. I can ride home from here. It isn't that far from my house."

The officer did not say anything. He didn't have to. The look on his face said, "Just do what I say."

"Okay, Sir, I'll be putting my bicycle in the trunk. Thank you for giving me a ride home." I must be in big trouble. He probably would talk to mother and father, and then I'd really be in trouble.

"Mark, you can ride up front with me."

"Really? This is going to be great!"

As the squad car pulled out of the park and headed down the street, a call came over the squad car's mobile communication's unit. The officer pushed the speaker button, "Captain Anderson here."

"Captain, we just received a call from a Russell Wilson stating that his son, Mark, had not returned home from school. He said that you and he were old friends, and could you keep an eye out for his son. He said you would know what he looks like. Mr. Wilson said his son is a spitting image of himself when he was 16."

"Control Central, call back Mr. Wilson and tell him our ETA is about seven minutes. I have his son and I'm bringing him home."

"That's a roger. Will call."

"That's right, Mark, your father and I were friends back in high school. We even worked for the state auxiliary police while in high school. Is your father still in the auxiliary police?"

"Yes, Sir; he works one weekend a month."

"It will be good to talk with him again. That is why I am giving you a ride home. This gives me a reason to look up your father. It has been a long time since we have talked."

"I'm not in big trouble, officer?"

"No, Mark; we do not jail kids for climbing on statues."

"There is my house, Sir, and there is my father waiting in the driveway."

The captain looked surprised. "Well I'll be. Your father is still living in the same house he grew up in as a boy. He must have bought it from the state. How long have you lived here, Mark?"

"I think we moved into the house when I was about four years old." That's why father would not let mother change anything in the house. This was the house be grew up in. I got out of the squad car.

"Hello, Father," I said. I was just waiting for him to start screaming at me.

"Hello, Mark. I'm glad to see you're okay. Your mother is inside with your supper on the table. I'll talk with you later." It was so strange. Father was so mellow - it was scary. I walked to the house wheeling my bicycle. I heard my father and Captain Anderson talking.

"Hey Mark!" Captain Anderson yelled.

"Yes, Sir."

"Remember, stay off the statues in the park."

"Yes, Sir."

I wheeled my bicycle to the garage and headed to the back door of the house. There my mother was standing with her face all red. I could not tell if she was mad or if she had been crying again. When I got to the top of the steps, she grabbed me by my shoulders and pulled me close and hugged me like she did when I was just a wee, little child. "Your father and I were so worried when you didn't come home from school. Your father called some people at the state police headquarters. Then a little while later we got a call back that they had found you."

"Mother, I just took a ride to the park. Captain Anderson saw me and gave me a ride home. He said he knew father back in high school. Is that true?"

"Yes, Mark. Your father and Steve were on the track team together. They were very good friends."

"They sure are talking a long time, aren't they mother?"

"They have a lot of catching up to do. It has been almost 20 years since high school. Let's sit down and eat supper and let them talk."

"What is for supper anyway? I'm starving."

"Meat loaf and mashed potatoes."

"Great, my favorite!"

"By the way, Mark, what were you doing in the park?"

"I was just thinking that I had never been to that park and thought I would explore it to see what was there. I met this older man named Ernie."

"Mark, you shouldn't talk to strangers."

"Mother, he was not a stranger. He was just an older man. He couldn't hurt me. Besides, he was a nice, old man."

"Well, nice old man or not, don't talk to strangers."

"We only talked a few minutes, and then there was this noise coming toward us. When I turned around, Ernie was gone."

Mother slipped a plate of hot food in front of me and said, "Eat your supper, Mark, before it gets cold. When your father is done talking with Steve, he will most likely have some questions for you."

"Mother, thank you for keeping my food hot for me, and thanks for not yelling at me."

"You're welcome, Mark."

"Mother, is father mad at me?"

"No, Mark, your father was just worried that you may have gotten hurt. Next time, let us know that you are going to be late."

"Yes, Mother. I'm sorry I frightened you and father. I should have let you know that I was going to the park."

While I ate, I found myself thinking back to the park and to all that had happened while I was there. Questions kept running through my mind. What happened to old Ernie? Where and why did he go? What about the first clue? I put my chin on the head of the statue, and all I could see was a lot of trees and that old church steeple. Then Captain Anderson came by and put a stop to the whole clue search. What was meant by the last line of the clue, "It will ring a bell?" Nothing seemed to ring a bell. I had never been to the park before, so what would ring a bell? Wait a minute! I was going about this all wrong. This letter was not written to me but to my father. I had to think as if I was my father at the time he would have received this letter from his father. I had to figure this clue out. What would ring a bell if my father had been in the park today? The trees that I saw wouldn't because they would have grown a lot. The only other thing I saw was that old church steeple. That was it! The letter spoke about God and stuff. That could have been the church my father went to when he was a child. That would ring a bell. The steeple, of course, the steeple. There were bells in the steeple. The second clue had to be in that old church, but where? Would the clue still be at that old church, and would I know the clue when I saw it?

Then I heard the back door open and my father walked in. He had a look on his face that was a half smile. "It sure was nice to see old Steve again. It had been such a long time since we had seen each other." My father seemed in a good mood. Maybe he would not question me about what I was doing at the park. It would be nice to know what Captain Anderson had told him. "So, Mark, Steve told me he found you climbing on a statue in the park."

What should I say? I couldn't tell him I was looking for clues to find Grandmother and Grandfather Wilson. I couldn't tell him that I found the first clue in a letter his father had written to him after they had gone into hiding. "Yes sir, I was." I sure hoped that was enough of an answer that maybe he'd stop asking questions.

"Mark, are you going to tell me why you were climbing on the statue, or do I have to guess?" Maybe if my father would guess, he would guess something a little more believable than what I could think of. "Well, Mark, I'm waiting."

"Oh, I thought you were going to try to guess."

"Don't be silly, Mark. What were you doing in the park?"

"Well, I had never been to that park before. Why is that father? Why hadn't I ever been to that park?"

"Your mother and I are very busy people and have just not had the time."

"I saw a lot of interesting things in the park while I was there." My father was starting to squirm a little, so I kept talking. "There were so many statues. I could see in the distance an old church with a steeple." My father was squirming even more, so I kept pushing. "I wondered if there was a bell up in that old church steeple. What do you think, father? Do you think there is a bell up in that old church steeple?"

"What I think, Mark, is that you ask too many questions. Don't you have any homework to do?"

"Yes sir, I do."

"Well, you better get going on it. It will be bedtime before you know it."

"Yes, father."

Father sure was quick to cut short theL questions once I started talking about the old church and the bell tower. The old bell tower certainly seemed to ring a bell with my father. I was going to find a way to get in that old church to find clue number 2. I went to my room to do my homework. I had to do that report on the flour mill industry for Mrs. Carlstrom because I was late for her class. Where should I start?

I found myself sitting at my desk in my room staring out the window into the night sky over the old mill and beyond. My mind just wandered. Were my grandparents still alive? Would they see the resemblance of my father and know that I was their grandson? Would my whole search for them be in vain because they were dead? Would just finding answers to so many of my questions make it worth my while?

As I continued to look out my window wondering, my mother spoke to me, "You're not going to get your home-work done sitting there at your desk looking into outer space. I don't want you up all night doing homework. You need to get your sleep. Oh, by the way, Mrs. Carlstrom e-mailed you tonight to remind you that your report is due Monday after your two week break. Now wasn't that nice of her to remind you about the report?"

"Yes, she is a nice teacher." (So nice, I said to myself, that all the kids in school call her the "dragon lady.")

"Your father and I had her when we were in school. I believe it was her first year of teaching. She seemed so mean; we had a nickname for her. We called her 'old dragon lady.' I see how wrong we were. She turned out to be a real nice teacher. E-mailing that reminder, that never happened back when your father and I were in school. Well, enough about the past. You need to get your report done. What is the report on, Mark?"

"The flour mill industry in town and what affect it had on our town."

"I see, the flour mill. That should be interesting. I'm sure you will do a good job on it."

"Mother, what do you know about the old mill?"

"Nothing, I don't know anything." Mother was squirming almost as much as father. I thought I'd push a little harder and see what would happen. "Did you know anybody that worked at the old mill, mother?"

"No, I've got to go now. I have some dishes to wash. Good night!"

As my mother hurried out of my room, I thought about how much fun it was to make my mother and father squirm just by asking a few questions about the old church and the old flour mill. What secrets did my mother and father have hidden away in the dark corners of their brains? What secrets were still hiding in the attic that made them squirm so easily?

CHAPTER 6

If Walls Could Talk

It was Saturday morning. The sunlight was filtering past the curtains of my room with a yellow glow. I pulled myself up into a sitting position and rested my back against the headboard. I wiped the sleep from the corners of my eyes and gave a big yawn. I said to myself, I sure dreamed a lot last night. I just couldn't stop thinking about clue number 2 and the part that read, "It will ring a bell." I had to get into that old church to have a look around to see if clue number 2 was somewhere in there. What reason could I give to mother and father so I could go into the city? Wait, I had it – my report! I'd go to the city information center, check in and then slide out the back door. Then I'd cut across town to the church and find the clue. After that I'd slip back into the information center, get some stuff for my report and check out. That way I'd have myself an alibi in case mother and father asked questions as to why I was gone so long.

"Mark, are you awake yet?" It was mother yelling loud enough to wake the dead. If I were sleeping, I would be awake because of her yelling. Who would think a little lady like her would yell like a high school football coach?

"Yes, Mother, I'm awake."

"I hope I didn't wake you up, but I wanted to tell you that your father and I are going to the state auxiliary police meeting. We will be gone most of the day, so you are on your own."

"Okay, Mother. Have a good time and don't worry about me. I'll be just fine. Goodbye."

"Goodbye, Mark. We are leaving now." I could tell in my mother's voice that she had already started to worry about me. I ran to the head of the stairs to say another good-bye and to reassure her I would be all right. When I reached the head of the stairs, Mother had started coming up the stairs. When our eyes met, she stopped in her tracks.

I said to my mother, "I'll be all right."

She smiled, started back down the stairs, and then turned around only to say, "Goodbye. We will see you later."

I went back to my room and watched mother and father get into the car. Mother opened her door to the car; before getting in she stopped. She looked up to my bedroom window. Father looked at mother wondering what she was waiting for. Then he followed her gaze up to my window. I waved and mother smiled. Then they got into the car and drove away. As they drove out of sight, I planned my day to search for the second clue. There were so many things I needed to bring: duct tape, a rope, knife, flashlight and lunch. I'd better bring some paper so it looked like I was going to do work on my report while at the city information center.

I quickly gathered my supplies and packed a lunch. I didn't want to waste any time. I grabbed a couple of bagels and went out the back door. With my search supplies and lunch in my knapsack, I strapped it on my back. I ran to the garage, got my bicycle and rode into town.

As I got closer to town, the excitement was building and my stomach was churning. There, just a few blocks ahead, was the park with the statues. The old church should only be a few blocks from there. As I slowly rode by the park, it seemed as if people in the park were staring at me. I could see the statue I had climbed on, so I stopped to get an idea of which direction the church was.

As I was looking for the church and its steeple, I heard a voice say, "It is two blocks down on the right side of the road." The voice was a familiar one; I turned and there was my new friend, Ernie.

"Ernie, it is you. Where did you go when the police came last time?" Just then I heard a car door slam. Oh no, it was the state police again. "Now Ernie, don't run off." As I turned back to talk to Ernie, he was gone again.

"Mark Wilson, you did not come back to climb on statues again, did you?"

"No sir!" I turned to talk to the state policeman; it was Captain Anderson again.

"That's good. I would hate to have to take you home again. It was nice to talk with your father, but we would not like to make a habit of it now, would we?"

"No sir!"

"Well, Mark, you have a nice day."

"Yes sir, I will. You have a nice day also."

A voice from inside the patrol car said, "Come on, Dad. They're calling you to come back to headquarters."

"All right, I'm coming. That is my son. You may know him, Kyle Anderson. He is about your age."

"Yes sir, I know your son. We have history class with Mrs. Carlstrom together."

Kyle opened up the patrol car door, and with a little smirk he said, "Well, if it isn't Markie Wilson. What are you doing here?"

"Hello, Kyle. I'm on my way to the information center to work on my report for history class."

"Yes, that's right. You got that assignment when you came to class late one day. We have to go. They are calling us back to headquarters."

As Captain Anderson got back into the patrol car, I was wishing I could have told him what his son did to my bicycle; but the sooner they went, the sooner I could get on with my search. Captain Anderson turned and waved goodbye. I waved back thinking, how could such a nice man have a son like Kyle?

Now that they were gone, where did Ernie go to again? Whenever the police showed up, he disappeared. Someday I'd have to ask Ernie where he disappears to and why. Speaking of why, why did Ernie say two blocks down on the right? How did he know what I was looking for? I searched the park hoping to find Ernie and ask him those questions, but he was nowhere to be found. I went back to the spot where I first heard Ernie say just two blocks down and to the right.

As I peddled down the road, I could see the information center. There was the church like my grandfather wrote about in the letter to my father. It was only a short ride, so it wouldn't be hard to get back to the church after I checked in at the information center to set up an alibi.

I stopped and leaned my bicycle up against a sign that said, "No Parking Except on Sunday." It looked as if no one had parked there at the church for many, many years. The front lawn was overgrown with weeds and small trees; there was a lot of trash mixed in with them. There were old tires leaning against the sign. The paint around the windows was peeling, and some of the windows were covered with boards or were so dirty you could not see in. Some of the windows were broken, and there were birds flying in and out making sounds as if they were talking to me or laughing at me. The building was a blend of stone and brick. The top was a steeple so tall it seemed to touch the clouds. The front door had a big chain and lock on it. There was a sign nailed to the door that said, "WARNING! This building belongs to the state land and water department. No trespassing. Violators will be prosecuted under Sec. 127-48."

It was not going to be an easy task to get into the church to look around. I'd have to see if there was a back door and a place to hide my bicycle while I looked around inside the church. I would have to find that later after I checked in at the information center. I'd better get over there and start to set up my alibi.

I grabbed the handlebars of my bicycle, swung my leg over and sat down. I started to peddle away when, out of the corner of my eye, I saw this little, old lady peeking around her curtains watching me ride away. Would she call the police, or was she just snoopy? I came too far to give up now. I'd leave for a while and then come in the back way to begin my search for the second clue. It had to be in there.

I rode up to the information center and spotted the bicycle rack. There was still one slot open. I locked up my bicycle and ran up the many stone stairs. I remembered mother and father saying that this was once called a public library, and it had thousands of books. Now there were only two old books under glass on display. The rest of the books were replaced with hundreds of computer terminals.

I swung open the big, heavy door, and I could hear a steady click of keys on the computer keyboards. There was a short line to check in at the desk to get assigned a computer workstation. I wondered who was at the desk checking people in. Oh, it was that nice lady, Mrs. Lang.

"Hello, Mark. What can I do for you today?"

"Hello, Mrs. Lang. I need a quiet spot. I have a history report to do."

"What is the report on, Mark?"

"It is on the history of the flour mill and the affects it had on our town. It cannot be less than a thousand words. It is for Mrs. Carlstrom's class because I was late for her class one day."

"Well, Mark, let me find you a spot way back in the

corner so no one will disturb you."

"Thank you, Mrs. Lang."

"I'll put you in number 258. That is way back in the corner by the back door. Is that all right with you, Mark?"

"That will be just fine."

I made my way to the corner right next to the back door. It could not have been any better planned. I would punch in my name and log in. Then I'd slip out the back door to the old church. If anyone came by my workstation, they would just think I was in the bathroom. I'd better have something started on my report showing on the screen so it looked like work was in progress. I quickly hammered out a few lines. Then I peered over the workstation dividers to see if anyone would see me slip out the back door. All the workers were busy helping people. Now would be a good time to make my move out the back door. I slowly backed up to the door still watching to see if anyone would see me leave and blow my alibi. As I twisted the doorknob, my heart started to beat faster. I could hear each of the mechanical devices in the door doing their job. The sound was deafening. I was sure everyone could hear me. There was one last big click. I stopped and looked around. Everyone was still unaware of what I was doing. I gave the door a slight push. I very quickly slipped out the doorway into a stairway. To make sure I could get back into my workstation, I put duct tape over the bolt on the edge of the door. I quickly shut the door and ran down a short flight of stairs to a set of double doors. Just beyond those was the outside. I reached for the door and stopped. I looked up just in time to see the door had a magnetic alarm system. It was a very old alarm system, but it worked. They were easy to bypass if you had some wire. That should be easy enough with the maintenance cart right down the hall. All I had to do was fool the system into thinking the door was closed even when it was open. I got the wire off the maintenance cart and within a few minutes, if everything worked like I'd seen in those old spy movies, I would be on my way.

I made my last connection with the bypass wire; but I heard someone coming. I had no time to double-check my work. I had to go out the door and hope the bypass worked, or get caught by whoever was coming down the hall. I grabbed the bar on the door, gave it a push and rushed out the door. Again I placed a piece of duct tape over the bolt and held the wires I used to bypass the alarm system so they would hang outside the door. That way no one would see the wires hanging and get suspicious. I ran and hid behind a dumpster to see if anyone was responding to the opening. I waited for about a minute or two. No one came. It worked. I didn't have much time, so I had to hurry to the church to look for clue number 2.

I went around to the front of the building where I had left my bicycle. There weren't many people on the street to see me leave. I would ride to the church and try to find a way to the back so nobody would see my bicycle or me. I could see the church from where I was. I'd have to circle the block and look for a way to get to the back of the church. If there was an alley, I could ride down that and check things out.

There was an old, fallen down garage next to the church. I'd put my bicycle in there to hide it. As I pushed back some boards that were hanging down in my way, I looked around at the junk that had piled up over the years. There was no way of telling when someone had last used the garage.

This side of town sure gave me a creepy feeling. It was like someone was watching me all the time. I could see it was not going to be a problem getting inside the church with the back door off its hinges and leaning up against the building. I walked quickly, glancing over my shoulder from the garage to the open back door of the church.

Just inside the doorway I turned and looked up and down the alley. No one was around. My eyes then searched up and down the houses to see if anyone was looking out their windows. Most of the houses were boarded-up, but there were a few houses that had smoke coming out of their chimneys. I could not see anyone in any of the windows for as far as I could see.

I slid my knapsack off my back to find my flashlight because it was so dark in the hallway that I was standing in. I did not dare move without fear of running into something or tripping over things on the floor.

With my flashlight in hand, I could carefully search for the second clue. I thought maybe I could find more answers to who my grandparents were, what they were like, and most of all, where they went. There was so much junk in the hallway. There were old ladders, windows and chalkboards. There was even an old wooden podium just like Mrs. Carlstrom had in her classroom. In another area there were tools. That must have been the area where the janitor's office was (if you could call it an office). It had a cluttered workbench, some old, rusty screwdrivers and an old mirror with a big part of a corner broken off hanging next to some dirty coffee cups. The janitor did have a table and one chair with a light overhead. It, too, was rusty and bent. The light bulb had been broken out of it. There was some paper on the table. Maybe it could tell me something. It was a page from a calendar with a Norman Rockwell picture on it. The month was April but the year was torn off. That did not tell me anything. I just had more questions. Why was that the only page on the table? Where was the rest of the calendar?

As I panned my light around the room, I saw two fuel oil tanks for the furnace. You should have seen the size of those things! I could see piles of boxes and other things that had been stored away and would never be used again. My light came across a fire door. It must lead into the church, I thought. Then I saw another door. As I stepped around the piles of junk on the floor, I brushed aside cobwebs hanging from the pipes and wooden beams. I reached for the handle to the fire door and heard something creak or squeak, so I quickly stopped and looked around. Was there someone else in the room with me? I listened for a moment. I did not hear any more, so I grabbed the handle. The steel was cold and damp. I pushed down on the handle that lifted the latch and pulled on the door. It would not open. I tried again and again, but the door would not open. I stood there and thought to myself how I would get the door open, because behind the door could be the answers to my questions.

I shut my flashlight off and put it in my pocket. Now with both hands free I clutched the handle, and with all my weight I was bound and determined to get that door open. I started to rock, and with each rock backward, I would count one, two and three. I used all my weight to pull open the door. It came open with a great rush of air. I stepped forward to walk through the door and something brushed against my cheek. Then there was another. Then something hit me in the chest. I reached for my flashlight in my pocket. I quickly turned on the light to see what hit me in the chest. As the light traveled across my chest, there with its beady, little, red eyes and mouth wide open and wings spread wide was a bat. It was clinging to my shirt. I jumped back from the door. Now I could see hundreds of bats flying out from behind the door. I took my flashlight and brushed the bat from my chest. While I was brushing away the bat, I tripped and fell over something. It made a squeaking sound. It was a large rat running away. I did not know who was more afraid, the rat or me. I just knew I didn't want to see that rat or any other rats anymore.

When I got up off the floor, I could still hear a few bats flying around the room; but they were not running into me anymore. Finally it was silent. All the bats had found a new resting place.

I slowly peered around the big, heavy, steel fire door

with my flashlight in hand. I saw that this door had lead me into another hallway. My flashlight searched the walls as I walked slowly down the hallway. I stepped into a room that had a large closet along one wall. Another light was shining back at me. I shut my light off. My heart was racing a mile a minute, but then I realized the other light turned off at the same time. I laughed and said to myself, I'm sure glad no one else was here to see this. I had found a large section of mirrors, and I had seen myself in them. It must have been some kind of changing room. I stepped over to the closet and slowly opened the door just in case some of my winged friends were living in there. No bats; that was good. There were all kinds of robes, and they were all the same red color. And books, real books! I grabbed at the pile of books as if I had found gold and I was an old prospector striking it rich. They were music books. They had a strange title, <u>Song Book for Saints and Sinners</u>. There was some sheet music to a song called, "Holy Savior." There was a big, fat book with a lot of songs in it. I also found a red songbook titled, <u>Great Revival Hymns</u> for church, Sunday school and Evangelistic services. I put the fat book and the red songbook in my knapsack. I would page through them later. I had to keep looking around to find my way to the steeple because that was all I could see from the park. That had to be part of the clue. Which way should I go?

At the end of the hallway there was a flight of stairs. I quickly walked down the hallway to the stairs. My light flashed across some pictures on the wall. The words over the pictures read, "Sunday School Graduation Classes Past and Present." I looked over the pictures and the year of each of the graduation classes. There was one from 1993, one from 1972, and there was one way back from 1955. There was no color on that picture. I wondered if any of those people knew Grandmother and Grandfather Wilson. Maybe they were in one of those pictures themselves. I didn't have time to look. There were too many pictures. I had to get to the stairs to find my way up to the steeple.

I started up the stairs. When I was only four or five steps up, something in my gut made me stop, run down the steps and down the hall to grab a handful of pictures off the wall. I took the pictures dated in the 1950's, 60's and 70's. I shoved them into my knapsack next to the books I had taken. Then I dashed over to the stairway and ran up the stairs until I reached the next floor.

At the top of the stairs was a set of big, wooden doors hanging crooked. I searched with my light, and I could see that the doors were damaged. There were big scuffmarks as if a battering ram was used to open them. Cobwebs hung from the lights on the ceiling. Off to my right was a door lying on the floor with the window broken out. The name-plate on the door said, "Office." I stepped into the office to look for clues. As I flashed my light around the office, I noticed that it had been burned and everything was black. If there were any clues, they would have burned in the fire.

I left the office and stepped over the door on the floor. I walked into a large room with a very high, arched ceiling. There were rows and rows of what looked like park benches with an aisle down the center. I walked down the aisle with my flashlight shining on the ceiling. My mouth was wide open in amazement at the grand architecture of the church. Sunlight was shining into the large room through the multi-colored windows making it easier to see, so I didn't need the flashlight anymore. I had never seen such windows before. This must have only been done in churches because I had never seen it in any of the government buildings. Each window had a different picture. One said, "Today in the town of David a Savior has been born to you, he is Christ the Lord." The next one said, "The child grew and became strong; He was filled with wisdom, and the grace of God was upon Him." There were so many windows, and each had something to say about the life of this person called Christ the Lord. The more windows I saw and read what was written on the glass, the more I wondered who this Christ was that each window showed a time of His life. I walked by many of the windows staring at the pictures and reading the words but not understanding. I walked across the room to even more of the multi-colored windows. One window had this man called Christ on a cross and the words under the picture said, "His blood was shed for the forgiveness of our sins." They killed him. Why? I found myself feeling sad and mad for this man who from all the pictures on the windows seemed like a good and kind man.

I passed by the next window with my head hanging down, too afraid to see what the next window would show and say. My curiosity got the best of me, though, and I just had to look. I just had to find out what the next window would say. To my surprise, that picture showed this man called Christ alive and floating in the clouds. The words under the picture said, "He is Alive. He has Risen just as he said." I didn't understand. He was dead and now he was alive. All this confused me.

I decided to continue looking for the stairs leading to the steeple. There was a doorway up ahead; maybe that would lead me upstairs. I walked through the door and could see a set of stairs going up and a set of stairs leading down to a set of doors with windows. While I was looking at those doors, I saw a long shadow coming up the sidewalk. I ran back to the doorway that I had come through. I peeked around the corner to see who was coming to the front door of the church. I knew the door was chained, but maybe the person had a key to unlock the church. Someone might have called and said they saw me. I slipped back up against the wall so I would not be seen.

The chains on the door rattled, and my heart skipped a beat. Then the door was being shaken and my heart skipped another beat. After a while it was quiet again. I breathed a sigh of relief. I raised my back off the wall and was ready to peek around the door when the front door rattled one more time. This time I thought the doors were going to come off the hinges. Quiet fell upon the church once more.

I ran back a few windows where a piece of the glass had fallen out. Who was at the door? Was it another person in search of answers, or was it the state police looking for me? It was a man all dressed in black. He was walking to a state patrol car. Why was he stopping? He was coming back and someone else was getting out. He was saying something. "Come back, Lieutenant. You know that little, old lady calls us out about once a week saying she sees lights on in the church and people walking around inside."

The lieutenant turned around and headed back to the car. Just then a bird flew by me and frightened me. I tripped over a piece of wood on the floor and hit a bench with my head. I jumped to my feet and looked to see if the state police had heard the noise. At the same time the bird flew out the broken upper window.

The man in the patrol car said, "See Lieutenant, that is what the old lady sees each time. Birds!"

As the patrol car drove off, I checked my head to see if I was bleeding from my fall. I had some blood on my hand but not much. I looked up then and saw I was standing in front of the window that said, "His blood was shed for the forgiveness of our sins."

I headed for the stairway leading upstairs. Each step I took creaked, moaned or popped as I climbed to the top floor. The sign at the top of the stairs read, "Jesus said, 'Let the little children come to me, and do not hinder them, for the kingdom of heaven belongs to such as these.'" Then it said, "Welcome to our Sunday School." Oh, those poor kids. They had to go to school on Sunday. I thought it was bad enough just having to go to school on Monday through

Friday without having to go Sunday also.

The first classroom I came to was for first graders. They had little chairs and a table in the middle of the room. Along the wall were taped the children's artwork. There was a big, pink heart with the words written, "Jesus loves all of us" and it was signed Marcus L. There was another piece of artwork that read, "Jesus is coming soon." What did that child mean by that, "Jesus is coming soon?" I left that room confused by what a first grader wrote. What did they teach in this school?

At the end of the hall, there was another set of stairs going up. I hurried down the hall passing up many more classrooms until I came to the classroom for ages 13 to 18. I slowed my pace to a walk. Hey, that was my age group. I was curious to see what kids my age were learning. To my surprise, there were no tables or desks in the classroom, only old couches and easy chairs along the three walls. On the other wall was a mural reaching from wall to wall and from floor to ceiling. It was a picture of that Jesus Christ man again with his arms held out wide wearing a white robe. The words painted in one corner of the mural read, "For God so loved the world that He gave His one and only Son, that whoever believes in Him shall not perish but have eternal life. John 3:16"

I stood and stared at the picture, then at the words, and then back to the picture trying to figure out how the picture and the words went together. Who was this John, and what did the numbers 3:16 mean? Was that some type of computer code? I did not understand. I left the classroom confused but with the picture and words burned into my mind. It must have been important to those people to let their kids paint it on the whole wall.

When I got to the stairs leading up, I took hold of the railing. The stairs were steep. I carefully placed my foot, testing each step to see if it would hold my weight. The steps creaked and popped until I came to a door. There was a sign on the door, "Notice to all bell ringers: keep this door closed at all times."

I reached for the doorknob and twisted it slowly. It was not locked. I started to open the door but remembered what happened with the door down in the basement with the bats. I stepped back away from the door and gave it a push. Nothing flew out as I flung open the door. Only a beam of sunlight filled the stairway. The bright yellow and gold light reminded me of the picture in the classroom. There were yellow and gold beams of light shining from behind that man's white robe.

I stepped into the room. It was a six-sided room with an iron ladder bolted to the wall. I walked toward the ladder. Dust had been stirred up into the air from the opening of the door. The dust particles were in the air rising up to the top of the steeple. As the dust would pass by each window, the light would light up the dust particles like stars at night. As I watched the dust rise in the room, my eyes came upon the ceiling. There was a piece of rope coming through a small opening in the ceiling.

I walked across the room to the ladder. I tripped on something, and my feet became entangled. I fell to the floor with a heavy thump and things went black for a moment. When I came to my senses, I was lying face down in the heavy dust. I tried to get up but I could not. Fear was rushing over me. Did I get hurt so bad that I couldn't get up? I looked at my legs. The fear that had rushed over me vanished when I realized I had tripped and gotten tangled up in some rope that was on the floor. As I untangled the ropes from my feet, I was thinking about the ladder and how high the ceiling was. I stood up and walked over to the ladder. My head started to hurt; my eyes went blurry for just a few seconds. I quickly grabbed the ladder and hung on. I looked up to the ceiling. That was the wrong thing to do. My head started to whirl, and my eyes started to blur again. I put my head down with my chin buried in my chest. I closed my eyes hoping it would pass.

After a few moments when my head felt like it had quit whirling, I slowly opened my eyes. I looked around and things seemed to be normal again. I must have bounced my head off the floor when I fell.

Once again I took hold of the ladder and slowly raised my head up to look at the ceiling. This time there was no whirling. I went up the ladder slowly at first, but as each rung passed by my face, I found myself climbing a little faster. Then I reached farther, skipping rungs to get to the top. The little windows seemed to flash by. Then there was a thump again. It stopped me cold. Rubbing my head with one hand, I looked up. I had run into the ceiling with my head, another lump on my head to match the one from when my head hit the floor. Oh yes, the floor. In my rush to reach the top, I had not noticed the floor was equally rushing away. I must have been 40 feet from the floor.

With the ceiling pressing against my head, I pushed open the trap door. A rush of fresh air came by my face. It was a welcome rush since I had been breathing and eating so much dust. I laid the trap door down quickly. I noticed it was an open bell tower, open for the whole town to see so I would not be able to stand up. There was a short wall that wrapped around with six large posts that held the steeple roof up. Hanging from the center was the bell. I finished climbing up into the bell tower. I crawled over to the wall and sat down putting my back up against the wall. As I rested, my eyes started to search for clue number 2. I did not see any writing on the wall or the crisscrossing beams of the steeple roof. Curiosity was getting the best of me. I just had to look over the wall to see how much I could see. Perched on my knees, I looked over the edge of the wall. It was amazing what I could see. I was looking down on the tops of trees and buildings as far as the eye could see. It was as if I was flying. My eyes floated over the treetops until they came to the park. I could see people walking around; they looked so small. I wondered if Ernie was still at the park.

Suddenly there was a flash of black and gray. The wind rushed by my face and stirred up dust and dirt into my eyes. It frightened me so I fell over backwards clutching my dirt-filled eyes. I heard another thump and then a somewhat muffled ringing. I lay on my back holding my head. I could not tell what was ringing louder, the sound in my head or the bell. I looked to see what had frightened me so much. There it was staring back at me, a pigeon. Now I had a lump on my forehead, one on top of my head and one in the back of my head. Every time I hear a bell ringing now, I'll remember this day.

Wait a minute, the clue! It said it would ring a bell. I got up off my back and started to search the outside of the bell to see if there was any hidden writing. Nothing, nothing at all, not even a scratch. I had really thought I would find the clue here. This was where the statue in the park was pointing. I was so disappointed I decided to lay down with my eyes closed and rest before climbing down the ladder. I laid there wondering where I went wrong in interpreting the first clue. Everything pointed to this church and the bell tower. Why wasn't it here?

I sat up to look around one more time hoping to see something I may have missed before. When I sat up, I found myself directly under the bell with my head just inches from the rim of the bell. I had never been this close to a bell before, much less inside the bell. You should have seen the size of that clacker! I reached up and took hold of the clacker with both hands but something felt strange. It was not as smooth as I thought it would be. I took a closer peek at the clacker. I found an envelope taped to the clacker with duct tape on the backside. Could that be the second clue that

I had been searching for? I carefully took the envelope off the clacker. It had yellowed just like the letter I found in the wooden box from my grandparents. I opened the envelope and then remembered that I needed to get back to the information center before anybody found out I was gone. I put the letter in my knapsack, strapped it to my back and crawled to the opening where the ladder was.

I put my feet on the first rung of the ladder and took one last look at the bell and the tower. With a big sigh I took hold of the ladder and began my descent down closing the trap door behind me. It seemed to take no time at all to reach the bottom. I hurried across the floor to the doorway remembering the pile of old rope that I had tripped on earlier.

I made my way through the church and remembered to put everything back the way it was when I came so no one would know that anybody had been there. (I put everything back, that is, except the items I had put into my knapsack to examine later.) When I came to the heavy, fire door, I looked around for more bats. It was quiet. I gave the handle of the door a quick turn. There was a tremendous crash and it startled me. The latch did not make that noise the first time I came through the door. There was another crash. Then I heard voices. "Tear this place apart. If there is anyone here, I want them caught." It was the state police. Someone must have heard the bell ring when I hit my head on it.

I pushed the fire door and quickly shut it behind me. I was making my way to the door that lead to the back alley when I saw some shadows moving across the wall. I turned to the window. There were more state police, and they were coming to the door. I rushed over to the two big fuel tanks for the furnace. I squeezed in-between the two tanks and worked my way to the back. I could hear the police rush in. They were knocking things over and smashing whatever was in the way. There was glass breaking all around me.

There were pieces of glass hitting the sides of the fuel tanks. Each time an item was smashed or thrown, you could hear the policemen laughing. What kind of people were they? Hadn't they done enough to chase these people into hiding?

I could hear one voice over all the rest. It was a somewhat familiar voice and he said, "Jesus is Lord. Watch this!" I heard the coffee cup hit the wall right above me. Then it ricocheted off the two fuel tanks and rolled down into my arms. It did not break after all that. That same familiar voice then yelled, "The cup didn't break. I'm going to get it and smash it into a thousand little pieces."

There was no place for me to run. I was caught for sure.

One of the other policemen said, "Just let it go, Corporal. We have to meet up with the rest of the group."

"It will only take a minute."

"I said let it go. Now move out, Corporal." The corporal was so mad he kicked the fuel tank because he could not smash the cup. The sound reverberated through the tank and was deafening. My head was pressed against one of the tanks. I quickly moved it away from the tank and then hit my head on the other fuel tank.

I could hear the policemen move toward the fire door. I worked my way to the front of the fuel tank to get a look at the policemen as they left. The last policeman took hold of the door and turned to look around one more time. When he turned to look in my direction, there was a small shaft of light shining through the window hitting his face. To my surprise it was Kyle, Kyle Anderson. That was why the voice was so familiar. What a little weasel! It was just like him to get angry and kick things all because some coffee cup didn't break. I watched Kyle, the little weasel, slide past the fire door. I waited a few seconds to make sure no one would be coming back. With the coffee cup in my hand, I squeezed out from between the two fuel tanks. The coffee cup was tapping on the back fuel tank. The tank sounded as if it was empty. That was so strange. You would think it would be full because it was the second tank. The first tank was still half full the way it sounded when Kyle kicked it.

I put the cup in my knapsack and then ran for the door. Once at the door, I stopped to see if there were any police posted in the alley. It was clear as far as I could see. I ran to the garage where I hid my bicycle. I grabbed the handlebars, swung my leg over, and was ready to ride. One more look to see if the alley was clear. I could hear the police inside the church still searching and still breaking things. That is when I heard a large window shatter. It was time to go. I rode out of the garage and down the alley as fast as my legs would take me. A voice yelled for me to stop. I just peddled all the faster. I didn't even look back for fear they might see my face and recognize me. I decided to take all the alleys back to the information center. I kept a watchful eye out as I rode in case the police pulled their squad car in front of me to cut me off. I could see the information center about a half block away. When I coasted up to the bicycle rack, I could hear the wail of police sirens coming my way.

I ran up the front steps to the information center with my heart pounding and fear that they would catch me. Suddenly I thought to myself, wait a minute. I cannot use the front door. That would destroy my alibi. I had to hurry to the back alley door where I sneaked out. I ran alongside the building, around the corner, past the dumpster and then up to the door. I pressed my ear up against the door to hear if anyone was in the stairwell. The police sirens were getting closer. I grabbed the handle and opened the door. I stuck my head in and looked around. There was no one there. I rushed up the stairs to the door that would get me back to my workstation. I slowly opened the door and crawled in on my hands and knees until I reached my chair. I slipped into my chair and started to take off my knapsack with one hand. I tried to type with the other just as if I was never gone.

I put my knapsack under my chair and tried to catch my breath, but I had this strange feeling like someone was watching me. I leaned back in my chair and looked to the right and then to the left. There was no one else in the work-stations next to me. I went back to work on my report, but I could not shake that feeling of someone watching me. It was hard to concentrate with all that had happened at the church. I leaned back in my chair to try to collect my thoughts. There were a pair of eyes looking straight into my eyes. My heart stopped, my mouth went dry, and my lips were moving but I was saying nothing.

It was Mrs. Lang. "You've been gone for awhile. Where have you been, Mark?" I was so afraid I could not say anything. How long did she know I was gone? Who did she tell? "What is the matter, Mark? Cat got your tongue?"

Why do older people say, "Cat got your tongue?" Who came up with that silly phrase anyway? "No, Mrs. Lang, I still have my tongue. You just surprised me."

Mrs. Lang came around from the front of the worksta-tion and sat down in the chair next to me. "So I surprised you!" Mrs. Lang said. (Her voice said, "Oh, I did not know that" but the look on her face said, "I know you were gone someplace doing something, but I don't know what it was.") "Mark, let's say we go back to my first question I asked you and you never gave me an answer to. Where have you been?" Fear was running rampant through my body; my hands were shaking and my brain had frozen her question in time. I'd played that question over and over and over. I could not think of a good, believable answer. "Well Mark, I'm waiting for your answer."

I could sense my mouth was opening up as if to say something, but I knew in my brain I had thought of no answer. I spoke anyway saying, "I was . . ."

Just then there was a disturbance in the front of the room by the main desk. Both Mrs. Lang and I looked to see what was going on at the desk. Mrs. Lang turned back to me and said, "Now what were you going to say, Mark?"

"What was the question, Mrs. Lang?" hoping to stall for more time so my brain could thaw and come up with an answer.

"The question was, Mark, where have you been?"

"Oh yes, that question. I remember now. Where have I been? That is a good question, a fair question."

"Mark, just answer the question!" I started to open my mouth when another worker came up from behind Mrs. Lang and whispered something in her ear. Her eyes got huge. She craned her neck to see over the workstations toward the front desk. She quickly got up from her chair and leaned over to me and said, "I'll get back to you and the question you are avoiding giving me an answer to."

Mrs. Lang headed up to the front desk almost in a full run. I felt a pair of eyes burning a hole in me. It was the other worker that had brought Mrs. Lang the message. I looked at the worker straight in the eyes. She did not move. "Well," I said, "Is there something I can do for you, or are you going to stand there all day like an old statue?"

She rocked back on her heels and turned to go back to work. Over her shoulder she said, "How rude!"

As she walked away I said to myself, "What does she mean, 'how rude'?" I jumped up from my chair and shouted back to her, "Me rude, you're the one that was staring at me. How rude is that?" I sat down at my workstation and noticed I had gotten the attention of the whole information center. I directed my next statement to all the people staring, "Well now, wouldn't you say she was rude the way she stared at me? One would wonder if she had ever seen a person work before. What do you think, mister?" The guy quickly focused back on his work and didn't answer my question. "What about you, lady?" She tried to pretend that she was not staring and went back to her work. I looked around and all the heads of the people went back to their work. I did the same.

Mrs. Lang was still up front talking to two men in suits. She was pointing and shaking her head a lot. I'd better get my work done and get out of here before she came back and asked more questions. I worked as fast as I could to gather as much information as possible for my report. I had the computer print it out. That way I could do my report at home and get out of here that much sooner. After waiting for the last sheet to come out of the printer, I started to pack up my things. When the printer was done, I could be on my way home. The printer stopped. I gathered the many sheets of paper, put them in my knapsack and walked to the front door.

When I approached the front desk, Mrs. Lang and the two men in suits were still talking. When I got nearer to them, they stopped talking and watched me walk by. They did not say anything. Ten feet more and I would be out the door and heading for home.

"Say, Mark." It was Mrs. Lang.

"Yes, Mrs. Lang," I said in my most innocent voice.

"These two gentlemen are with the state police." I walked over and reached out to shake their hand as a kind gesture. All I got was a cold, blank stare. Mrs. Lang continued to say, "They were wondering if you had seen anybody go in or out of those back doors where you were working."

"No, Mrs. Lang, I did not see anybody. Why? What happened?"

The one officer said, "We had a report of a break-in at the old church just a few blocks from here."

I was curious to know how much they knew, so I asked as if it was news to me, "What did the person or persons look like? Maybe I could help. My father is on the auxiliary state police, you know."

The officer said, "We are not sure. Our source was a

little, old lady, and she said it was a young man about your size."

"What kind of a car was he driving?" I asked the officer.

"He was riding a bicycle."

"Well, if I see anyone or anything strange, I'll give you a call. I hope you can find him." I walked to the door hoping they would not follow me and see me ride off on my bicycle. I glanced over my shoulder to see if anybody was watching. I saw no one peering out the windows. Just in case, I decided to ride in the opposite direction of my house to throw them off.

CHAPTER 7

It's In The Bag

W hen I rode down Old Mill Road toward my home, I frequently looked over my shoulder to see if the state police had followed me. There was no one behind me. My riding around town for a while must have given them the slip, or it was the fear getting the best of my imagination.

I rode into the driveway and saw that mother and father were still gone. That was great because I could go through and examine the things I picked up at the church. I would be able to take a good look at clue number 2 to see what it could tell me. I leaned my bicycle up against the side of the garage and started walking to the house. At that moment a car pulled into the end of the driveway and stopped. I froze in place wondering who it was. Then the car slowly backed out of the driveway and drove back down Old Mill Road toward town. They were gone, and I could relax again. I shouldn't jump every time there was a noise or a car that drove by. I would be a gray haired, old man at 16.

I ran to the back porch and took the key from under the planter and unlocked the door. Then I replaced the key, looking around to make sure no one was watching me.

Once inside, I headed to my bedroom to eat the lunch I had packed. With the arrival of the state police at the information center and with Mrs. Lang asking so many questions, I didn't have time to eat. I was so excited that by the time I got to the stairs, I was almost running. For just a moment I could hear a voice in the back of my head saying, "No running in the house," and, "Mark, take one step at a time or you could fall and hurt yourself." It was my mother's voice. I looked around as a cold chill ran up my back; there was no one there. I took hold of the banister and ran up the steps taking two steps at a time. I was laughing as I took each giant step. When I reached the top, I spun around and looked back down the steps as if I had climbed Mount Everest. I spun around again and walked to my room. There were so many things I wanted to do. What should I do first? Do I inspect the items I picked up at the church, eat lunch or look at clue number 2? I could do them all at the same time.

I went over and sat on my bed, pulled the knapsack off my back, opened up the top flap and poured everything I had in there onto the bed. I could not believe all the stuff I had put in the knapsack. I found my lunch all squished; but as hungry as I was, I'd eat anything. I snatched my sandwich. As I unwrapped it from the plastic, I noticed a circle had been pressed into the bread. I was confused for a moment as to what had made that mark. Then it dawned on me, the coffee cup. I searched through the pile on my bed for the coffee cup that Kyle tried so hard to break. I found it and placed it on the ring in my sandwich to see if it matched. It was a perfect match. I sat there staring at the cup wondering whom it belonged to and where that person was now. That was one tough coffee cup. There was not a chip or even a crack in the cup. There were only a few scratches across the words, "Jesus is Lord." I continued to eat my lunch and pick through the items on the bed.

I reached for the red songbook. The cover was faded, and it was ragged around the edges. I could tell it was well used. I opened to the front page, and there was a name written on it. The first name was Grace. The last name was too faded with age, but it started with Tub. The title was <u>Great Revival Hymns</u> for church, Sunday school, and Evangelistic services. Copyright, 1911, Rodeheaver-Ackley Co. The pages didn't tear as I turned them. They made more like a crackling sound because they were so brittle and yellowed. The first song was called "Repent!" Copyright, 1910, By Rodeheaver-Ackley Co. I just stared at the notes. My thoughts bounced between fear and curiosity as to what the words would say.

Verse 1 said: "Repent! 'tis the voice of Jesus Now sounding in your ear; The message of God rings loud and clear, Now seek Him, for He is near." As I read the words, it was as if they were reverberating in my ears. I didn't know if I wanted to read anymore. I closed the book and pushed it aside and stared out the window. I could still hear my voice reading the first verse: "Repent! 'tis the voice of Jesus Now sounding in your ear; The message of God rings loud and clear, Now seek Him, for He is near." I tried to think of other things, but it just kept getting louder. I snatched the book and opened to that song. That song was calling me to finish reading the rest of the words.

Verse 2 said: "Repent! while the Lord invites you; Before the Savior fall; The wages of sin is death to all Who heed not the Gospel call."

Verse 3 said: "Repent! while the Holy Spirit Is striving with your soul; The burden of sin on Jesus roll, Surrender to His control."

Verse 4 said: "Repent! for the days are flying; The final hour draws nigh; No pleasure have I, saith God on high, In seeing the wicked die."

Verse 5 said: "Repent! for He made atonement; He took

the sinner's place; O turn to the Lord, and seek His face, And trust in His saving grace."

Those words seemed so strange, and they confused me; but in the first verse it said, "The message of God rings loud and clear." Why did I not understand? It was not clear to me at all. Somewhat disappointed, I turned the pages and read more titles to other songs, "At the Cross" and "Jesus is Calling." There were so many songs talking about grace, love, God and this Jesus person. As I turned more pages, I came across Number 154, "Jesus Loves Me." How could the writer of that song say that? Verse 1 read: "Jesus loves me! This I know, For the Bible tells me so; Little ones to Him belong, They are weak but He is strong." There were more words that I did not understand, "For the Bible tells me so." What is the Bible the writer talked about? Maybe it would help me understand what the writers of those songs were talking about. I closed the book and put it in my knapsack; then I found myself pulling it out again and opening it up to the first song, "Repent!" I read the words of the song one more time and then quickly closed the book and put it in the knapsack. I sat at my desk questioning myself as to why I read that song again. I did not understand it the first, the second or even the last time. I couldn't understand what kept drawing me back to that song.

I reached into the pile of stuff and pulled out those old black and white pictures of the Sunday school classes from the 50's, 60's and 70's. I was hoping to see someone familiar, but none of the faces looked like anyone I knew. I was hoping to see the resemblance of my father's face in one of the pictures. I was hoping to see my grandparents so I would know more about them besides their names. It would be nice to put a face with their names. I slipped the pictures back into my knapsack and pulled out the yellowed envelope with clue number 2. It was so old that I carefully opened it up. I tried not to tear the paper that was inside.

Once again there was nothing written on the outside of the envelope. I pulled out the paper inside and found there were two pieces of paper folded separately. The one piece of paper had small holes in it and groups of letters scattered across the page. The other had just writing.

As I unfolded the paper with the writing, it started to tear where it had been folded. The paper was so old and dry; I had to slow down and be more careful. When the last section was unfolded, I carefully smoothed the sheet out so it would lay flat. That way I could read what it had to say. The clue read like this: "Congratulations Son! You have found clue number 2. I was hoping that you would remember the good times we had ringing the bells on Sunday mornings to start the worship service. I remember the time when you were so small that when I would pull on the rope, the weight of the bell would lift you off the floor, and you would laugh and laugh. Your mother and I hope for those kinds of days again.

Continue on with this clue. Take the Bible your mother and I gave you on your 12th birthday and turn to page 1010. Place the second sheet of paper that was in the envelope on that page. Be careful to make sure the corners line up or the message will mean nothing. Each hole in the paper will reveal a letter or number to match up with the letter already on the paper. This will take you to the next clue. Each clue will get harder, but put your trust in God to lead you."

As I read the words that my grandfather had written, I could feel only sadness come over me. How could I finish the search without the Bible that my grandfather had written about? Who was to say if my father still had that Bible or if he burned it with all the other things in the attic? My grandfather said that each clue would get harder but that I should trust in God. I didn't even know this God. How could I put my trust in him? If I did want to put my trust in him, how would I do it? Would I just call out, "Hey God, are you out there?" Would he call back? I sure wish I had met my grand-father and grandmother. I would have asked them so many questions. I would never meet them without my father's Bible. It could be anywhere or in ashes.

Just then there was a crash in the attic. How could that be? No one was up there. I wondered what made that noise. If I could only find the key to the attic, I could see what fell up there. I wondered if father would have hid the key some where in the hallway. It would be worth a look. I hurried out to the hall and looked around wondering where they would hide a key. I would start at one end of the hall and work my way to the other end until I had searched everywhere or until I had found the key. I carefully ran my hands across the molding around my door. There was nothing there but some dust and hard, dry bugs. I worked my way over to the picture of the old mill. I felt around the frame, nothing. I ever so slowly lifted the wire off the nail that held the picture on the wall. To my surprise, tucked in the corner of the frame was a skeleton key. I grabbed the key, held it out in front of me and just looked at it. I thought that the key could open not just the attic door but a whole lot more.

I hung the picture back on the wall and went down the hall to the attic door. Then I stopped and ran back to make sure the picture was straight. My mother would notice if it was hanging crooked. Now with the picture hung straight, I ran down the hall to try the key in the lock. I listened as I slipped the key in the hole. I heard each piece of the lock working to pull the bolt back to let me into the attic. I took a deep breath, grasped the doorknob and gave it a twist. It worked, the key worked! I pulled the key out of the keyhole and put it into my pocket.

I quickly climbed to the top of the steps. There I found two boxes had fallen on the floor. They must have been sitting on the old rocking chair. But why, after all this time, did they fall? I went over to the boxes to see what was in them that would make such a loud crash. I opened the first box. In it there was some old, handmade, wooden toy trains. You should have seen them all! There must have been a dozen of them. There were the engine, boxcars, flat bed, coal car and the caboose. Why would they keep these up in the attic? I would have liked to play with these when I was little. Wait! I would like to have it in my room. It would be so nice on the shelf. But if mother and father would see them in my room, they would just about die, and then they would ask a hundred questions. I'd just have to put it back in the box and wait for another time. What was in the other box, more trains? Oh man, it was heavy! It was certainly not more toy trains. I set the box right side up and pulled back the flaps. They were books. I was always told that the state had taken all the books and burned them. My father must have hid these for some reason. Maybe the titles of these books would give me a clue as to why my father would want to keep them. There were two books titled <u>Boy Scouts of America Handbook</u> and <u>Tom Sawyer</u> by Mark Twain. Then there was this old, dusty book. The cover was half torn off. I couldn't even read the title because there was so much dust on the cover. I would have to look inside. When my eyes came across the words on the page, I froze. My hands began to shake. I couldn't even say it out loud. I had to whisper it. It was a Holy Bible; but was it the one that my father was given at the age of 12? I flipped the page, and there on the top of the page it read, "This Bible is presented to Russell F. Wilson. Happy 12th Birthday, Son. Love, Mother and Father." It was the book that the clue talked about. I'd take it with me. I hurriedly put the rest of the books back and closed up the boxes. Then I put things back in order. I had to get the attic door locked and the key back behind the picture of the old mill before mother and father came home. I went down the stairs locking the attic door behind me. With the Holy Bible under my arm, I walked toward the picture on the wall of the old mill. I lifted the picture off the nail and placed the key back into its hiding place.

Now with the Holy Bible in my possession, I would be able to place the paper on the page that my grandfather told me about. That would get me to the next clue. I sat at my desk and carefully laid the yellowed and brittle paper next to the Holy Bible. I opened up the Bible and looked for page 1010. There were so many pages. As I flipped through the pages, I got a few glimpses of words. I stopped flipping pages and read Psalm 5. "Give ear to my words, O Lord, consider my sighing. Listen to my cry for help, my King and my God, for to you I pray. In the morning, O Lord, you hear my voice; in the morning I lay my requests before you and wait in expectation. You are not a God who takes pleasure in evil; with you the wicked cannot dwell. The arrogant cannot stand in your presence; you hate all who do wrong. You destroy those who tell lies; bloodthirsty and deceitful men the Lord abhors. But I, by your great mercy, will come into your house; in reverence will I bow down toward your holy temple. Lead me, O Lord, in your righteousness because of my enemies-make straight your way before me." Those words were how I felt. I felt alone in my search for clues. I needed help. Grandfather talked about trusting in this God. He trusted in this God, and he was a very wise man. I saw my grandfather's wisdom with each clue. In each message that he wrote, he told of his love for my father and how he trusted that the Lord would bring my father back to him. Did I dare reach out to this God to help me in my search for my grandparents?

I had to continue on to page 1010 to get directions to the next clue. I was getting excited about figuring out the message with the missing letters or numbers. Oooops! I went too far. I had to turn back. When I got to page 1010, I told myself that I had to line up the marks on the paper to the same marks on the page. It was not working. Why wasn't it working? I was too high on the page. I had to line up the big letter P on top of the P on the left corner of the page and the page 1010 on top of the page number in the book. It worked; I did it! Then I had to write it down on another piece of paper so I didn't have to keep matching it up each time I needed to look at the clue. I took pen and paper from my desk and carefully wrote the clue down: "Go into the church basement and enter the number two fuel tank. Follow the tunnel until you get to the fork. Take the right tunnel to the end. There another clue will be in a box."

I had to go back to the church, but that is where I came the closest to getting caught by the state police. The clue said there was a tunnel, but I had to enter the number two fuel tank. I do remember it did have a strange sound when Kyle threw that coffee cup at it. When would I find the time to get back to the church? Mother and father would not have all day meetings whenever I needed to look for a clue. I couldn't always go to the information center and sneak out the back door. Sooner or later somebody would see me either coming or going.

I sat at my desk staring out the window when a thought came to me. What if I would cry out to the God that my grandfather and the Bible talked about? Would he help me find the time to look for the next clue? It said, "I should lay my request before the Lord and wait in expectation." Could this God of grandfather's make it so that I would have the time to continue my search? It would be worth a try; there was nothing to lose. What would I say? What if I didn't say it right? Then what would this God do to me? I sat there pondering what to say to this God that I didn't know anything about. I was just looking out the window up in the sky when I heard a car coming down the road. It was my mother and father coming back from their meeting. I had to pick up all the things I got at the church and hide them so they would not know what I had been doing all day. I put the coffee cup, songbooks, envelope and my father's Holy Bible in my knapsack. Then I remembered that I had not made my request to my grandfather's God. I stopped for a few seconds and said, "Okay God, I don't really know if you're out there or here or where you hang out. I don't have much time to figure out the right words to say, so I'm just going to say it. I need all the help you can or will give me in helping me find the clue so I can find my grandmother and grandfather. I know you probably are wondering who I am. I'm Mark Wilson, and you know my grandfather and grandmother. They are William R. and Frieda R. Wilson. In the clues I have read they talk about you all the time. My grandfather told me in one clue to trust in you." My father's car door slammed shut, and I could hear the click of my mother's high heels on the driveway. "Okay God, I have got to go now. My mother and father are coming. I'll wait for your answer." I put the knapsack under my bed to hide it. "Wait a minute, God. How am I going to know if you answered me or not?"

"Mark, are you home? Mark, are you upstairs?" It was my mother yelling at me again, but this time she didn't sound mad.

"Mark, if you're up there, answer your mother!" Yep, that was my father, always coming in at the last minute to get his two points in.

I yelled back down to them, "Yes, I'm up here. I'll be down in just a few seconds. I want to hear all about your meeting." If they only knew why I wanted to hear all about the working of the state police, they would just die. The more I understood the police, the better I could stay ahead of them when searching for clues.

When I came out of my room and got to the head of the stairs, there were mother and father waiting for me. My heart sank down into my stomach. I was in trouble now. Their eyes were all big. Wait a minute! They were smiling, and that could be really bad or really good. I couldn't tell. "Hello, Mother and Father. Did you have a good meeting?"

Mother seemed the happiest because she blurted out, "Yes! I'm so proud of your father and what he did. Tell him Russell. Go ahead and tell Mark what you did."

The strangest thing happened then. My father's mouth opened and I saw his lips moving, but my mother's voice was all I heard. "Well, let me tell you, Mark, what your father did. He volunteered to start a citywide watch group to report any strange things happening in the city. Go ahead, Russell, tell Mark what that little, old lady reported just today."

"The little, old lady said that . . ." Mother cut father off because he was taking too long, I guess.

"She said that she saw lights on in the old, abandoned church. That is when your father volunteered to start the citywide watch. Isn't that great, Mark?"

"Yes, Mother, that is a great idea." That would only make it harder for me to get around town to look for clues with a thousand or more eyes watching everything I was doing. "How soon will this citywide watch dog thing start?" I asked, hoping to have some time to get my search done before it started.

"Mark, it is not a citywide watch dog thing, but you know, that would be a great operational nickname for this project," my father said as he stood next to my mother beaming as if he thought of it himself.

"But father, when will the citywide watch dog project start?"

"It will take some time to get volunteers trained. We volunteered to go first, but another couple was chosen to go instead for a week of training in the capital city. Then that couple will train the rest of the volunteers here in our town. Other than that good news, nothing much happened." Father turned and walked to the computer to see if there were any e-mails while they were gone.

"Mother, whatever happened with the report of lights in the church that the little, old lady saw?" I asked hoping to get a clue as to if the police knew it was me.

Mother said, "They found nothing, but they did see someone riding away. If your father would have been there, he would have caught that person."

"I'm glad you and father had a good time at the meeting, Mother. I'm going up to my room until supper is ready."

I was upset when I went to my room. I trusted in my grandfather's God, and I made my request to him. I wondered more and more about this God with each step I took up to my room. Did he not hear me, or did I not say the right words? With the state police starting the citywide watch soon, I would have to move faster. It was too bad mother and father couldn't have gone on that one-week training to the capital city. That would have given me plenty of time to search for clues.

"God, if you could have worked it out so mother and father would have gone to the training, that would have been the kind of help I needed. Now I've got a thousand more pairs of eyes watching my every move. To top it off, I gave father a nickname for the project."

Just then I heard father yelling for my mother. I had not heard him yell like that for a long time (at least not since I had broken the front window of the car with a rock). I ran downstairs into the study where I saw my father on the computer. Mother was entering the study from the kitchen. Father looked to my mother and exclaimed, "They can't make it!"

"Who can't make what?" mother questioned father.

"The other couple can't go next week to the training for the watch group, and the state police are asking us if we can get things in order to leave first thing next week." Father jumped up and hugged mother. It took me by surprise, and it must have surprised mother, too, because she dropped the wooden mixing spoon on the floor.

Mother asked, "When does the state need to know for sure whether or not we can get things arranged?"

Father replied, "It is as good as done. I have four weeks of vacation coming."

"Oh dear! Russell, what will we do with Mark?"

"Mother, I'm 16, almost 17. You're not going to get me a babysitter, are you? Just go and have a good time. I'll be just fine."

"Are you sure, Mark?" mother asked with worry in her voice.

I assured her, "Yes, I'll be fine."

Mother faced father and said, "Great! E-mail back to the state that we will be ready to go as requested."

The word requested just bounced around in my head as I slipped out of the study and went back up to my room. I made a request to my grandfather's God that my parents would go on the weeklong training to the capital. Now, somehow, the other couple couldn't make it. I didn't know what to think now. Was my grandfather's God listening to my request, or was it merely coincidental? If it were God and he helped me with getting my mother and father out of the way for a week, maybe he could help me in other ways. This God could make it so the state police would not ever catch me.

I decided I'd better get to work on my report for Mrs. Carlstrom. Maybe by handing it in early I could get on her good side, if she had a good side. What did I do with the printout sheets from the information center? Oh, I found them. They had fallen on the floor under my desk. When I bent over to pick them up, I saw a pair of feet behind me. It took me by surprise, and I stood up to see if it was mother or father. (It was so hard to tell when they were wearing their auxiliary police uniform.) When I stood up, I had forgotten to back away from the desk and banged my head on it. (As if I hadn't done enough damage to my head while at the church.) The person behind me came rushing to my aid. With one touch I knew it was mother.

"Mark, are you all right?"

"Yes, Mother, I just slightly bumped my head."

"Let me take a look at it, Mark."

"I'll be okay, Mother."

The next thing I knew mother had me in one of her motherly headlocks that was impossible to get out of without losing an ear, nose or some part of my body. "Mark, that is a pretty big bump on your head for just slightly bumping it." Mother was so worried about one bump on my head. She would die if she knew half the trouble and damage I did to my body today.

"Mother, I heal fast; before you know it, it will be gone just like that." I tried to snap my fingers but, of course, they failed to snap. She gave me the look, the "are you sure" look. "Really, Mother, I will be fine. Is supper ready yet?"

"No, Mark, supper is not ready yet. I have only been here a few minutes. I am not a magician. I don't just snap my fingers and the food appears. I will call you when it is ready." Mother turned to leave my room snapping her fingers. It was bad enough that she got her fingers to snap on cue with her "I'm not a magician" statement; but she also had this little smirk on her face as she entered the hallway.

I'd better get to work on my report. I looked at my printout from the information center and saw that if I rewrote the information and added a few comments of my own, I would have plenty of stuff for a report.

SNAP! SNAP! I jerked my head around so fast to see what was going on I could hear my neck crack. It was my mother again. "By the way, Mark, I would like you to clean up your room."

I must have been working on my report for a long time

because mother was at the bottom of the stairs yelling up to me. "Mark, wash your hands because supper is ready!" Why did she tell me to wash my hands? I was 16 years old. I would think I got that part of the daily routine down after all these years. The sad thing is she still checked to see if I washed both sides. Next thing you know she would be telling me not to forget to use soap.

"Mark, and don't forget to use soap."

What did I tell you? Do I know my mother or what? That week that they would be gone on their training would be a dream come true. I would be able to work on finding more clues, and I could eat whenever or whatever I wanted.

CHAPTER 8

Freedom At Last

I did not think that this day would ever get here. It seemed as if the days dragged on and on. Finally it was packing day. Mother and father were packing their suitcases to go for a week to the capital city for their training, and I would be free. With school's first quarter over and two weeks off before the start of the second quarter, I'd be free to do and go anywhere.

Waiting for this week was not a total waste. I did get to read some of my father's Holy Bible. It was so different to read a book where you actually turned the pages by hand and not just click your mouse on the computer. Yet, it was neat. Just think, back in the olden days everybody had books; and now they were rare and only two were kept under glass at the information center. I had three books of my own! I wondered how many other people had books hidden away up in their attic like my mother and father did. How many had a Bible? I found myself drawn to the book. I remembered it was just a few days before when I opened my father's Bible for the first time. I had never read a book before, so I did not know where to start. I figured I'd start at the beginning. There was a table of contents page. The first section was labeled: "The Books of the Old Testament." The next section was labeled: "The Books of the New Testament." There were so many books with strange words, and some had people's names like Ruth, Daniel, Luke and John. I turned to page one and there in big, bold print was the book titled Genesis. I had never seen that word before, so I looked it up on my computer dictionary. One definition was "creation of the universe." In school the teacher in the science lab told us a different story than what I read in the first few pages of Genesis. This God created everything in just six days and not over thousands and thousands of years of evolution as the teacher had said. The teacher said the world started with a big bang and then formed from sea slime into complex humans. I never did really believe the teacher's version of creation. There was so much that was left up to chance. I liked the Bible's version better. This God created things in an orderly manner, and he did not make any mistakes. The Bible said God created something, and God said that it was good.

Mother and father had been so busy packing I had hardly seen or talked to them. I saw mother flash past my bedroom with her arms full of things to pack. You would think they were going for a month instead of just one week. In less than 24 hours mother and father would be on their way to training, and I would continue the search for my grandmother and grandfather. I would find them and have all my questions answered.

The hours slipped by faster and faster. It was 6:30 p.m., and mother had not started supper yet. Just then the doorbell rang. From down the hallway my mother yelled, "Mark, could you get the door? It should be the pizza. Your father has scanned his number into the pizza company so it is paid for already."

"Okay, Mother!" Wow! Mother and father must be in a

great mood. Pizza! They had not ordered out pizza since my 14th birthday. Father always said it was highway robbery what they charged for a pizza nowadays.

I ran down the steps to the door. I caught a glimpse of father carrying things from the bathroom medicine cabinet to their room where mother was packing. Father just looked at me and smiled as I made my way to the front door. I could see the silhouette of the pizza man. For a few seconds my mind flashed back to the church and the time when the state police came crashing into it looking for me. When I reached the front door, I had come back from my flashback of a few days before. I took hold of the doorknob and flung the door open to get the pizza. I could not believe my eyes. The pizza man had the lid open on the pizza box and was looking inside. I frightened him so much that he slammed the lid shut and almost dropped the pizza on the ground. As our eyes met, this time he frightened me. It was he, the lieutenant from the state police that was trying to rip the doors off the hinges. I froze in place just as I did a few days back when I looked out the window of the church to see a man all dressed in black. "Hey kid, do you want this pizza or not?" asked the lieutenant.

"Yes, I sure do." I took the pizza and hurried back into the house. I peered out the window to watch the lieutenant, or should I say pizza man, head back to his car. Before he got in, he turned and looked back at the house. He pulled out a small tablet of paper from his back pocket and wrote in it. Then he stopped all of a sudden. He looked at the window where I was peering around the curtain, and he pointed his finger at me as if to say, I know it was you, and I'll be watching you.

"What are you doing, Mark?"

"Mother, don't do that. You scared me."

"What were you looking at?"

"The pizza man, he was writing something in a little

tablet and . . ."

"Where? I don't see anyone," answered mother.

I quickly dove back to the window and pulled back the curtain but he was gone. "The lieutenant is gone."

"Who?" mother inquired.

"I mean, the pizza man is gone."

"I think you must be hungry. You are starting to sound stranger than usual. Mark, call your father and let's eat."

I went to the foot of the steps and yelled, "Father, the pizza is here. Come and eat." I turned around to walk toward the kitchen table, and there was mother with her hands on her hips staring at me.

"What?" I asked.

"I could have done that. I wanted you to go up and tell your father it was time to eat. Now go tell your father it is time to eat, and don't forget to wash your hands."

I spun around toward the stairs. Father was at the top looking down at me. I never really noticed what a big man my father was. I wondered if he got his big size from his father. Would I look like my father someday? Would my children see my father in me? I must have been staring because father said, "Mark! Hello . . . earth to Mark. What are you staring at?"

I snapped out of it and said, "Nothing, Father!"

Father kept prodding, "It sure looked like you were staring at something."

"I was just . . ."

"You were just what?"

"I was just . . . um . . . thinking. Do you look like your father?" My father's eyes grew as large as basketballs and his mouth dropped open. I could not believe I said that. My eyes grew larger and my mouth dropped open too. I quickly tried to cover up my mistake. "No, what I meant was, do I look like you, Father?"

"Why . . . of course you look like me," he said as he

passed me heading to the kitchen to eat. I stood at the bottom of the stairs still in shock that I had asked my father if he looked like his father. "Mark, are you coming? The pizza is getting cold," father yelled with a mouthful of pizza.

I ran to the kitchen but slowed to a walk as I entered the doorway. It was very quiet during supper that night. The only sounds you could hear were the three of us licking our fingers, and the rustling of napkins as we wiped the pizza sauce off our faces. The silence was broken when father said, "Mark."

"What, Father."

I must have said it with fear in my voice because father said, "Mark, take it easy. All I wanted to ask you was if you wanted to split the last piece of pizza with me."

I was so relieved that there were not any questions about what I had said earlier at the bottom of the steps. I was also glad mother didn't ask me any more questions about what I was staring at earlier. I said to father, "Sure, I'll split the last piece with you."

Father grabbed a knife and cut the piece in half. I raised my plate so it was ready to receive my half of the pizza. All was going well until father said, "Yes, Mark, if you keep eating like this, you could grow up to be big and strong like me." I fumbled my plate because of the shock of his statement. I recovered my composure but not until after I had knocked over the salt and pepper shakers.

"It looks like you have to work on your coordination, though, Mark," father replied with a hint of laughter in his voice.

All I could do was agree and say, "I will start working on that tomorrow."

I finished my pizza and asked mother and father if I could be excused from the table to go to my room to play computer games. Mother answered, "Sure, that would be fine. Your father and I still have some packing to do, so we will see you in the morning before we go."

"Okay, good night. I'll see you in the morning." I left mother and father sitting in the kitchen. Once I was out of sight, I stopped just around the corner to see if father was going to talk to mother about when I asked him if he looked like his father.

"Russell," Mother said, "Do you think Mark has been acting strange lately?"

"Ramona, Mark is a teenager. All teenagers act strange."

"I suppose our mothers and fathers thought we acted strange, too."

"Oh yes, Ramona, my mother and father at times did not know what to think about the strange things I would say or do. I remember the time when I told my father that I . . ."

Oh no, the computer in the study was beeping. Someone must be e-mailing something to our house. Father stopped his story, and I could hear his footsteps coming toward me. I had nowhere to run or hide. I darted for the stairway, and then turned around as if I was coming down the stairs to get the e-mail. I had spun around in time to see my father coming through the kitchen door.

"Mark," father said, "I'll get the e-mail. Most likely it is for your mother and me about our trip to the capital city."

"Okay, Father. Good night."

"Good night, Mark."

I went up the stairs to my room, this time for real. I fooled my father into thinking I was coming downstairs for the e-mail. It was too bad I could not hear him finish the story he started to tell my mother. It may have given me more clues and insight into who my grandparents were.

Father called for mother to come and see what was being e-mailed. He seemed happy about the news. By the time I reached the top of the stairs, mother and father were hugging each other. Mother said with tears in her eyes, "I can't believe we are going to meet with the governor at his office tomorrow afternoon. It is all because you had the idea to start the citywide watch dog project."

Father replied, "I will e-mail his office to confirm the exact time and location of the meeting." Mother and father thought that this next week would be exciting for them. If they only knew what I had planned for that week since we had no school.

Early the next morning I heard all kinds of noise. Mother and father were running up and down the stairs and doors were slamming. I looked out the window, and the sun was just barely starting to peek over the hillside. My clock on the nightstand said 6:30. Mother and father must have been planning to leave early in order to get to the capital city. All I could think about was trying to get more sleep; but with all the commotion, I could see that getting more sleep was out of the question. I sat up in bed and turned on the nightstand light. I rubbed the sleep out of my eyes. I could hear mother coming down the hall humming some tune I had never heard before. Then again, I don't remember ever hearing my mother hum anything.

"Good morning, Mark!" Mother surprised me, and I almost poked my eye out when I was rubbing the sleep out of it.

"Good morning, Mother. You and father are up early. How soon before you take off to the capital city?"

"Your father still has to put a few things in the car, and I'm going down to the kitchen now to fix breakfast. Your father would like to be on the road by 8 o'clock. Mark, would you like to have breakfast with us before we leave?"

"Sure; I think that would be nice. What are we having?"

Mother pondered a few seconds and then answered, "I think we'll have pancakes, sausage and some juice. How does that sound?"

"That sounds good. I'll be down in just a few minutes." Mother must have been in a really good mood. She had not made pancakes for a long time.

I got dressed, but I couldn't find my shoes. I looked everywhere, but I couldn't find them. Someday I should clean my room and then maybe I could find things. They had to be somewhere. I looked under the bed for the tenth time hoping that the shoes would have walked there after the ninth time. There, at the end of the bed, was a pair of father's shoes. What were they doing there? I crawled under the bed and swam past all the junk to get to my father's pair of shoes. My shirt got stuck on a bedspring as I was crawling under the bed. I could not move so I had to back up and unhook myself.

Once I was unhooked, I turned back to get the shoes but they were gone. I laid there amongst all the stuff trying to figure out what happened. A light pierced the darkness and my father's voice said to me, "Mark, what are you looking for?"

"I'm looking for my black shoes, but I can't find them."

"That is because you probably left them in your closet with the rest of your dirty clothes."

"Thanks, Father."

I swam out from under the bed and stood up in front of my father. He had this look on his face. First it was a look that said, "Is this really my son?" Then he got a smile that turned into a quiet chuckle.

"What are you chuckling at?"

Then my father started to laugh loudly. He grabbed me by the shoulders and walked me to the mirror. When my eyes caught sight of what my father had seen, I started to laugh too. I had swept the underside of my bed with my body, and there were clumps of dust hanging from every part of it. The one that made us laugh the hardest was the one dust ball hanging from my ear. It looked as if I had taken one of mother's earrings and put it on. Father and I must have made quite a ruckus because mother was soon standing in the doorway to my room.

"All right, what's so funny?" mother questioned. It surprised father and me so much that we were speechless. When mother saw all the dust balls hanging from my body, she started to laugh. That got father and me laughing again. Father then pointed out the one hanging from my ear. Mother laughed even harder. She laughed so hard she had to sit down on my bed and wipe tears from her eyes. After a few moments we all settled down and Mother said, "Let's go eat breakfast."

Father and I both said, "Okay."

Then out of the blue mother said, "By the way, Mark, do you think someday I could borrow that lovely earring of yours?"

Father and I were so stunned by my mother's question that, for just a moment, we looked at each other. Then the laughter burst forth again, and we laughed all the way to the kitchen. Mother, of course, picked most of the dust balls off as we walked down the stairs. There had not been that much laughter in the house for a long, long time.

The breakfast time went fast, and before I knew it, it was 8:15. Mother and father rushed off to their week in the capital. I stood on the sidewalk next to the driveway and waved goodbye.

Mother called out, "Be good, and we will see you in one week!"

My father saluted me and then pulled his right ear and smiled real big. He put the car in gear and began to back down the driveway. I watched the car drive down Old Mill Road toward town until I could not see the taillights anymore.

Out of the corner of my eye, I saw a black car pull out of the woods and drive by slowly. I looked to see who was in the car, but the windows were tinted blue. I went back in the house keeping one eye on the mysterious, black car and one eye on where I was walking. When I reached the front door, I quickly walked in and ran to a side window to see if the car would turn around. The driver went past a few houses down the road and then stopped. I watched for what seemed like an eternity. Then the back up lights came on. I jumped back from the window so they would not see me watching them watch me. I peered around the curtain just in time to see the car race past the house. They must have received a call to do some "real police work" instead of watching some kid who was home alone.

I went to the kitchen to wash the breakfast dishes. Then I packed a lunch so I would be able to search most of the day without having to return home. As I washed the dishes, I planned a couple of different routes I would take to get to the church. I also planned a couple of different routes to escape if the state police would get a tip that someone was in the church. I had to avoid that little, old lady that tipped off the state police the first time I was at the church. I had thought so hard about the routes in and out of town, I was finished washing dishes in a very short time.

I opened the refrigerator to see what I was going to pack for lunch. Mother didn't want me to go hungry. There was enough food in the refrigerator to feed a small army and me. There were fruits, luncheon meats, bread, cheese and a big bowl of my favorite noodle salad. She even got me the individual juice bottles. I thought that maybe they should go away more often. I never got so many of my favorite foods in one week. I reached in the refrigerator to grab a juice bottle. That is when I saw the note. It was from mother. It said: "Dear Mark,

I know this is your favorite juice. Try not to drink them all in one day. There is enough for one a day. Don't sit in the house all week and do nothing. Get out and enjoy the nice, fall weather.

Love, Mother"

If she only knew what I had planned, I think she would rather I stayed at home. I had to pack my knapsack with a lot of stuff. I had to be careful not to bring anything that would help the state police find my grandmother and grandfather. I also had to make sure that I did not bring anything that would get me thrown in jail. I was glad I memorized the last clue just in case there was trouble and I ran into the state police. I would have to double-check the clue one more time so I didn't make a mistake. It said: "Go into the church basement and enter the number 2 fuel tank. Follow the tunnel until you get to the fork. Take the . . . Take the right . . . No, the left tunnel." Was it the right or the left tunnel? It would be best if I looked at the clue one more time, or I could be lost under the city in a maze of tunnels and never find my way out. I looked at my notes. I was right the first time. "Take the right tunnel and go to the end. There another clue will be in a box."

My knapsack was packed and I had enough food for the day. The time was 9:40, and if the day went well, I would be home in time for supper. I went to the living room and peeked out the slit in the curtain to see if that car that was cruising by was back or if the coast was clear. I carefully looked up and down the road making sure they were not parked off the road hiding behind some trees. I thought I would not rush anything and make sure I was in the clear before making any moves. This would be like a chess game. I would be the white knight in search of the white king and queen, who were my grandparents. The state police would be the black opponent. The governor was the black king, and my mother and father were just two of his many pawns. As the white knight, I would have to be as wise as an owl, as cunning as a fox and as swift as a deer.

I checked out the back door to make sure there were none of the black king's pawns watching me. I slowly pressed my face up to the screen and surveyed the tree line and looked over at the garage. All was clear. I slung my knapsack over my shoulder and headed for the garage to get my bike. I would start out with route number one until I felt it was getting too dangerous or if someone started to follow me. Then I would switch to one of my three other routes.

I rode down the driveway and then turned back to look at my house. I got this strange feeling in my stomach. As I turned out onto the road, I tried to shake that strange feeling by telling myself that I would be back in time for supper. I hoped.

I rode down Old Mill Road and passed by the Zabling pig farm. I hoped their dog wouldn't come out and chase me. When I got closer to the farm, I could see that someone was walking out of the flower garden by the road. It was Mrs. Zabling. She was a nice lady. It wouldn't hurt to stop and talk so I would have an alibi.

"Hello, Mrs. Zabling. How are you this morning?" I stopped and a cloud of dust that I had just stirred up passed between us.

Mrs. Zabling was spitting and sputtering and fanning the dust away. "Well, I'm doing just fine, Mark. That is very nice of you to ask."

"How is Mr. Zabling doing?"

"Well, Mark, between you and me, I think he moves a little slower each day. He is not a young man like you anymore."

"Did he ever tell you the story about when he let me ride on the back of Big Bertha, the biggest pig on your farm? All was going well until Big Bertha saw a hole in the fence and started to run straight for the opening. Mr. Zabling saw what was about to happen and yelled for me to jump off. I was so afraid that I just froze. The fence was getting closer. The next thing I knew Mr. Zabling was running across the pen. He dove and knocked me off the back of Big Bertha just in the nick of time before she crashed through the fence and fell ten feet into the empty manure pit and died. I thought Mr. Zabling was going to be mad, but he just started to laugh. Then I started to laugh as we both were covered with mud and manure from head to toe. Mr. Zabling said that he guessed it was time for Big Bertha to go to market."

"No, Mark, he never told me that story." Mrs. Zabling had a puzzled look on her face. "Mark, you have a nice day. I have to go in and take a look at my bread to see if it is ready for the oven."

"Say hello to Mr. Zabling for me."

"I will do that, Mark."

"Oh, Mrs. Zabling, what time is it?"

Mrs. Z reached into her dress pocket and pulled out an old pocket watch. The outside of the watch was tarnished, but when the cover opened up, the inside was still as shiny as if it was new. "The time is 10:05, Mark."

"Thank you, Mrs. Zabling."

When Mrs. Z turned to head back to the farmhouse, I pedaled on down the road. I wondered how much the Zablings knew about what happened to my grandparents. I came to the intersection of Old Mill Road and the County Highway. I stopped at the stop sign and scanned the area to see if anybody was around. I looked back down Old Mill Road, and there on the side of the road was a black car. Two people were walking out in the field where Mr. Z was picking his corn. They were waving their arms trying to get Mr. Z to stop the tractor. Didn't they know Mr. Z had bad eyes, and if they wanted him to stop, they would have to stand in front of him and not on the side? Otherwise he would not see them. Sure enough, Mr. Z drove right on by. When he turned around to make the next pass, he would see them. Yep, he did! A big, black puff of smoke shot into the air, and the tractor came to a stop. The cab door of the tractor opened, and the two people walking in the field started talking and pointing. That told me that it was time to get moving while they were talking to Mr. Z. I could make my getaway and lose them once I was in town.

I rode down through part of the old warehouse district area. I wanted to rest at the park, so I rode until I reached the front gate. I thought maybe Ernie would show up. It had been a while since I had last talked with him. I looked toward the statue of the child looking heavenward. If Ernie were around, it would be only a short while before he would show up. I could see a person sitting on the park bench next to the statue, but I could not tell who it was from where I was. I rode up and called out Ernie's name. The person didn't move. I got closer and called out Ernie's name one more time. I was almost positive it was Ernie. Still there was no response. I hopped off my bike and let it drop to the ground. I asked Ernie what was up and why he didn't answer me when I called to him. The head of the person on the park bench quickly rose up and our eyes met. It was not Ernie. It was a state police officer; the same one that delivered the pizza to our house.

"I'm watching you, Mark Wilson, and now I'll be watching your friend, Ernie, whoever he is."

The policeman walked away laughing. After taking a few steps, he spun around and gestured that he would be keeping an eye on me. He did that gesture several more times before he walked out the front gate of the park. I collapsed on the park bench with my eyes closed and my hands covering my face in disbelief of what had just happened. Now that Mr. Super Snoop policeman was watching me, did I dare make a trip to the church?

"Hello, my friend."

I peeled my hands off my face and opened my eyes to see Ernie sitting next to me. "Ernie, how long have you been sitting there?"

"Mark, quiet down. I have only been here a few seconds." I must have been talking loudly, but I was so surprised to see Ernie sitting next to me when the state police had just left.

"Ernie, a state policeman was just here, and he said he would be keeping an eye on me and my friend, Ernie."

"I know. I watched him leave."

"Maybe we should go someplace else?"

"No, Mark; we will be okay here."

"But Ernie, that policeman could come back, and I have so much to tell you. There have been a lot of things that have happened since the last time we talked."

"Tell me, Mark. What has happened since our last meeting?"

"Well, I haven't told anyone this, but I'm looking for my grandparents. I feel I can trust you with what I am about to tell you."

We talked for what seemed to be hours, but nothing I said really surprised Ernie. When I told him about finding my father's Bible, Ernie just smiled. He didn't talk much. I did most of the talking. Ernie would only say, "That was good" or "Be careful." He was a good friend. Not once did he say stop, or forget about looking for your grandparents, or stop looking for anymore clues.

I had one more question to ask Ernie, so I said, "Ernie, I have a question for you."

"What is that question, Mark?"

"Do you believe in this God that my father's Bible talks about and that my grandparents wrote about in their letters and clues? Or is it just a big story?"

Ernie didn't say anything. He just looked away for a moment. Then he said, "Mark, from what you have told me, it is not so important whether I believe in God but whether or not you believe."

"I don't know what to think about God."

Ernie replied, "It sounds like your search for clues will also include searching for answers to the question you asked me. Do you believe in this God of your father's Bible and that your grandparents gave up all that they had to find freedom from the state's persecution?"

"That is the other thing. What if, Ernie? I'm just saying, what if I do maybe believe? What do I do then? Do I tell my mother and father? Sure, my father let my grandparents go when he could have turned them in. This time he may not close his eyes. He could turn me into the police, and they could make me talk about where the others have run off to. My 17th birthday is coming up and I must decide whether to take the mark of the state. My grandparents refused the mark, but what do I do?"

"Mark, take your time and search for the answers to your questions. When the time comes, I know you will make the right decision." There was something in Ernie's voice that was so calming.

"When will I see you again, Ernie?"

"I'm not sure, but I plan on being around for a long time."

"I really had a nice time talking with you, Ernie, but I must go to the church and follow-up on the last clue I got."

I reached for my knapsack that was on the ground next to the park bench. I grabbed the handlebars of my bike and set it upright on its wheels. Then I turned to say goodbye to Ernie.

"Ernie?" Why was I not surprised he was gone again? I sure would like to know how he did that.

The time was 11:48. If I could get over to the church when most people would be eating lunch, then there would be fewer eyes looking out windows and doorways. I would have to be extra careful to avoid that little, old lady that called the state police last time.

CHAPTER 9

How Did I Get Into This?

When I looked at the church, I began to get excited about what I would find in the tunnel on the other side of the fuel tank. This time when I went into the church, I would take my bike with me. I would hide it under or behind the junk down the basement.

I was only one block away from the church's back door. I decided to ride down the left side of the alley. That way if there were people in the high-rise apartment buildings, it would be harder for them to see me. I would be straight down from them. They would naturally look out across the skyline and not down at a dirty, old alley. Once I was across from the back door of the church, I would dart across the alley and into the back door. That sounded like a great plan.

I pedaled my bike slowly and got as close to the buildings as possible only moving out to get around trash cans. Things were going as planned, so far, and I saw no one in any of the buildings on the right side of the alley. Oh no! They had put the back door of the church on and boarded it up. Now what was I going to do? I couldn't waste this day. I only had a week before mother and father came home. I'd tuck myself in-between the two big dumpsters and think of a new plan. There had to be another way in.

I squeezed my bike into the back behind the big apartment dumpsters. Just when I reached for my knapsack, I heard a large number of cars racing down the street in front of the church. I dashed to the back of my hiding spot and pressed myself into a corner. There were more cars that came speeding down the alley kicking up dust. I watched what was going on through a small space between the dumpsters. It was the state police dressed in their black uniforms. They exited the four squad cars, and the men spread out over the alley just like the pieces to a chess game when you dump them onto the game board before you line them up to start the game.

There was one more car coming down the alley. It must be the "black knight," Captain Anderson. His pawns were scrambling to get in line. The car slowed to a stop and one pawn rushed forward to receive orders from the "black knight." As Captain Anderson drove off down the alley, I got a good look at one of the pawns. It was the same policeman that I saw in the park that said he would be keeping an eye on me. Just seeing him again so soon frightened me. I jumped back away from the peephole and hit my head on the side of the dumpster. The officer heard the noise and started walking toward the dumpsters. I froze hoping that he would not see me. Just then two cats ran out from behind the dumpsters chasing each other. The policeman was so close I could almost read the nametag on his uniform. He turned around and yelled to the rest of the men to start the search.

"If there is someone in the area that does not belong here, I want them. Move out!" I closed my eyes and breathed a sigh of relief.

Then there was a crash and a bang. My eyes opened and my heart started to race. Somebody was trying to move the dumpsters. I grabbed both dumpsters next to me and held on with all my strength because if I were to be found, who knew what trouble I would be in. I was straining to hang on, and I could hear the officer straining to get them apart. He was frustrated that the dumpsters would not come apart, so he kicked them. Then he walked back to the rest of the search party.

My arms were throbbing from the strain of holding my hiding place together. I slumped to the ground and rubbed my arms hoping the pain would soon go away. Here I was sitting on the ground with no way to escape and the area crawling with police. I decided that now would be a good time to eat my lunch. With each bite of my lunch, I could hear the police smashing more of the things in the church. I looked now and then to make sure no one was searching the alley again. One of the times I peeked out I saw a chair flying out through the basement window of the furnace room. As the chair landed on the lawn, I realized that in the trashing of the church, they had made a better way for me to get in. The basement window was on a more hidden side of the church, so I could go in and out without being seen easily. The state police searched until 1:24. Then they got into their squad cars and cruised down the alley. With the search complete, they shouldn't come back.

I gathered my stuff together to make my move to the broken out basement window. I couldn't get my bike through the window, so I had to find a new hiding place for it. There was a big pile of trash that was thrown out the church windows during the search. I could bury it in amongst the trash. I looked up and down the alley to see if it was all clear. I ran alongside my bike, and when I reached the corner of the church, I rested only for a few seconds. I lifted up an old chalkboard and slid my bike under it. Then I piled a chair on top of the chalkboard. I kept low to the ground and carefully made my way to the basement window. There was broken glass from the window all around. Each time the police came to the church, they destroyed it more. Soon there would be nothing left of the old church. That was maybe what they were working towards. What was with this church and God thing that had the state so mad that they would do this? At one time it must have been a great looking building, but to look at it now, it would be hard to imagine the beauty it once had.

I found an old curtain on the ground next to the foundation and spread it over the window ledge so what glass was not broken out would not cut me or tear my clothes. That would be hard to explain to the police if they were to question me. Worse yet, what would I say to mother? "Oh, by the way mother, I tore my clothes to shreds while crawling into the basement window of a church the state had said was off limits to everyone."

I dropped my knapsack in through the window and it landed on a workbench right below. I carefully crawled through the window, first one leg and then the other. I searched for the workbench with my feet. Once I was sure I had firm footing, I lifted my upper body over the window ledge. While I was slipping into the basement, I looked around outside one more time. I couldn't be too careful. All was quiet.

There was still enough light that I did not have to use my flashlight. I didn't need to draw any more attention to myself while I was searching for clues. I walked carefully over to the number two fuel tank and ran my hands along the seams looking for a way in. I found nothing. I got a chair and looked on top to see if there was a hole cut in. Once again, nothing that looked like a way in. I tried to remember back when I had to squeeze in-between to hide from the police the first time I was in the church. It could be between the two tanks. I squeezed between them and worked my way alongside the tank feeling for any sign of an opening. I found nothing. Disappointment was setting in. What if? No,

I was not going to go into all the "what ifs." The clue told me there was a way into the fuel tank, and I would find it. I'd start from the front of the tank and systematically search.

When I turned to go back out to the front of the tank, my pant leg got caught on something, and I could not get free. My flashlight was in my knapsack, so that was not handy. I reached down and found a piece of metal sticking out from the end of the tank. I freed my pant leg and went to get my flashlight. As I worked my way out between the tanks, I thought about how that had to be the way in. Once again I squeezed between the tanks with flashlight in hand. I saw that the sides of the tanks were getting cleaner, and my clothes were getting dirtier with each pass in and out. I could see the metal piece that I got my pant leg caught on. This time I stepped over that piece and got around the corner to the back of the tank. I scanned my flashlight over the backside of the massive fuel tank. There, in the bottom corner, a piece of the steel had been cut away. The opening was not very big, but as skinny as I was, I should not have any problem getting into the fuel tank. I got down on my hands and knees, and with flashlight in hand, I poked my head in to see what was in store for me. I took a quick look around but couldn't see any tunnel entrance. Then again, I almost gave up looking for the entrance to the fuel tank. I pulled my head out and sat in the dirt thinking, do I go in and look closer? And if I do find the tunnel, then what? I had to find the tunnel entrance first; then I would worry about what to do next.

I grabbed my knapsack and flung it into the tank; then I crawled into the tank, trying not to get cut on the sharp edges. Once inside the tank, I could smell a slight hint of fuel oil, but otherwise the tank was mostly oil free. The tank was large enough that I could stand up without hitting my head. I wanted to find my knapsack. It shouldn't be too far from the entrance. While I felt around for my knapsack, I got preoccupied with some handwriting on the walls of the tank. Some of them were names, some were dates, but most of them were too hard to read. One marking was very clear. It was a large arrow pointing to what would be the front of the tank. With my flashlight trained on the wall, I walked to the front of the fuel tank. Then I saw a second arrow. That one had a 90-degree bend down. I walked over to where it was pointing so I could get a closer look. Would it be another hole in the wall to crawl into or would it . . .?

At that moment my question was answered. I found myself dropping down, bouncing off dirt and rock walls until I came to a sudden stop on something soft but lumpy. It was my knapsack. I must have flung it into the hole. As I sat there looking up, I decided I had dropped 10 to 12 feet down the shaft. I scanned my new surroundings to see what I had dropped in on and if there was a way out of there. The shaft was about four feet across, and there was no ladder or rope to climb out. There was only one way to go—like the clue said. "Follow the tunnel until you get to the fork. Take the right fork to the end. There another clue would be in a box." Maybe there would be a way out, too. I carefully stood up, checking to see if I hurt myself during the fall or the sudden stop at the bottom. Everything checked out okay. I took one more look up the shaft. Why, I don't know. Was I hoping a ladder would grow out of the side of that wall for a way out?

I turned and faced the tunnel entrance. The entrance was large enough for me to walk through without any problem. The walls looked as if hand and not a machine dug them. Large, rough cut timbers supported the walls and the roof of the tunnel. I walked down the tunnel making sure I didn't hit any beams. They did not look too stable. Cobwebs hung from the beams like long curtains reaching from the roof to the floor. From time to time I would see broken shovels and empty food cans. The people who dug this must have worked long hours, not even taking time to come up to the surface to eat. There had to be great dedication to achieve their goal, and if my grandfather's story was true, the state police provided plenty of pressure to get the tunnel done quickly.

When I looked ahead, I could see the tunnel was coming to a fork just as my clue said it would. When I approached the fork in the tunnel, I could see that the tunnel structure had changed into smooth cement walls and floors. I scanned down the right tunnel, then down the left and then back to the right. I could feel the excitement starting to build as I walked down the dark tunnel. I walked and walked. I could feel the tunnel getting colder and damper. I glanced at my watch and to my surprise, I had been walking for almost 1 hour and 28 minutes. I could hear the sound of running water coming through the walls. Then the tunnel would bend and the sound of water would fade away. As I listened to the fading sound of water, I tripped on something. It was a cement block. I walked a few steps more and tripped again. This time it was a clump of dirt. I shined my flashlight down the tunnel, and it shined on a huge pile of dirt. My heart sank as I looked over the pile of dirt from the floor to the roof, or what was left that had not caved in. A flood of questions rushed into my head. What do I do now since I could not reach the end of the tunnel to get the next clue? How would I get to the other side to find the next clue? How was I going to get out of the tunnel? Did the state cave the tunnel in on purpose, or was it a natural occurrence? Maybe I could climb to the top of the pile and dig to the other side. I climbed up the pile of dirt using my hands to pull myself to the top. I was getting nowhere because with each handful I would scoop away, more dirt would fill in its place.

I slid down the dirt pile and wondered how I was going to get out of the tunnel and up the shaft that I had dropped down into. I knew I had a long walk back to the shaft, so I found myself walking fast. Before I knew it, I came to the fork and entered the section of tunnel that was hand dug. I slowed my pace down so I would not hit any beams and start another cave in. I found myself at the beginning of the tunnel. I shined my flashlight up the shaft to see if I could find a way up. I scanned the walls and I could see where it looked as if there were hand and foot holds carved into each side of the wall. How was I going to reach the first set of holds without a ladder? I could go back and get some old beams and lean them up against the wall. Then I could climb up to get a start. I ran back and found a few beams. One was lying on the ground and the other was wedged under a crossbeam. It should be okay to move because there were three other beams holding that one up. I dragged the first beam through the tunnel back to the shaft. I could get a feel for what the people went through to make the tunnel. I went back for the second beam and hoped I was right about it not being that important in holding up the roof. I slowly twisted the beam. Dust and dirt began to fall so I stopped. I looked around to see if there were any other beams to use, but there were none. I had to use that beam. Otherwise I would not reach the start of the carved handholds to get up the shaft. I wrapped my arms around the beam and took a couple deep breaths. With one big jerk, I pulled the beam out. It fell to the floor, and a cloud of dust and dirt rose up. I grabbed one end and dragged it down the tunnel and placed it with the other beam.

I strapped on my knapsack. Carefully I climbed up the beam, hoping I would not fall and the beams would stay in place long enough to reach the first set of hand holds. After a few minutes of working my way up the beams, I found myself perched on the very top of them. I leaned over and grabbed onto the hand hold to my right. Then I reached with the left hand and grabbed onto that hand hold. Then came my right foot. As I was getting ready to bring my left foot up, I could feel the ground begin to shake. The two beams began to slide out from under my foot so I pushed off and hung onto the shaft wall. I could hear rocks, dirt and timbers falling down. The tunnel was caving in again. I could feel a rush of air coming up the shaft, and dust and dirt filled the air. It was making it hard to breathe and impossible to see. I had so much dirt in my eyes, but I could not wipe them. I had to blindly feel for each hand hold all the way up the shaft. I moved slowly. I could feel the muscles starting to ache in my arms. My legs were twitching uncontrollably up and down like a jackhammer. I could not tell how much further I had to go to reach the top with all the dirt in my eyes. I didn't know if I should wait for my legs to quit shaking or if I should continue on.

I decided to press on and reached the top with just a few more steps. I pulled myself onto the floor of the fuel tank and collapsed. My eyes had teared up enough to wash the dirt out, but my body ached so much I just laid there listening to the ground moan. I could tell the tunnel had caved in more because clouds of dust billowed up the shaft. I lay on the fuel tank floor and wondered what my next step should be. I didn't have the next clue and the tunnel kept caving in more. I stared up at the top of the fuel tank with my flashlight getting dimmer the longer I lay there. This put me back to square one. (Okay, maybe not that far back.) I felt my grandparents were alive because of the letters and clues. I found no death certificates in the city records. Wait a minute! That was it! If I could get back into the city computer and download the map of all the tunnels under the city, I could find another way in on the other side of the part that caved in. Once inside the tunnel again, I could find the next clue. That was what I would do, but I had to remember to move quickly because the city had a tracking security system on their computer network.

The new plan of action seemed to give me a burst of energy, and my muscles didn't ache as much. I sat up and gathered my stuff. There had to be more than one entrance. I tossed my knapsack out the back of the fuel tank and looked around one more time. I decided to put my mark on the wall as the others had done in the past. I used the back end of my flashlight and wrote, "I am the white knight." Then I squeezed through the hole and between the two fuel tanks. I slowly peeked out around the edge of the tanks to see if the coast was clear to come out. Once out in the light, I noticed I was dust and dirt from head to toe. I would have to clean some of the dirt off so I would not draw attention to myself when I rode home. I beat the dust off my pants and shirt with my hands; a cloud of dust formed around me. After several minutes of beating the dirt off my clothes, I decided I looked better than when I first crawled out. I didn't have to look at my watch to see that it was later in the day. The sun was setting. That was good because I would be able to ride home and not be that noticeable.

I walked over to the window that I crawled through to come into the church. I tossed my knapsack out the window first, and then I carefully inched my way out headfirst. I got half of my body out the window and I was just about to pull my legs up and out. Then I felt a pair of hands grab me by the arms, jerk me up and out of the window, and set me on my feet in a matter of seconds. I could not believe my eyes. There were two men dressed in black uniforms standing right there. I couldn't think of anything to do, so I tried to make a run for my bike. Before I could get close enough to my bike, they grabbed me and pushed me down to the ground. One officer put his big boot across the back of my neck so I could not get up and try to run again. The other officer laughed as he put handcuffs on me. As the officer tightened each handcuff around my wrist, you could hear the enjoyment in his laughter. Once I was handcuffed, they stood me up and grabbed my bike from where I had it hidden. The officers didn't say a word to me or to each other. They just grabbed me and dragged me toward their squad car. They didn't ask any questions, and I began to panic. Why weren't they asking any questions, or did they have the answers to why I was in the church? If they weren't going to ask questions, then I would ask them questions.

"Hey, what are you guys doing? Why am I handcuffed?" There was no answer. They just stared straight ahead. "Why don't you answer my questions, or don't you have any answers? Well? Why don't you answer me?"

One of the officers grabbed me, spun me around and slammed me up against the squad car. He got his face right in front of mine and said, "I'll be asking the questions, not you! I'll ask the questions when I'm ready to ask you and not before."

Then he opened the squad car door, pushed me into the back seat and slammed the door. As I lay in the seat struggling to get into a sitting position, fear overwhelmed me. I had so many questions. What did they know? What would they do? Would they call my mother and father? I could hear them putting my bike in the trunk. In between the clanging and banging, I tried to listen to what they were saying, but they were not talking loud enough. Both police officers walked alongside the car slowly and looked in. They gave me the strangest look. What that look meant I don't know, but it made me worry all the more. I didn't know what was going to happen.

The driver got in first and adjusted the rearview mirror so he could watch me. Once he had the mirror adjusted just right, he gave me a little smile. But it was not the kind of smile you would hope to see when you were handcuffed in the back seat of a police car. It was more like the smile a cat would have after eating a prize-winning parrot. The other officer . . . well . . . he did not look just once. Oh no, he looked once every block all the way to headquarters. It was the longest ten blocks of my life. The driver gave me one last evil eye look in the rearview mirror when we arrived at headquarters. Then he got out, rushed to the back door and flung it open. Meanwhile, the other officer slammed his hand several times hard against the cage that separated us. Then he spoke with a rough, gravelly voice. He had his teeth clinched together and growled, "Are you scared, boy?"

Before I could answer, the other officer said, "You better be!"

I felt a thump in my chest, and then a thump on my back. Was my heart beating that wildly with fear? Then a voice in my ear said, "What are you waiting for, boy?" I turned to see if the voice was just in my head or if someone was talking to me. When I turned my head, the face of the officer driving was only inches from my face, and he had that silly smile on his face.

I was about to answer his question when he pulled me out of the back seat. I wasn't even sure how he did it. He pulled me from the middle of the back seat away from the squad car without touching the car seat or sidewalk until my feet landed about three feet or so from the car. Then with each officer grabbing under my armpits, once again I was airborne. My legs were moving as if I was walking, but they were going nowhere. After a few steps I just left them dangling. I was hoping they would not suddenly drop me to the ground. The officers seemed to be having fun. They were smiling that silly smile and laughing as if they were crazy. I felt the grip under my armpits change as we approached the main doors of the headquarters, so I figured I was coming in for a landing. I started to walk in the air preparing to hopefully land on my feet and not my face. When both officers reached for different doors at the same time, I thought to myself that they didn't seem too bright. They flung open their doors and still hanging on to me, they each walked through their own door. The center post caught me on the side of the face very hard, just missing my nose. I would have broken my nose if I had hit the center post with that much force. Both officers laughed very loudly as they stepped back out their doors. I hoped the next time they would walk through the same door. To my surprise and horror, they rammed my face and body repeatedly into the post until I could feel blood running down my face. That seemed to make the officers even more determined to either get me in the door through the center post or kill me. I was getting weak from the repeated slamming into the post. The last time I remember hitting the post, I heard a loud popping sound. Then everything went black.

When I came to, I had a huge headache. I went to rub my head and noticed my world had changed. I was in a cell where it was cold, dark and damp. It smelled really bad, worse than the boys' locker room at school. I found myself lying in the middle of the cell floor. I struggled to sit up, but the pain was so tremendous that I decided to roll over and try to get up that way instead. I had a hard time seeing my hands. They had dirt from the tunnel and dried blood on them meaning that I had been in the cell for a while.

I stood up with the aid of the cell bars. My head began to pound even harder, and my vision was still blurry in one eye. I scanned the cell to see what I had gotten into, and I noticed a small mirror hanging on a nail over by the sink. Walking over to the mirror, I could feel that my ribs were either bruised or cracked, or some of each. I found it painful to breathe too deeply. When I got to the sink, I hung onto it to steady myself. With one hand I wiped the years of dirt off the mirror only to see a horrible face all dirty, bloody and bruised looking back at me. The worst part was that it was my face. The one eye had swollen shut except for a small slit. That would explain the blurry vision in that eye. My nose was bloody, my lips were both still bleeding, and I was missing a front tooth. I tried to see what other physical harm they had done to me with my one good eye. I could see that my right ear was red and beginning to swell. As I was moving around to get a better look, I saw another face in the mirror. It frightened me at first, and then I remembered whose face it was. It was one of the officers that brought me in. The fear went away and anger came rushing in.

Before I even turned around, the officer said in almost baby talk, "Oh, it looks like Markie fell down and go boom many times."

My anger increased even more, but I knew he was trying to make me mad so that I would say something that they could use against me. I slowly turned to the officer with my busted up face and said, "I must be careful and watch where I'm walking next time. Thank you for your concern." Then I smiled my best smile.

The officer was taken back by my response. The smile he had left, and his true color came out. Red! He got so mad even his ears turned a dark red. He grabbed the cell bars and pushed his face up close and growled, "Your days are numbered, kid. It will only be a matter of time." He slammed his fists against the bars and walked away.

I listened to the heels of his boots hit the cement floor as he walked out of the cellblock. I began to laugh a little, but it hurt too much. I headed over to the sink when I heard a muffled voice say, "I would not make him too mad if you want to make it out in one piece."

I froze in my tracks and raised my eyes slowly to look in the mirror to see who was behind me saying that. I could not see anyone. My shirtsleeve was half torn off. I figured I might as well finish the job and use it as a washrag to clean off some of the dirt and blood. I was thinking out loud to myself and said, "I thought for sure I heard a voice, but I must be hearing things. Maybe I hit my head harder than I thought."

"No, you're not hearing voices."

"There's that voice again. I knew I heard a voice." I spun

around and stumbled to the cell door. I looked up and down the hallway of the cellblock, but I didn't see anyone. "Okay, that's it. First I'm hearing things and then talking to myself. And I lost the argument besides. I need some rest, and maybe I'll clean up later."

I scuffled over to the bottom bunk and sat down. Immediately the covers flopped back and there was the face that went with the voice I was hearing. I stood up quickly, a little too quickly, because I hit my head on the top bunk. It knocked me to the floor once again. While I was lying on the floor looking up, I saw first one hand grab the edge of the bunk and then the second hand. I could hear some rustling, and then a head popped over the edge. The cell was dimly lit, but from what I could see, the man had been here for a long time. His hair was dirty, and it looked like it had not seen water in months, maybe even years. When he would breathe, there was an odor I had smelled before; but what was it?

"Hello, boy. My name is Jerome Stein. I have been here for a long time, and I know it does not pay to make the officer mad." When Jerome finished speaking, that unidentifiable smell was not the damp, musty smell I thought it was; it was his breath.

"Well, Mr. Stein, my name is Mark and I'm glad to see that the voice I heard was not in my head, but that it has a body to go with it."

"So, Mark, what are you in jail for?"

"I don't know. I was just hanging out riding my bike and those two, big apes called police officers decided to grab me and rough me up a little."

"Mark, they more than roughed you up a little. It appears as if they tap danced on your face. You had to have done something wrong."

"Let me ask you the same question. Why are you in jail, and how long have you been here?"

"Mark, you may not believe this. I have been here so long I don't remember what I did wrong."

"What? You've got to be telling me a story. You don't remember what you did wrong?"

"Let me refresh your memory, Mr. Stein," came another voice from behind. When I turned around, I saw that it was the other officer. "Mr. Stein here was caught trying to get a second account number from the state since he had used up his year allotment of credit in just four months."

"I had six kids to feed, and my wife was blind, so she didn't have an account number."

I turned to look at the police officer to ask him how they could let those kids go to bed every night hungry. The police officer must have read my mind because he said, "Boy, don't believe a word this man says. He is lying through his green teeth. He doesn't have six kids. He's not even married."

I was mad Jerome had fooled me. "How could you lie to me? Why?"

"Mr. Stein does this to all the new inmates hoping to get them to let him use their account to support his gambling habit."

"Is that right, Mr. Stein? Well, the joke is on you, Mr. Jerome Stein. I don't have an account number. I'm not old enough yet."

"Okay, Mark, grab your stuff. You're moving out."

"You're letting me go?"

"In your dreams, kid."

I reached for my knapsack on the floor in the corner by the sink. When I bent over, old Mr. Green Teeth said, "Watch out for the good cop, bad cop trick."

I questioned, "What do you mean good cop, bad cop?"

"Trust no one, Mark, no one." As those words were burned into my mind, the smell of his breath burned in my nose.

"Come on, kid. I don't have all night!" The officer swung open the cell door. I walked past the officer and peered back at Mr. Stein. He mouthed to me to trust no one. Then he covered up his head again, just like a spider would crawl to the corner of its web waiting for the next unsuspecting victim to land. I stepped outside the cell into the hallway and looked each way wondering which way to go. Shortly after that thought was in my head, the officer grabbed the front of my shirt and pulled me to the right. Then with a push in the back, I knew which direction to go. We walked past people in their cells, and they would slowly raise their head to look and see who was walking by. Some would say nothing and some would shout insults at the officer.

One person I remember the most was the guy in cell 7C. He shouted, "Trust only in Him." Then with one finger, he pointed up and looked up also.

The officer grabbed my shirt again and gave me a push to get me moving. "Don't listen to him. He is a nut case. He says that to everyone. It doesn't mean a thing. He is just crazy. Isn't that right? You're crazy!" the officer screamed at the man in cell 7C. We had only taken a few steps and the officer lunged at the man in cell 7C and retorted, "Lunatic. It is because of people like you . . . ." The officer stopped in mid sentence.

I wasn't sure about the sanity of the man in cell 7C, but the officer was a little crazy himself. As my father would say, "The man has slipped a few cogs in the head, or the lights are on but nobody is home."

The officer pushed me in the back again to get me moving, and I could feel his anger toward the other man by how hard he shoved me. We walked down a narrow hall with many doors. All the doors had small windows with bars on them. We came to the end of the hallway where a door to my left was open. I slowed my pace to get a look inside to see what was in the room. There were three chairs and a small, square table. With a sudden grasp on my shoulder, the police officer directed me into the room and told me to sit in the black chair.

As I pulled the chair away from the table, the heavy door with the barred window slammed behind me. I looked back to see where the officer was. He was gone, and I was locked in the room alone. There was a large mirror on one wall, and I knew that it was not to see if your hair was in place, but that it was a one-way mirror. Most likely there were a group of police officers watching me and listening to what I would say and do. I would play along with their game until I found out what I was in here for. I sat down in the black chair just as the officer said to do. To speed things along I pretended to be calm, and I rested my head on my arm to make it look as if I planned on taking a nap. It had only been about one minute that I had my head down, and I could hear footsteps in the hallway. I had to stay in control at all times and not let them get me flustered and say the wrong things.

The same two officers came in and sat down across the table from me. One officer pulled out a tape recorder and put it in front of me in the middle of the table. The other officer just glared at me like an old, junkyard dog just waiting to bite.

The officer said, "Hello, Mark. I'm Officer Sam Dixon and my partner here is Officer Rufus Barrington." It was so hard not to laugh at the name Rufus. It sounded like an old person's name from way back when my grandparents were young.

To keep from laughing, I pinched myself in the leg and at the same time said, "Hello Officer Dixon, Officer Barrington." I figured that if I just said their last names, I wouldn't be so apt to start laughing at the name Rufus.

Officer Dixon reached for the tape recorder and started to record. "I'll be recording this interview. We would like you to speak clearly and loud enough so we can hear and understand everything that is said, okay, Mark?" I nodded my head.

"Hey kid, the tape recorder doesn't hear that little pea in your head you call a brain rattle. Answer yes or no," Officer Rufus barked at me.

"Yes sir!" I yelled.

Officer Dixon quickly jumped in and told us to calm down. "Let's make this as easy as we can." He looked in the direction of Officer Rufus "Old Junkyard Dog" Barrington. "Okay, I'm glad to see we are all calmed down so we can get some answers to our questions, and maybe we can get home at a decent time."

"That sounds good to me," I said.

Rufus leaned forward in his chair forcing the table to hit me in the chest. It slightly knocked the wind out of me and scared me half to death. "He was not talking about you, kid."

Jumping in between us again was Officer Dixon, "Now let's not jump to conclusions. If Mark answers the questions right, I see no reason why he can't go home tonight. That is, if I ever get to the questions. Now Mark, for the record, state your full name."

"My name is Mark Royal Wilson."

Officer Dixon wrote something on his notepad, but I could not see what because his hand was in the way. "Royal for a middle name. That is unique. Is that your father's name or something?"

"No, I don't know where that name came from."

"Is it your grandfather's name?"

"No, I don't think so."

Officer Barrington jumped to his feet and slammed his hand on the table, "What do you mean, I don't think so? You either know or you don't."

"Okay, no."

"Okay, no what? Is that no, I don't know my grandfather's name; or no, I do know who I'm named after?" By now I was so confused, I didn't know what to say.

"Okay, kid, what's your answer?" I just sat there staring at the tape recorder.

"Kid, I asked a question and now what is your answer?"

"I don't remember the question."

Officer Barrington really got mad now. He kicked over his chair and slammed his hands on the table. With his face just inches from my face, he said, "This kid is hiding something, Sam. I know it. I can feel it in my bones."

"Rufus, get your chair and let's go on to another question." Rufus picked up his chair and sat next to Sam. He glared at me with his arms folded.

"Mark, what were you doing at the church?"

"I was just looking around."

"What were you looking for, Mark?"

"I was not looking for anything in particular. I was just, you know, looking around."

"He is hiding something, Sam. I know."

"I know, Rufus. You can feel it in your bones."

"Let me have this kid for five minutes. I'll get him to tell us everything he knows." Rufus rushed over and clutched my shirt, pulled me out of my chair, and started to drag me over to the door.

I was getting real scared now. What was this psycho officer going to do to me? Officer Dixon ran over and rescued me, "Rufus." He pried Rufus' hands off my shirt. "Mark, take a seat at the table."

"Yes sir," I said, and hurried over to the table. As I sat at the table, I could see the two officers in the mirror. They talked for a while, and then Rufus left the room. Officer Dixon came back to the table and sat down.

"Now, Mark, where were we? Oh yes, what were you looking around for?"

"Nothing, I was just goofing off."

"Now, Mark, I'm your friend. I was the one who peeled Rufus off you and sent him away for awhile." I just gazed at him, and all I could hear was the voice of old green teeth saying that I should trust no one. He said there was a good cop, bad cop trick. "Okay, Mark, just to show you what a good guy I am, I'll shut off the tape recorder and we can talk off the record."

"It is like I told you; I was just looking around the church. I was just goofing off and doing nothing in particular, and that is the truth."

"Mark, my friend, how can I help you if you don't tell me what you were doing in the church? What or who were you looking for? Did you take anything from the church?"

"No, you can search my knapsack if you would like."

"No, that would not be necessary to do."

"No, really, look. I have nothing to hide."

"That is not necessary because we already searched it when you first came in. I'll tell you what I'll do. I'm going to the bathroom, and that will give you some time to find the truth of why you were at the church."

"Officer Dixon, I told you the truth. I was just there goofing off. I was not really doing anything."

"I'll be back in a few minutes and we can talk about the truth of what you were doing at the church." I watched Officer Dixon walk out of the room and lock the big, heavy door behind him. There I sat all by myself. I couldn't say or do anything, because I didn't know who or how many were on the other side of the mirror watching me. Time seemed to drag; minutes seemed like hours and hours seemed like forever. Officer Dixon was only going to the bathroom. What was taking him so long? I no sooner had that thought, and I could hear the key rotating in the door's lock. I turned to see not Officer Dixon but Officer Rufus "Old Junkyard Dog" Barrington. What was he doing back? Did they send him in to beat the truth out of me?

"Grab your stuff, kid, and follow me."

"Where are we going?"

"You are going back to a cell to have more time to think about what you were doing in the church."

"I told you the truth, but you don't believe me."

"Kid, I guess you have a problem then, don't you. You better ask your God to help you out of this trouble you're in now."

"What God? I don't know any God."

"Yeah sure. Just like you were at the church goofing around. You better come up with a better story the next time we talk. And kid . . . , start with the truth. We are going to find out one way or another, so make it easy on yourself. Now get your stuff and follow me."

I thought for sure I would be going home tonight. What did I say to make them keep me in longer? I followed Officer Barrington down the same hallways that we came from. There it was - cellblock C. Oh no, I hope I don't have to spend the night with Old Green Teeth. As Officer Barrington swung open the door, the smell of the cellblock rushed out at me. A wave of fear came rushing over me. How long would I be here? No one knew I was here, so there was no one working to get me out. What would mother and father think when they got home and found the house empty? Then they would report me missing, and they would find me sitting in jail.

I stood there in the hallway frozen in place. Officer Barrington's voice was growing quieter as the seconds ticked by. The slamming of the cellblock door awakened me, and I found myself in the hallway. Officer Barrington was on the other side of the door walking into the cellblock without me. What should I do? Do I make a run for freedom and take the chance to escape? What would happen if they recaptured me? I would be in even more trouble and would never see the outside world again.

The cell door swung open and banged up against the wall. There was Rufus, the "Old Junkyard Dog." His face was twisted up with anger and his nostrils were flaring. Even his ears were red with intense anger. Times up! Rufus had just decided what I was going to do. He had his billy club drawn, and he rushed and got behind me. He put the billy club up against my throat and gave me a sharp, powerful jerk. Instantly it cut off my air supply. Rufus barked in my ear, "No one has escaped from me before and you, kid, are not going to be the first!" I was beginning to feel lightheaded from the chokehold Rufus had on me. If I didn't get air soon, I felt that I would black out. Rufus walked me through the cellblock to make sure I got in this time.

Once inside, I heard the door slam and lock behind me. He gave me a push down the walkway between the cells. I was weak and dizzy from the lack of air. I fell to the floor, but there was no time to rest. Rufus barked at me to get up and start walking. I tried but fell to the floor again. That was when I felt a kick to my ribs and one to my back. My head hit the bars to one of the cells, and I blacked out. I must have been out for only a few seconds because the next thing I remembered was being dragged down the walkway and deposited in front of cell 6C.

Rufus pulled the keys from off his belt. I thought I would be locked up with Old Green Teeth again in cell 5C. Rufus unlocked cell 6C, and when he swung the door open, it struck me in the side of the head. Rufus seemed to enjoy that. He reached down with his billy club and put it under my chin. With a handful of my hair, he wrenched my head back and said, "This is just a small sample of what will happen if you don't give us the answers to the questions." As quick as he wrenched my head back, he thrust it forward slamming my forehead into the floor and everything went black again.

CHAPTER 10

Who Can I Trust?

———◆◆◆———

W hen I came to, there was a bright light shining in my eyes. The light made my eyes hurt, so I covered them with my hands. My head was throbbing with each beat of my heart. Was I alive or dead? Or was I somewhere in between?

The question was answered when old green teeth, Mr. Stein, said, "Hey kid, if you're not going to eat your food, give it to me."

I was still alive, and Mr. Stein was not going to get my food no matter what it was. When I uncovered my eyes, I found the bright light was simply a light bulb hanging from the ceiling. I turned away from the light and opened my eyes again. What I saw was almost as painful as looking into the bright light. I saw Mr. Green Teeth with his hand reaching between the bars of his cell. He was not reaching to help me, but he was trying to get my food. The pain I felt was not just because I had been kicked around but that I was hungry also. I had not eaten for several hours. I was too sore to move, so I looked around the cell for the food that Mr. Stein was wanting. I could not see any food, so I figured he was just playing a cruel joke on me.

As I lay on the floor, my eye caught a glimpse of the man in 7C. "Hello kid, I'm glad to see you moving. I thought maybe Rufus had gone too far and killed you."

I struggled to sit up so I didn't have to talk to the man sideways through the jail bars. I didn't know a person could hurt so much. "Hello, my name is Mark."

"Well, Mark, Mr. Stein is right. There is a plate of food on the shelf just behind you. They brought it in a few hours ago, so it might be stone cold; but if you're hungry, cold food tastes pretty good." I leaned back and saw the shelf and the plate of food. "Go ahead, Mark, eat and we can talk later."

I lay there trying to figure out the best way to get to my feet in order to get to the food. After several seconds of thought, my plan was to drag myself over to the bed and pull myself up. Then I would try to walk over to the shelf. There was one thing missing from my plan. I did not account for the pain and how difficult it would be. Another thing I did not see in my plan was that there would be two inmates watching my every move, one hoping I would make it to my feet, and the other hoping I didn't so he could get my food. I was determined to get to that food; I would have to just look past the pain. I got to my feet without making a sound and walked over to the shelf with the food. I could hear Mr. Stein moan as I got to my feet because that meant he would not have a chance to get my food. My eyes then focused on the plate of food. There was macaroni and cheese, green beans and a roll. I grabbed the roll and attacked it.

I don't think I even stopped to take a breath from the first bite until I heard the man in cell 7C say, "Mark, slow down. No one is going to take your food."

I felt a little silly about the way I was eating, so I slowed down and finished every spoonful. I did not realize how hungry I was until I had nearly finished all the food. I pushed the plate away. I could see Mr. Stein had fallen asleep. Only the man in 7C was awake. "Hey, Mister in 7C, I didn't catch your name when I came in. I can see that Rufus is not too good at introducing people."

"My name is Felix Jenkins. Welcome to cellblock C. Normally the state puts their guests up in the Ritz Hotel, but they must be full tonight."

I was dying to find out why Officer Barrington wanted to kill this guy earlier today. I could not think of a smooth way to ask so I said, "Say, Felix."

"Yeah, Mark, what is it?"

"Does Officer Barrington always show hospitality by screaming at the inmates, or are we just lucky? If he shows me any more hospitality, I will probably end up six feet under taking a permanent dirt nap with the worms. What does he have against you and me?"

"I suppose I should first ask what you are in here for, Mark."

"I was just goofing off in some old church just for something to do."

Felix leaned forward to the cell bars and pointed at me, "That is it."

"What is it?" I questioned innocently.

"You are one of us trying to find them."

"Wait a minute. What do you mean us and them and find what?"

"Don't worry, Mark. I am one of them searching for the way to freedom also."

"Felix, do they drug this food, because you are not making any sense with this talk about us, them and we stuff. What freedom are you talking about?"

"Freedom to worship God and His Son, Jesus Christ." I gave Felix my best blank look as if I had never heard of such things before just in case the cellblock was wired for sound.

Felix inquired, "Mark, you do not know what I'm talking about?"

"I'm sorry to say they didn't teach that in school. Maybe it's in one of my next quarter classes. I think there is a class called 'Ancient Greek Mythology.' Is that what you're talking about?"

"Okay, Mark, I understand you're afraid the cellblock is wired, but be assured there are no microphones in here. I have talked a lot about this with other inmates, and I have never had any problems with the guards. I feel it is the least I can do for my God by spreading the 'Good News' about His Son, Jesus Christ."

"Felix, who is this Jesus person? Is he a friend of yours here in town?"

"He is everybody's friend, Mark."

"Even Officer Rufus 'Old Junkyard Dog' Barrington's?"

"Yes, Mark, as mean as Officer Barrington is, Jesus Christ loves him also, just like he loves you and me."

"Now wait a minute; I got you there. How can Jesus love me when I have never met him before? Tell me how that works."

"God sent His Son, Jesus Christ, to earth to die for us and to save us from our sin."

"No way! You're trying to tell me that this Jesus was an alien but is dead, so you want me to be friends with a dead alien? Next thing you know, you'll say they have a secret base on earth. That story is a little hard to believe. By the way, Felix, how many times did the guards hit you in the head?"

Felix appeared to me a little mad. I could tell by the tone of his voice. "It is true, Mark."

"Okay! Okay, just take it easy. So your friend, Jesus, has a secret base on earth. Where is it, and why aren't you there?"

"I waited too long hoping some of my family would

follow me, but they turned me in instead. That is why I am in jail. The police think I know where the freedom community is."

"You don't know, do you, Felix?"

"No, Mark, I don't know."

"Tell the state police you don't know anything about this freedom community, and they'll let you go."

"I did tell them that."

"When did you tell them that you didn't know anything?"

"About three or four months ago."

"What? Why didn't they let you go?"

"They said if I sat long enough, I would remember." I must have had a look of worry on my face because Felix said, "I'm sure they will let you go sooner than that."

"Yeah, besides, I'm just a kid. My mother and father will be back from their meeting with the governor at the capitol city. They went there to talk about my father's new watch dog program."

"Yeah sure, kid." Jerome, old green teeth, was awake. I wondered how much of Felix's and my conversation he heard. "I'm here waiting to have a meeting with the King of England too."

"Really, Jerome, my mother and father will be back in a week. They will get me out if I'm not out sooner."

Felix yelled, "The guards are coming. Get back away from the bars."

"Why?" I asked.

"Don't ask why, kid, just do it," Jerome barked at me.

They both dove to their bed, so I did the same. You could hear the door unlock and then swing open. There were two sets of footsteps coming down the walkway. I looked up slightly to see who it was. It was two new guards. I must have lost my mind for a moment, because I stood up and walked over to the bars to my cell and asked, "Excuse me, where are Officers Dixon and Barrington?"

One of the guards looked at me and asked, "Are you talking to me?"

"Yes, sir, I was wondering where Officers Dixon and Barrington have gone."

"They have gone home for the night, but they did have a message for you."

"Oh yes? What is it?"

"We hope you have a good night's sleep. We'll be back in the morning to see if you are ready to answer some questions. Lights are out in five minutes!" The guards left as fast as they came. I stood there stunned, not believing that I had to spend a night in jail.

Jerome called out to me, "Hey, Mark, word of advice, make sure your arms and legs are not hanging off the edge of the bed when you sleep. The rats like to nibble on fingers and toes." Then Jerome laughed like a crazy man until Felix told him to be quiet.

"Mark, don't listen to him. There are no rats. Just try to get some sleep, because they'll be in early to start questioning you again."

"Yeah, okay. Thanks, Felix."

I laid there in my bed thinking about the day when the cellblock went black. The only light was from the exit sign, and there was a light at the end of the walkway of the cellblock. Just then a thought came across my mind. It was something Felix said about the officers being back early to question me again. How did he know that? He was talking to the other guard for a while. There I go again, letting my imagination run wild. Next I'd be thinking he was an undercover cop. He most likely remembered what happened to him when he first got put into jail. Yeah, that was it. He couldn't be a cop. He talked too much about God and the freedom community and stuff. The best thing for me right now was to take Felix's advice and get some sleep. I laid my head down on the old, flat, stale smelling pillow and covered up with the wool blanket. That was all it took; I was asleep.

I was awakened the next morning by the sound of the cellblock door unlocking and hearing voices whispering. I opened one eye and looked toward the cellblock door. To my surprise, it was Dixon and Barrington. They were standing in front of Felix Jenkins' cell. I couldn't understand what they were saying until Felix said, "Check on the kid and make sure he is sleeping."

I closed my eye just as one of the officers flashed his light into my cell. The light was so bright that I could see it even with my eyes closed. I heard the officer turn back, and I opened my eye again. I continued to watch and listen to what was happening and being said. Officer Dixon asked Felix if he was ready for a break.

Felix said, "I was not sure if you two would remember to come and get me. I hope you got some real food, because this jailhouse slop is nasty. I wouldn't even feed it to my dog."

I couldn't believe what I was hearing. Felix was a state undercover policeman planted in here to get me to talk about what I knew about the freedom community. They must have thought I knew something and planted Felix in here to check out my story. Boy, was I glad I didn't spill my guts. It was good to play the part of clueless and say I didn't have a clue about what he was talking about. If they were to find out about the clues and the tunnels, I would be in jail forever; and my grandparents and the freedom community would be in danger of being found. Who knew what the state would do to them? Felix sure had a convincing story about God's love. Man, was he good! I wondered if at one time he was a Christian like my father and mother and turned his back on it. I lay there in my bed replaying the conversation Felix and I had the day before. One thing stuck out. God sent His Son, Jesus Christ, to earth to die for us and to save us from our sin. I played it over and over in my head until I drifted off to sleep.

I awoke to my cell door slamming as two guards entered into my cell. It had to be a dream. If I pinched myself, I would wake up and those two, hairy apes would disappear. I didn't have time to pinch myself, before the two, hairy apes grabbed me by my arms and just about jerked them out of their sockets. The pain I felt was enough to know that this was not a dream. They dragged me out of my cell and gave me a push toward the cellblock door. When I walked by Felix's cell, he was sitting on his bed. He did a poor acting job by trying to show that he had concern for me. It would have been believable if there hadn't been powdered sugar and jelly filling on the corner of his mouth. I didn't let on that his cover had been blown and I knew he was a policeman.

I said to him, "It is okay, Felix. I'll be going home. Thanks for being such a good friend."

As the guard gave me a kick in the backside, I had hoped I hadn't overacted myself with that "such a good friend" stuff. I turned to the one guard and said, "You look like a friend of mine. Maybe you know him. Captain Steve Anderson?" There was no response from the ape, just another kick in the butt. "You should get to meet him someday. He is a very nice man."

As I was talking to the two apes behind me, I ran into a brick wall, or so I thought. It was another policeman even bigger than the other two. He pushed me into the interview room with the mirror and slammed the door behind me. "Hey, didn't your mother teach you not to slam the door? If my mother was here, she would make you go in and out the door 50 times to teach you not to slam the door."

The door opened, and I hurried to the table and sat in the chair facing the door. I waited but no one came in. The door was still open. According to the clock on the wall, I had been sitting for only ten minutes, but it seemed like hours.

When were they going to come in and question me?

The door moved slowly. Who would come in, the three big apes or Dixon and Barrington? I could hear voices outside in the hallway, but I couldn't tell how many there were. The door swung open and to my surprise, it was Captain Steve Anderson.

"Hello, Captain Anderson. Boy, am I glad to see you. Now maybe I can get out of here."

"Not so fast, Mark. I have a few questions for you."

"I told the officers everything."

"I know, Mark, but I would like to hear it straight from you. What were you doing at the old church?"

"I was goofing off."

"Do your mother and father know that you like to goof off at this church?"

"No."

"Did you get tired of climbing on statues?"

"No."

"No, you didn't get tired of climbing on statues, or is it, no, I don't climb on statues anymore?" I was getting confused because Captain Anderson was asking the questions so fast, and I didn't have time to think. "Well, Mark, what is your answer?"

"No, I don't climb on statues anymore."

"You just sneak around in old boarded-up buildings that the state has posted with an off limits sign."

"No, I was not sneaking around."

"What were you doing in the church, Mark, praying?"

"No, Captain Anderson. All I was doing was just goofing off at the old building. There was no sign to say "Keep Out"; so how could I know it was off limits by order of the state police?"

"So that is your story?"

"Yes sir!"

Captain Anderson made a motion toward the mirror and

then turned back to me and said, "All right, Mark, here is what the state is going to do with you. You will go back to your cell and get your belongings. Then a guard will bring you up to fingerprint you, and you will have your picture taken. Just in case we should have need of this information, we will have it on record."

"Is that all, Captain Anderson?"

"No, when you get done with that, you will come back to my office where I will give you more information. The guard is here now, so go get your belongings, and I will see you in my office shortly."

The guard was waiting at the door to take me back to my cell. He didn't say a word. He just gave a nod of his head. When we walked into the cellblock, I saw Felix sitting on the edge of the bed muttering something. When he saw me, he jumped to his feet and exclaimed, "Praise the Lord! You're all right, Mark!"

I was tired of his little game, so I said nothing to him and did not even look his way. My cell door was still open, so I walked in and grabbed my knapsack. As I walked toward the cell door, something struck me as odd; well, maybe not so much odd but out of place. When I left my cell, my knapsack was under my bed at the head end, and just now I picked it up at the foot end. I was sure glad I had not brought anything of importance that would aid them in their search for people like my grandparents. I decided I would search the bag later to make sure they didn't put any listening or tracking devices in it, hoping that I would lead them to the freedom community.

I saw Mr. Stein was still doing what he does best, and that was sleep. "Goodbye, Mr. Stein," I yelled. A hand came out from under the blanket and waved.

The next cell was Felix's, if that was his real name. I knew he was going to say something to me as I passed by. What would I say to him?

"Mark, are they letting you out?"

"I think so. I have to talk with Captain Anderson to get more information, and then I think I'll be free to go home."

"May the Lord bless you in whatever you do, Mark."

The guard looked at me with the strangest of looks, so I did the only thing I could think of. "Oh look, there is the Governor!" The guard spun around on his heels and popped a crisp salute. Felix jumped to his feet and gave a salute also. Then he realized what he had done and tried to cover his mistake by pretending to scratch his head. I just looked Felix straight in the eye and said, "Have a nice day . . . Officer." Felix looked at me with the expression that he had just had his cover blown, and by a kid no less.

The guard finally realized that the governor didn't pass by the cellblock, so he dropped his salute, grabbed me by the shirt and flung me into the hallway. He took me to be fingerprinted and to have my picture taken. Then we were off to see Captain Anderson and find out the details of my release. We walked through a jumbled maze of hallways. We walked up and down stairs until we came to a door with the state seal and the name Captain Steve Anderson on it. The guard knocked firmly on the door.

"Enter!" was shouted to us from behind the door. The guard opened the door and there sat Captain Anderson behind his huge desk. I walked in and to my surprise, Officers Barrington, Dixon and Felix were there also. Captain Anderson motioned for me to come in and said, "Take a seat, Mark. This will not take long. We have decided to put you on a six-month probation. In those six months, you will meet weekly on Monday with Officer Lorraine Appleby. If for some reason you fail to meet with her or are found to be in trouble in any way, we will then set you up for a one year stay at juvenile boot camp."

"Is this the boy, Captain Anderson?"

"Yes, this is Mark Wilson."

The voice of the lady behind me sent chills up my spine. It was a gruff voice, but maybe she was a really nice lady. I turned around to see what she looked like. She stood at least 6 foot 5 inches and was about 300 pounds. Her hair was pulled back tight in a bun. Maybe that was why she looked so unhappy.

She walked over to me and put her face within inches of my face. I didn't know what she was going to do - kiss me, bite me or just sniff me like a dog when it meets someone new. I wasn't sure, but it sounded like she growled first and then spoke, "Boy, if you are so much as a minute late, you might just as well be an hour late; because that will be your last hour of freedom. Do you hear me, boy?"

"Yes Sir, I mean, Ma'am."

"That will be all for now, Officer Appleby."

She gave me one last glare and turned to leave the office. When she reached the door, she turned with a jerk and said with her finger pointing at me, "I'll see you on Monday at 4:00." I could hear the heels of her shoes pound the tile as she walked down the hallway.

Captain Anderson said, "Mark, you are free to go now, and I don't want to see you in here again. Stay clear of the church. If there are no problems, I see no reason to tell your mother and father."

"Thank you, Captain Anderson. There will be no problems."

I grabbed my stuff and headed for the door, and I didn't look back. Once I got outside the police headquarters, I looked for my bike. I had a lot of work to do in the next few days before my mother and father came home.

CHAPTER 11

Home At Last

A s I coasted to a stop in the driveway at home, I surveyed the neighborhood to see if the police had followed me. Everything looked clear. When I leaned my bike against the garage, I noticed a very small wire sticking out of the plastic handle grips. Should I remove it, or should I leave it in place? I slipped the handle grip off to see if it was a tracking device or a microphone. It appeared to be a tracking device. I put the handle grip back on and left the device in the garage on the shelf with some old jars and dusty bottles. That way I could still use my bike and they would think I was at home. Maybe by the time they found it, it would have as much dust on it as the rest of the junk around it.

The first thing I did when I got in the house was to check my knapsack for any listening devices that may have been planted there. I had said nothing verbally for fear that there might have been a listening device somewhere. I didn't find any devices in my knapsack, so I sat down for a few minutes and enjoyed the freedom of not being behind bars.

Just sitting in jail for one day made me think about what

little freedom we had. When I finally came back to earth, I went straight to the refrigerator. I needed food. I reached for an apple, the bread and some jelly. I closed the refrigerator door and went to the cupboard. Oooops! I ran out of hands to grab the peanut butter. I put the apple in my mouth so that a hand would be freed up to get the peanut butter jar. While I made my sandwich, I looked around the kitchen to see if anything was out of place. As far as I could tell, everything looked fine. I would have to make sure I checked the rest of the house for listening devices. I had to be careful.

While I ate my sandwich, I sauntered into the study and over to the computer to see if we had any messages. I turned on the computer with my one free hand and checked my e-mail for messages. There were four messages, and they were all from mother. Good grief! Why does she worry so much about me? Three of the messages arrived yesterday, and they were only a half hour apart. The other message came today. I'd better see what she needed to tell me. Beep, beep, beep. It was another message. Surprise, surprise! It was my mother. I'd better let her know that I was still alive. She'd probably ask where I'd been. I'd tell her I'd been out making new friends. She'd love that.

The message read: "Mark, this is your mother. I'm calling for the one-hundredth time to see if you are okay. The least you could do is return my call. Where have you been?" (I knew it. I knew she would ask. Oooops! There was more.) "Your father and I are having a good time. We will be home late Sunday night. If you run out of food, I made arrangements with the Zablings down the road. They said they would be happy to have you over for a few meals if needed. If you are home within the next 30 minutes, you can e-mail me at www.GovMansion.org. I'll wait a few minutes just in case you are reading this message now."

Well, I better let her know I'm here. I started to e-mail her back when I heard an unusual tone coming from the computer. Good, I got her before she left. My message read:

"Hello, Mother. I am alive and doing well. I have been busy meeting new friends. The food supply is just fine but if I need anything, I'll stop in to see the Zablings. I'm glad you and father are having a good time at the governor's mansion. If I'm in bed sleeping Sunday when you get home, wake me up. I would like to hear all about your trip while it is still fresh. Love, your son, Mark."

There, that should make her happy. Oh, now what? Mother always had one more thing to say. "Mark, don't forget to put the garbage out on Thursday. Don't put it out too soon or the raccoons will get into it. Good night. Love, Mother."

Okay, she was done now, or would there be one more little message. Nope, that was it. I shut the computer off and checked the rest of the house for police "bugs." When I reached for the off switch on the monitor, I noticed grease marks on the side of the computer. I looked at my hands to see if I had put the grease marks there. My hands were clean, and there was no way my father would have left any marks like that. When I turned the computer off, I heard that strange tone again. The police must have put a tap on the computer. Now they knew I was not just blowing smoke when I told them my parents were with the governor. Now that the police were tapping the computer, I would not be able to use it unless I wanted them to know what I was doing. The bad thing was that I needed to get back into the city water works file on their computer to get a better look at the map of all the tunnels that ran throughout the city. I would have to start with the areas around the old church. I needed to find out where or if I could get back into the tunnel on the other side of the cave-in. The last clue said I had to get to the end of the tunnel in order to find the next clue.

There were four things I had to work on. First I had to find a computer to get access to the city files. Next I had to get the information and a printout without getting caught. Third I had to stock up on supplies and equipment before heading back into the tunnel. And last I had to finish searching for the "bugs" the police may have planted in the house while I was in jail.

While I was sitting on the sofa thinking, I decided that I should "de-bug" the house first. That way I'd know what, if any, rooms would be safe for thinking out loud. I also wouldn't be putting myself in jeopardy with the state police. I conducted a room-by-room search moving in a clockwise circle around the main floor. I did the second floor the same way. I picked up items that I would take with me to help in my search for my grandparents as I searched the house for "bugs."

One hour later I found myself in the bathroom upstairs. I had found no other devices other than the tap on the main computer downstairs. I only had the bathroom to search, so I decided to run a nice hot bath to get the layers of dirt off of me. I looked in the mirror over the sink to see how dirty I really was, but it was a little too dark in the bathroom. I turned on the ceiling light. Wow! I was almost as scummy-looking as Mr. Stein. I was trying to tell what was dirt and what was bruises or cuts given to me by my new friends as I called them when e-mailing mother. One of the biggest bruises was the one on my chin. It looked as if they had used it as a footrest or something to clean the mud off the bottom of their boots. My head was tilted back and my eyes were looking into the top edge of the mirror, and I could see the reflection of the light on the ceiling. There was a small, dark square about the size of one of father's prize, toy cars he would never let me play with. I ran to get a chair from my bedroom to reach up and see what it was. I positioned the chair under the light and reached up with my finger. I fished for the dark square and finally grabbed it with two fingers. I pulled it to the edge of the light where I got a better grip on it. It was a listening device, in the bathroom, no less. Is there no privacy?

I carefully put it back, and with it I put a note on the door and mirror that this room was "bugged." Once I had the device back in place, I noticed the tub was getting very full. A thought occurred to me as I shut the water off. I could use this room as a way to give them the false idea that I was a police cadet want-to-be. No, I'd better not. It may draw even more attention to me, and I didn't need that, not with Lorraine Appleby as my new shadow for the next six months. Just looking at the lady was enough to send chills down my back.

I put my hand to my chin and felt whisker stubbles so I went to my room to get my shaver. I went back to the bathroom and looked in the mirror. Today is the day I will stop shaving and start my first beard. That way it would give my face time to heal from all the cuts and bruises. I got undressed and stepped into the tub. The hot water felt nice. As I sat down, I could see more bruises on my legs, upper arms and around my rib cage area. A nice, long soak in the tub would help the sore muscles and clean out the cuts I had. I lay back, leaned my head on the back of the tub, and closed my eyes for just a few minutes, or so I thought. When I opened my eyes, I looked for my watch to see what time it was. I had been in the bathtub for almost two hours. My skin was white, and my hands and toes were all wrinkly from being in the water so long. I'd better wash and get out. I decided that with as dirty as I was, I'd better wash the tub out afterwards to get rid of the dirt ring. My mother would nag me to death otherwise. Washing out the tub, I could see how really dirty I was by the mud left on the bottom. Toweling myself dry proved to be a painful ordeal with all my cuts and bruises. I tried not to leave blood on the towel. I didn't want my mother to think I was murdered or something when she washed the towel.

Once I was washed up, I felt like a new man. I thought I'd head up into the attic to see what supplies I could find. Some of that camping equipment would be real handy. I got the key from behind the picture and headed for the door at the end of the hallway. This time going up in the attic was not as much fun because I had the key, and the danger of being caught by mother and father was not a possibility. With a quick turn of the key, the door was unlocked and I opened it. The smell of dust and mothballs overwhelmed me for just a moment. After the wave of attic smell passed, it was onward and upward where I hoped to find a major portion of my supplies that I needed for my trip down the tunnel and back . . . Wow! That was something I had never thought of before. What would happen when I got back? Who would be looking for me? What would the police do when they could not have me in their sight everyday? I pondered those thoughts while very slowly climbing the stairs. The sight of my grandfather's uniform made up my mind. I wanted to see them, meet them and get to know them. I wanted them to know me. When I touched the sleeve of the coat, it was like electricity was running through my fingers and throughout my body from my head to my toes. "I will find the next clue!" I said out loud scaring myself just a little with the volume and intensity at which I said it.

If I remembered right, the other time I was up here there was a pile of camping stuff over by the window. That would be a good place to start. There were three boxes marked camping equipment. I opened the first box to see what was in it. There were four sleeping bags, a couple of wide brimmed hats and a pair of boots with the toes slightly curled. I grabbed the boots and put them next to my feet to see if they would fit. If I was going to be digging around in tunnels, I needed better footwear than these old, worn out tennis shoes. The boots looked like they would fit, but it was hard to tell with the toes curled up. I forced the boot on my right foot and tried to walk around in it. It was stiff and hard to walk in; but if I was going to wear them, I'd better get them broken in. I squeezed the other boot on and continued to look in the boxes.

I started a pile of possible items I would take with me. I should plan as if it could be a one-way trip, but with the possibility of coming back. I'd need a sleeping bag, so I put that in the pile.

I opened the second box, which was the biggest of the three. Inside I found a large backpack with all kinds of stuff already packed. I pulled it out of the box to get a better look. I saw there was another backpack just like the first one, and it too was already packed with items. Just then I felt a chill run up my spine and a breeze blow across the attic. Who had these belonged to, and who pre-packed them and did not use them? Did they plan on still using them someday? Was it mother and father? Had they planned on making the same search that I was on? What stopped them, or were they still planning? What were they waiting for? The great stuff I found in the backpack was taking a lot of the guesswork out of what I needed. They had everything: cups, silverware, plates, a small saw, a lot of dehydrated food packets, sheets of plastic, rope and even two rolls of toilet paper. Now that was a must! I put the whole backpack on the pile of stuff to go.

The third box was opened already from the other time I was up here. There was the small, folding shovel. There were two canteens that I would need for drinking water and a box of eight candles. Wow! They must be two inches in diameter and six inches long. They would help save on batteries in my flashlight. Someone had gone through a lot of planning to get all this stuff together. Now if I could get it all packed up, I'd be ready to go when I got the information on alternate tunnels, entrances and exits. I gathered together all my supplies and thought about how I could get the information from the city file without drawing attention to myself. That would take some heavy thinking to come up with a perfect plan so I wouldn't get caught.

As I picked up the backpack to go down the stairs, I stopped on the top step a moment to look around at the piles of things in the attic. One could only imagine the hundreds or thousands of stories that had been locked up here for so many years. What other secrets were there up here that may go undiscovered? I turned, made my way down the stairs and shut off the light. I shut and locked the door behind me and went to my bedroom. I dropped the camping supplies in the middle of the room and turned to the hallway to put back the key to the attic.

When I got back to my room, I thought about how I needed to get on a computer to get the information about the tunnels. How and where to do it was the question. I lay down on my bed and stared at the ceiling trying to think of a plan to get what I needed. I could feel my eyes getting heavy. Sleep was just around the corner, but my need for information was what kept me going.

Later that night I rode my bike into town. I had no lights on my bike, and I was dressed in black. I even took ashes from the fire pit in the backyard and smeared them on my face as the state police commandos do. I cruised to the back alley of the information center and slowed to a stop by the dumpster. I parked my bike behind the dumpster and checked to see if I had been followed. All was clear, but it was not time yet. I still had 38 seconds before the two computers at my house started an e-mail barrage to keep the state police busy. The two computers would talk to each other for the next two hours. They would make bogus calls to fake e-mail addresses, all of which were my different e-mail addresses not registered with the state. They would not be able to figure that out.

Fifteen seconds until "Operation Crossfire" started, and then I would hit the back door of the information center that still had the tape over the lock and the alarm wired to show that the door was closed even though it was open. Count down 5,4,3,2 and . . . Oh boy! I must have fallen asleep while thinking of a way to get my information, but that dream I had was a great idea and should work. I should have the computer set up like in my dream by tomorrow night. I'd start first thing in the morning. I'd use the computer downstairs to make the calls. That way the state police would watch the e-mail transmission to a bogus e-mail address, which would be the computer in my room. I surely was tired and could hardly keep my eyes open. Maybe I should just go to bed and get up early.

CHAPTER 12

The Zablings Are
A Big Help

———◦◦◦———

I was awakened by the sound of gently falling rain hitting the window of my bedroom. I opened my eyes, and for a time I watched the rain run down the window. It was so peaceful. It looked as if it was an all day rain, but that was okay because there was so much yet to do before I went into town.

I got dressed and made my way to the kitchen for breakfast. I was trying to decide if I should have my usual cold cereal, or if I should make some scrambled eggs, bacon and toast. If I had cold cereal, there would be fewer dishes to wash. I pondered for a moment and decided to have the cold cereal.

With breakfast out of the way and my dishes washed, I began working on "Operation Crossfire." I used the main computer downstairs to make all the calls to the other computer in my bedroom. Since father and I ran our own wires to link the two computers together, the state police didn't know that our computers could talk back and forth without using the state controlled Internet lines. I would program "Operation Crossfire" on an old computer disc. My bedroom computer would send a coded message to the main computer to start the calls and to send the pre-programmed conversation back and forth between the two computers. I worked on my programs for "Operation Crossfire" for the next 3 ½ hours. The scary thing was that there was no way to test my program without tipping off the state police since they had a tap on the main computer. I would just have to believe that the idea I got in my dream would work.

I had been working so hard on my program that I didn't notice that the rain had stopped and there were a few breaks in the clouds. I walked over to the window and looked down Old Mill Road to what was left of the old mill. The old, wooden building had lost most of its paint and the sun bleached the wood out. Back in its earlier years it was most likely a fine looking structure, but now it was just a shell after the fire two years ago when lightning struck one of the grain silos.

As I looked out, black clouds began moving back in. It looked as if it was going to rain again. Then the strangest thing happened; a shaft of light came down through the black clouds and illuminated the old mill. The light was kind of yellow, but it was also a little golden. I had never really seen a color like that before. As quickly as the light appeared, it disappeared back into the sky. I stood in front of the window wondering about the strange light and if it had a meaning, or if it was just a part of nature I had never seen before. There was a great flash of lightning that streaked across the sky, and then a clap of thunder so loud it made the window rattle. I could feel it in my chest. It frightened me so much I jumped back from the window, tripped over my shoe and landed softly on my bed.

When my eyes got back to normal after seeing that flash of lightning, the fat songbook from the church was there. I had somehow opened it up. I started to read the words of a song, "Our God is an awesome God; He reigns . . ." I no sooner got the words of the song out of my mouth and there was another flash of lightning and a clap of thunder. I went to the window to watch the sound and light show. The rain began to fall hard again, and I could see small, pea-sized hail hitting the window.

Then my eye caught some movement in the tree line across the road. It was a person next to a black car with the trunk opened. I slowly backed away from the window, found my father's binoculars, and took a closer look from another window downstairs. I carefully pulled the curtains apart just enough to get a look at the car and the person outside it. To my surprise, there was another person in the back seat with a high-powered lens on a camera. I took a look at the tires of the car and they were fine, even though one person was pretending to be changing a flat tire. It was a smoke screen for them to take pictures of the house and me. I'd better get back up to my room before they get suspicious as to where and what I was doing.

I decided to make lunch instead. With the day being rainy and cool, I thought I'd have soup and grilled cheese sandwiches. It would bore the socks off them if they had to watch me stir the soup on the stove. Then maybe they would leave and I could get back to packing for my next trip to the tunnels.

I turned the light on in the kitchen so they could see me. I prepared lunch while the men in the black car were still trying to fix the same flat tire for 45 minutes. My lunch was prepared, and I decided to take it up to my room where I could watch them watch me. I found myself a tray and loaded up my soup, two grilled cheese sandwiches, and a glass of milk and headed up the stairs. I was on the second step when there was a knock on the back door. It surprised me so much I almost dropped my tray of food. I set my tray on the dining room table as I made my way to the door. I could see two people standing outside. Before I could get to the door, the person on the other side knocked harder and longer. I reached for the door, but before I got there, the knob turned and the door opened. A hand curled around the edge of the door and then a head popped in. It was Mrs. Zabling and her husband. What a relief it was to know it was them and not the state police.

"Hello, Mrs. Zabling. Come on in. I see Mr. Z is with you. I didn't hear you drive up in your truck."

"No, we came over on the John Deere through the hay field. What happened to you? You look like a big truck hit you. Are you okay?"

"I'm just fine. I ran into some guys that were bigger than me. Thank you for checking to see how I am doing."

Mrs. Z smiled real big and said, "Your mother and father asked us to keep an eye on you and to check in on you every so often."

"Well, as you can see, I was about to have lunch. You are more than welcome to stay and talk if you would like."

"No, no. That's okay. We were just a little worried because we could see this black car parked outside the front of the house. Dwayne and I think they are the state police."

"Yes, you are right. They are the state police. I have been watching them watch me for the last hour or so."

Mrs. Zabling squeezed my shoulders and leaned forward. Her mouth switched to one side. She said quietly so that no unwanted ears could hear what she had to say, "Now Mark, what bad thing have you been up to that would cause the state police to sit outside your door?"

"Now Mr. and Mrs. Zabling, you know me well enough to know that I'm a good kid. As for the state police, they don't have to have a good reason to sit outside someone's home and spy on them."

"You are so right, Mark. I remember them sitting

outside our home for weeks a few years back. They thought Janice and I were in the black market."

"Well, that's silly of the state to think that. With their credit system, what would you use for money?" I asked Mr. Z.

"The state said we would sell our pigs and grain on the black market and receive items or services of equal value. Many people went to jail because of the state's fear that the black market would take away some of their power and control over the people in the state."

"Did the state try to jail my grandmother and grandfather?" The Zabling's eyes almost popped out of their sockets. "Don't be so surprised. I know that the house I live in at one time belonged to my grandparents. I also have found out that they lost it to the state and had to live on the streets for a while. My source says that a few friends helped them out by letting them stay a while and would feed them. I wonder who those friends might be . . . hmmmmmmm?" Then I gave them that big-eyed look. "I know it was you two so spill the beans." They said nothing. They just looked at each other and then looked around. I looked them both straight in the eyes; first at Mr. Z and then at Mrs. Z. They were good. It looked like I was not going anywhere with this line of questioning. I would have to give them something that would let them know they could trust me and that I didn't work for the state police. "Okay, I'm going to trust you with something I know. That way you can trust me. I just want to know more about who my grandparents were. I know some of why they left." Mrs. Z took hold of Mr. Z's hands and pulled him closer to whisper in his ear. "I found a letter written to my father from his father saying why they left. My grandfather wanted to give my father a chance to find his way back to them." My words startled the two of them and they banged their heads together.

"You know, then, that the state police are still looking

for them, Mark."

"No, I didn't, but I do now. Please sit down. I think we have a lot to talk about."

They pulled out chairs and we sat at the dining room table. They talked and I ate my food. We talked for hours about the good old days before the government collapsed and the state police took over. Then there was a quiet spot in the conversation, so I injected some questions, "Why did you folks stay? Why didn't you follow my grandparents?"

"We decided we would help others find the way to Jesus Christ and become Christians. We felt that if all the Christians would leave, who would spread the word of the Good News of Jesus Christ?"

"Do you know where my grandmother and grandfather are and how to get there?"

"No, I'm sorry, Mark. They didn't tell us because if the state was to get that information, all would be in danger."

"I see. I had hoped you could help me find them."

"Mark," Mrs. Z said, "Do you know Jesus Christ?"

"No, not really. I have read only a few pages of this book my grandfather gave my father. The book is called the Holy Bible. When I was in the old church, I saw a lot of pictures of him. That's how I know this Jesus Christ. I saw a picture on a window where these people killed him."

"Did you see the window that showed Jesus Christ alive again, where he rose again from the dead?"

"Yeah, but that is where the story I saw on the church windows got a little hard to believe. When you're dead, you're dead. The End! It is not that I don't believe there was a guy named Jesus Christ, but it is just some of the things they say he did when he was alive."

Mr. Z jumped in the conversation, "But he is alive! He lives in heaven with God the Father!"

"Okay, there is a story I can believe a little more than the one that my science teacher has us study about in class."

00000000

0

"This same God who created the world raised His Son, Jesus, from the dead."

"So that would make Jesus the Son of God."

"Yes, that's right, Mark!"

"Where was the Mother God in this story?"

Mrs. Z said, "There was no Mother God. Jesus' mother was Mary, but she was not a god. She was a human like we are."

"Okay, let me get this straight. There is a God the Father, and He has a son named Jesus Christ."

"Yes, that's right, Mark."

"And Jesus' mother is Mary Christ and she is not a god."

"No, her name is just Mary."

"I'm getting more confused. I have to think about this stuff for awhile."

The Zablings had big smiles on their faces as they stood up from the table. Mr. Z replied, "We better go back to the farm before it gets too dark. We don't want to have to use the lights on the tractor and attract attention to us."

I walked them to the door. "Thank you for telling me more about my grandparents. I feel I know them better."

They both said at the same time, "Be careful, Mark!"

Then Mrs. Z added, "We will be praying for you to find Jesus and your grandparents. Like your grandfather said, 'Trust in God and let Him lead you.'"

We said our goodbyes, and I watched them walk to the tractor. With one more wave from the cab of the tractor and a big puff of black smoke, they went back across the field to their farm. I watched for a while until they drove around the tree line.

I went back into the house to the front window to see if the state police were still sitting outside. I pulled back the curtain just enough to see the road. The state police were gone for now. I had this feeling that they would be back. Then it hit me that maybe they went over to the Zabling farm to question them. There was no extra car on the road or in their front yard, but a cluster of pine trees blocked some of their yard. I just had to believe that they made it back all right.

I was ready to put "Operation Crossfire" into motion tonight. Just in case my plan to get information from the information center would fail, I would have time to work up a plan B before my parents would get home at the end of the week. There were still a couple hours before I could go into town with sunset not until around 5:30 and real darkness for an hour after that. The cloud cover would help speed that timetable up a little.

As I waited for sunset, I packed up some of the items that I would take when I went back into the tunnel. I found the compass and map pouch I had hidden away and put that in my backpack. I ran from room to room picking up items like more candles, string, tape and odd items like an empty coffee can, coat hanger and a plastic, watertight container where I packed as many wooden stick matches as I could. Why was I packing so much? I was only going into the tunnel to find the next clue, and then I would be back home. I stood and stared at the items for a moment. Then I hurried off to the kitchen to see what I could use in there. Some times I scared myself by what I did, but most of the time it worked out fine.

Evening came quickly. It would soon be time to go into town to gather information on another entrance to the tunnel. It was 7:30 p.m. before I had everything ready to go. My bike had all the light reflecting parts taped over with dad's black electrical tape. I was dressed in all black from head to toe. What skin was showing, I covered with ashes from the backyard fire pit.

The information center closed at 8:00, and by 8:15 the last employee would leave the building by the front door. By 8:30 "Operation Crossfire" would automatically start. As I rode down Old Mill Road toward town, I felt the rush of adrenaline. I peddled faster and faster. I had to tell myself to slow down or I'd get to my first position too early, and that would attract attention. That was something I didn't need.

When I rode past the Zabling farm, I could see two figures in the window. I saw two long flashes of light and a short flash. I didn't know what they meant by that, but I gave them two long and a short back. It would be good to know that if something should go wrong, they would come looking for me. I watched to see if there were more signals, but the windows remained dark until I could not see the farm anymore. Time seemed to be rushing by as I continued to ride. My first stopping point would be the city park. That is where I would rest for a few minutes before moving into my position in front of the information center. I could see the front gates to the park just a few blocks ahead of me. I'd find my usual park bench and look to see if Ernie was in the park. I rode through the front gates and watched for any signs of the state police. I parked my bike in the trees just behind the park bench where I usually would meet up with Ernie.

I made myself comfortable under the outstretched branches and blended in with the surroundings. The time was now 8:11. I'd rest here for a few minutes, and then I'd proceed to the alley behind the information center. I scanned the park from my hiding spot. I could see most of the park from my spot. There were no police around that I could see. In fact, the park was almost empty except for an older couple feeding the pigeons over by the fountain that the city filled with dirt. They made one big planter of it. I suppose it was cheaper than pumping water into it.

I sure was hoping to see Ernie. I missed the old guy. I couldn't remember for sure when we talked last. I looked at my watch; it was 8:16. Ooops! I was a minute behind sched-ule. I'd better get moving. As I stood up, I felt what seemed like a hand pushing me down to the ground. I looked around but saw no one, not even Ernie. Then I heard footsteps and I crawled deeper into the cluster of pine trees. I pushed a branch over to get a clear shot of the sidewalk. Standing there was the park ranger and a state policeman with his police dog. I began to panic. What was I going to do now? I was dressed like a commando and hiding in the trees this late at night. My probation officer, Lorraine Appleby, would hang me out to dry. Then something dawned on me. Why wasn't the dog barking and going crazy to tell his handler that I was in the trees? Maybe I'd be okay. I started to relax and tried to hear what they were saying, but they were too far away. I waited for them to leave so I could continue on with my mission.

Just then I heard a branch snap. It was so loud it sounded like a cannon going off. The dog started barking and jumping around. I'd been caught now. I best just give up and not make things any worse. I stood up and started walking toward the police officer, but I felt something on my shoulder again. I quickly looked to see who had a hold on me. To my surprise, the branch I had backed into and snapped was hooked on my shirt.

By now the dog was barking very loudly, and the K-9 handler was having a hard time getting him to settle down. That was when the K-9 handler exclaimed, "Oh no, Caesar just broke his leash! I feel sorry for that rabbit over there by the gate. Well, I better go get Caesar back under control. That's all I need is for someone to get all uptight and call the captain. I'll see you later, Hank."

"Okay. I hope you can get Caesar back on his leash."

"So do I. Caesar, come here!"

As the K-9 handler ran after his dog, the ranger turned to walk back the way he came, but he stopped for a moment. It was as if he thought he saw something. I froze in place and didn't even breathe. My eyes were fixed on the ranger's face. He walked near the cluster of trees, but he stopped and shrugged his shoulders. Then he walked to his park ranger golf cart.

With the police and the park ranger out of my way, I had to hurry to the alley and get into position by 8:30 so "Operation Crossfire" could begin on time. I dragged my bike out from under the tree branches and swung my leg over the center bar of the bike. I scanned the park one more time. There were no police, no Ernie, and no strange feelings of something holding me back. I could feel a little chill in the fall air, and it didn't help to have sweat soaking my shirt from the fear of being caught. I rode out the side entrance of the park and made my way to the alley behind the information center. While I was riding, I thought about that strange feeling of something holding me back. I would have walked right into the waiting arms of the law if that strange feeling hadn't stopped me. I really thought it was Ernie. That was something he would do to surprise me. I hoped Ernie was all right, wherever he was.

I turned off into the alley and slowed my pace down to take time to look around and make sure there were no stake-outs. I found my spot between the dumpsters and glanced at my watch. The time was now 8:28. I had made good time coming over from the park. I'd wait until 8:32, and that would give enough time if there were any lag time between the computer and my watch. While waiting, I went through the steps that I would take to gain entrance. Once I was in, I hoped to find a computer quickly to gain access to the city files. I had to remember to set my timer for 2 minutes and 45 seconds to give me enough time to exit the file before they could trace the break-in to their computer files at city hall.

I peered out between the dumpsters to see if any state police were cruising the streets and alley. All was clear. The time was 8:33. I ran in a crouched over position hoping to not be seen by anyone. I reached the back door and could still see the wire I used to fool the alarm last time. I hoped it was still hooked up, or this could be over before it even got started.

The door opened easily, and I wasted no time slipping

into the building and shutting the door quietly. I moved up the steps to the door leading to the information center computer area. The room was very dark. Only small beams of light broke through the darkness from the streetlight. I reached into my pocket and pulled out my small flashlight to help me locate a computer terminal to gain access. I looked for a computer along the wall opposite the big windows so no one would see the light from the computer screen. I was hoping to locate a computer that had not been put away because that would be easier. I had searched through half the room and still found no computer terminal that had been left out. What a time for people to be neat! I knew the computer at the main desk would not be put away, but it was by the big windows. I ran over to the main desk and just as I thought, the computer terminal was not put away. I had to figure out how to block the light. I looked around for something to act as a shield. I tried to stay calm while I searched, because there was no real time pressure until I got into the city files. I scanned the room for a shield and noticed an old flag propped up in the corner. I rushed over to get it and saw some lights streak across the room. I quickly dropped to the floor and shut my flashlight off. I lay motionless on my back as the lights streaked across the room walls and ceiling. It had to be the state police patrolling the area. They would move along in a few moments, and then I could get back to my task at hand.

The front doors began to rattle and I could hear someone yelling something, but it was too muffled to understand what was said. I was hoping they did not have a key to get in. Since when did the city start doing door checks? Oh no! If they check the back door, they would find it unlocked. There would be more police here than I would want to see. I couldn't rush to the back door now. The person out front was still rattling the door, but he would see me run across the room. When would that person get a clue that the door was really locked and go away? Then the door quit rattling. I peered over at the door from my position on the floor. I could see the person had left. I dashed across the darkened room running into tables and chairs, but I could not let that slow me down. I had to get to the back door before they checked it and found my duct tape across the lock.

I was at the back steps taking two or three at a time to reach the door. I opened the door only a few inches and frantically searched for the tape with my hand. When I found the tape, it didn't want to peel off. I could feel my heart beating faster as fear was starting to overtake me. Would I get the tape off in time, or would I feel a hand on top of my hand? Finally, a corner of the tape peeled up, and I grabbed a hold and pulled it off and shut the door. I heard the door latch. I leaned on the door with my shoulder trying to calm my heart down. As I scanned the door and hallway, I noticed the wire was still hooked to the alarm. It was hanging partly on the outside of the door. I reached up and tried to pull the wire in but not to disconnect it, because I would need to exit the same way I came in. I tugged on the wire, but it must have gotten pinched in the door. With my fingers only inches away, I heard footsteps outside the door.

The door began to rattle just like up front. "The door is locked, sir," the voice on the other side of the door yelled.

There was a reply, but the door rattling stopped me from understanding what was said. If I were lucky, he would not see the wire hanging there. I waited to hear them walk away. I still had my fingers on the wire. The person tried the door one more time. Then, in an instant, the wire was ripped from the grasp of my fingers. "Hey look! I found this wire hanging on the door!"

This time I heard a voice in the alley plainly say, "Rookie, don't pull on it. Let me see it first."

"Ooooops! Too late, sir!"

"Did you not learn anything in the police academy?"

179

"Yes sir!"

"Throw the wire in the dumpster and let's continue on with our door check patrol."

I heard the footsteps walking away from the door, and then I heard the lid to the dumpster open and close. As the voices faded away, I breathed a sigh of relief until I remembered that the wire on the alarm system was part of my exit plan. I couldn't think about that now. I had to get my information first, and then think about how to get out of here. I went back to the computer terminal at the main desk to get the maps of the city's tunnel system. As I crossed the room, I kept an eye on the doors and the windows to make sure the patrol didn't come back for a second check.

Once at the main desk, I stopped and looked around. I had the strangest feeling as I stepped behind the desk, because this was where Mrs. Lang stood. I felt that somehow she would find out that someone other than herself had been standing behind her desk. That would be silly. How would she know?

I put the flag over the computer terminal and made a tent to block the light of the screen to anyone that may be passing by. I stuck my head inside and turned on the computer. The large, color monitor came on, and there was Mrs. Lang's face greeting me. I jumped back a few steps because it frightened me. I quickly recovered, though, and clicked to get to the main menu to find my way to the city files. In just a few seconds, I was in the city file menu; but before I clicked to get into the file, I needed to start my timer so I didn't overstay my time and have the city's security tracking system locate me.

After the timer was set, I clicked on the section called maps. For the next 2 minutes and 45 seconds I clicked in and out of files to find the right maps with the layout of the underground tunnels. I finally found the maps of the section of the city I needed with only 1 minute and 17 seconds remaining. I needed to print the maps out and exit the site in 48 seconds. I hit the key to print and leaned back to wait for the printer to start. A flashing red square appeared on the screen that said to insert paper in the printer and re-enter. I scrambled to find some paper in the drawer of Mrs. Lang's desk and nervously put it in the printer and hit the print key again. Time was ticking down. Now there was only 27 seconds on the timer. The printer began to print. Would there be enough time to get the maps printed, and would I be able to exit the file in time?

I watched the timer tick off the seconds as the printer slowly printed out the maps. It seemed as if the printer was slowing down and fear was coming over me. I found myself telling the printer to go faster, and my voice was getting louder. I snapped out of it when I heard my own voice echo in the room. I lifted the old flag and peered around the dark room. Calmness began to settle in. The printer was working at the normal speed. Beep! Beep! The timer went off and I needed to exit now, but the printer was not done. I looked at the printout. It had the map, but the key that told what all the symbols were had not been printed out yet. I needed that or the map was worthless. I held my breath for the next few seconds until the printer was quiet. The moment the printer finished, I exited and then stopped. I reached under the desk, grabbed a handful of cable and wire and ripped them from their connectors. Sparks flew out from under the desk and the monitor went dead. As I gazed down at the wires in my hand, I said to myself, "Well Mark, that is one way to exit a file, but I would not recommend that as a normal practice." Not knowing if I had made my three minute time limit, I had to get out of the information center and as far away as I could. The place could soon be crawling with state police. I had no time to waste. I grabbed my map, dropped the handful of cables and wires and ran toward the back door. I stopped because I saw an open window. If it were already opened, it wouldn't set off any alarms.

I ran to the window and opened it up more. I stuck my head out to survey the possibility of an escape route. There it was - a way out. I could crawl out the window onto the stone ledge, and with a few steps I would be able to reach the lightning rod grounding cable running down the side of the building to the ground. I had to make a decision to go out the window and down the side of the building, or crash out the door and make a run for it hoping that the state police wouldn't catch me. I decided to go for the window. I had been chased by the police enough. I strapped on my stuff and slipped out on the ledge. I remembered to close the window down to the same amount it was opened. I faced the wall and slowly shuffled my feet along the ledge trying not to look down. I didn't remember that the ledge was so long when I first looked out the window. I reached for the lightning rod grounding cable, and all I found was a wall. I began to panic because there was supposed to be a cable and not a wall. I looked around to see what to do next. There was no choice. I had to make it around the corner and reach the cable. After a few more steps, I could feel my hand on the cable leading to the ground. I pulled myself to the cable and began climbing down the brackets that held the cable to the building. It acted like a ladder and before I knew it, I was on the ground.

I searched up and down the alley but saw no one. Then I listened and there were no sirens, so I must have made the three-minute time limit. I dashed over to the dumpster and got on my bike. As I pushed off the curb in the alley and rode for home, I decided to take my alternate route just to be on the safe side. There were less homes and more vacant buildings on the alternate route. I would still have to hide when I saw a car approaching, because I wouldn't know who was in the car or if it was an unmarked state police car. When I got close to a streetlight, I wanted to check my watch, but I knew I had to stay out of sight. If I rode hard and fast and didn't come across many approaching cars, I'd be home in no time flat.

Heading into the driveway, I slowed my peddling down and sat up straighter on my bike. I had made it back home without any problems. It was a long, hard ride home, and now I could rest. It would feel good to take a shower and wash off the sweat, dirt and ashes I used as camouflage. I put my bike back in the same spot just in case the state police came by. If I didn't, they would wonder why their tracking device they planted on my bike didn't show I moved it.

I hurried into the house to see how the computers were doing with "Operation Crossfire."

I put my printout from the information center on the dining room table and went to check the main computer. When I looked at the screen, it was into its fourth Internet call. I would stop the operation at the completion of the fourth call and save the rest of the program in case I needed it again. As I sat at the computer desk watching the computers talk to each other, I looked over at the printout on the table. I was eager to examine the map so I could find a new route into the tunnel to get to the next clue and be that much closer to finding my grandparents.

As I turned back to the screen, the fourth call was just ending, so I got ready to shut "Operation Crossfire" down. I hit a couple keys and I was done. Now if anyone would need to e-mail or talk to me, the line would be open. I grabbed the disc and made my way up the stairs to my computer to get the other disc. I popped the disc out of my computer, put them in a large envelope, and taped it to the bottom drawer of my desk. There were no labels, access information or secret passwords written on the disc; it would take someone weeks to get into it. With the discs safely stored away, I sat on the edge of the bed to rest a few minutes before getting cleaned up. Someone calling with an e-mail broke my enjoyable time of resting. I ran to the stairs and quickly swung a leg over the banister and slid down.

At the bottom I swung my leg off the banister and ran to see who was e-mailing so late at night. It was mother. She wanted me to call her as soon as possible. I decided now would be as good a time as any. It would help seal my alibi to have a conversation with my mother at the capital city. The Internet address I could reach her at came up on the screen. I'd better write it down so I got it right, www.KingstonMotel.center.com. I should call mother while she was still there. As soon as she's done with her e-mail, then I could get on line. What was she waiting for? I had the address written down. Of course, one last little note. Don't forget to water the plants. Okay, are you done now, mother? Now get off so I can call you back. Then you can remind me another time to water the plants. All right, she was off. Now I could call the chat line of the place she e-mailed me from. I could type in my mother's name and wait to see if she was still there waiting for me to call her back. It took only a few seconds, and my mother was giving me a list of things to do. She rattled on for what seemed like forever. I could not get a word in edgewise. Finally she slowed down and asked me how I was doing. I typed in that I was doing just fine. Father must have been telling her to get off the line, because she ended our little chat abruptly.

I hurried upstairs and ran water for a bath. It was going to be a quick bath, because I was anxious to study the new map I had printed out at the information center. After I got cleaned up, I laid the map on the table and stared at all the tunnels running from one end of the city to the other. This could take some time to figure out the best place to re-enter the tunnel. As I looked over the map, I located the church. There were two tunnels that ran near the church, but which tunnel did I want? One was numbered 0038 and the other was 0707. I ran my finger across the map following the line of 0038. It appeared to end about five blocks away from the church. When I walked in the tunnel, I walked for well over an hour so tunnel 0038 was not the tunnel I was looking for. As I studied the line representing tunnel 0707, I could feel the excitement grow as my finger moved along the map. I thought to myself that if I started at the end of the tunnel, I would be right at the next clue. My finger raced along the red line of tunnel 0707 until it ran off the paper. That was when I got a sick feeling in my stomach. I read the words, Part 1 of 2. I didn't look to see if there were any other parts to the map. The map I had didn't even show my house or the old mill. The tunnel was out in the middle of nowhere. Disappointment slowly crept over me, and my finger slid down the page. I closed my eyes, because I could not stand to look at the map anymore. That was to be my best hope for getting to the tunnel and finding the next clue. Wait a minute! So I didn't find the end of the tunnel. All I needed to do was get back in the tunnel on the other side of the cave-in, and then find the end of the tunnel and the next clue. My head was still hanging down from being disappointed. My eyes opened wide, and my face was only inches from the map. My eyes focused on the map and there, in the shaded area in very small print, it read Lot A and B of Section 12. Next to that in parentheses it said Zabling farm. My head popped up like a bagel in a toaster. There it was, a black dot in the middle of the Zabling farm. I had never seen a manhole cover on their farm. Tomorrow I would have to ride over to the Zabling farm and talk to Mrs. Z. Maybe she could tell me where the manhole cover was so I could get into the tunnel. For now, there was nothing I could do until I talked with the Zablings, so I went to bed.

Morning came quickly, and my sleep ended abruptly when I heard someone pounding on the back door. I grabbed some clothes and ran downstairs. I peered out the window next to the door and to my surprise, it was the Zablings. I opened the door and was about to say good morning when they rushed in and quickly shut the door behind them.

"Mark, go up to the front window and see how many state police cars are parked along the road."

Mrs. Z had such fear in her voice; I found myself running to the front room window. When I reached the edge of the window, I strolled on by, as it was the natural thing to do. I couldn't show the state police I feared them or even noticed they were there. Once past the window, I counted eight black state police cars along the road. It was so hard not to run away from the window in fear. I crawled on my hands and knees back to the other room to tell the Zablings what I had seen.

"There are eight squad cars along the road. What do we do?"

The Zablings said nothing for a moment. Then Mr. Z said, "I think your grandparents had a hiding place out back for when the police made their raids."

"Yes, they did. I wonder if it is still in one piece or not," replied Mrs. Z.

By now all the hair on my arms was sticking straight up with fear, and all I could ask was, "What do we do now?"

Mr. Z said, "Grab anything you don't want the police to find, and we'll see if your grandmother and grandfather's hiding place is still there."

"And if it isn't?" I questioned.

Mr. and Mrs. Z said at the same time, "We just keep on running until we get to our farm, and we can hide there."

I ran around the house with my backpack in hand grabbing all the information I had found. I grabbed the knapsack with the pictures, books from the old church, the Bible and the coffee mug that said, "Jesus is Lord" and stuck it inside the big backpack. I put the clues I had found in my search, the map of the city tunnels and the two discs from the computers in the backpack also.

I could hear knocking on the front door as I ran down the stairs. I stopped in mid stride. There was another knock. The Zablings said, "Come on, Mark, we don't have all day. They will be smashing in the door next time."

We ran to the back door and down the porch steps. At just that moment when I hit the bottom steps of the porch, I could hear the window breaking. Then a second hit on the door and the lock gave way. I could hear the police rushing in as the three of us ran across the backyard to find the hiding spot. The Zablings seemed to know where they were going, so I just followed and didn't ask any questions. We ran just as fast as our legs would take us. For as old as the Zablings were, they sure could move fast when they had to. We headed out behind the garage to an old, wooden shed.

I told them, "You're not going to get in there. My father locked that up a long time ago, back when we first moved in."

Mr. Z had a look of determination and fear all over his face. He wrapped his big hands around the padlock. With a twist and a jerk, I heard something snap. Then he pulled open the door. He said, "Come on! Get in!"

Mrs. Z hurried in the shed, and I could hear the police coming out on the back porch. I froze in place with fear. My feet were like lead, and I could not move them, as hard as I tried. Mr. Zabling grabbed me by the collar and pulled me in and shut the door. I looked around the shed to see where Mrs. Z was, but she was gone. The shed was only 5 feet by 6 feet, and most of it was full of wood and junk. I turned to ask Mr. Z where his wife was, but he put his hand over my mouth and pushed me to the floor. Then a trap door opened and out popped Mrs. Z. She motioned me to come into the place where she was. I slid on my belly like a snake. It was dark, but there was enough light to see that Mr. Z was crawling in now also. He shut the trap door quickly, and then wedged a stick up by the door.

We could hear the police searching the garage and the backyard. Footsteps ran past the shed, and there were all kinds of yelling back and forth. It seemed to go on and on. The shed door opened, and the light filtered through the spaces between the floorboards. I could see only parts of Mr. and Mrs. Z's faces. They looked as scared as I felt. As the policeman searched the shed, he caused dust and dirt to fall. It was getting into our eyes and making it hard to breathe. We had to cover our faces until he was done searching. When the policeman left, he didn't say a word. He just slammed the door and more dust and dirt fell.

I started to get up and reach for the trap door, but I felt a big hand on my back pulling me down. Mr. Z got his face real close to mine and said, "Sit! Get comfortable because we will be here for a long time."

"But why?"

Then the door of the shed flew open again, and this time there were three or four police up above tearing the place apart. With my shirt pulled up over my face and the noise above, I had time to think that the Zablings knew more than I thought. I think they had been through this before with my grandparents.

One officer yelled, "Let's go!"

"No, not before we find that kid."

"He is not here!"

"He is here. I can feel it in my bones."

"Why does he always say, 'I can feel it in my bones'? He has never been right yet," one of the officers questioned.

"We're leaving," the sergeant said, "You told us to search the shed again so we did. We're done. You and your bones can do what you want. Come on guys, let's go back to the house." We could hear the other officers walking away laughing at the one officer. Little did they know that this time he was right. We were only inches away at times. After a few moments, the last officer walked back to the house muttering something about one of these days I'll show them.

The three of us just sat in the dark for a long time not saying a word and not knowing if there were any more police around in the area. Finally Mr. Z said, "Here is what we will do. We stay down here until after sunset. Then we will go over to the farm."

"Hey, I've got to see what they did to my house, Mr. Zabling."

Mr. Z grabbed my shirt and pulled me close so he could yell at me in a whisper, "You just don't get it yet, do you Mark? The police were looking for you for a reason, and it was not to sell you tickets to the 'Policemen's Ball'!"

Mrs. Z grabbed a hold of Mr. Z's hands and tried to pry his fingers open to let go of my shirt. She talked real softly to Mr. Z, "Dwayne, it's okay. He is just a boy. He doesn't know."

Slowly his fingers uncoiled from my shirt. I sat back down in my seat and looked at him. There was some deep down fear in that man's heart, because I had never seen him get like this until the police started coming around. Mrs. Z kept talking to Mr. Z to get him back to normal. "It will be okay, Dwayne. Now look at Mark; he probably thinks you're a mad man."

"No, I don't think that at all. Mr. Zabling, you're a real nice man. Mr. Zabling, a really nice man."

I must have been babbling because Mr. Z patted me on the arm and whispered, "You're okay, Mark; you can stop talking now."

"Okay," I said.

Then Mr. Z leaned forward, and I leaned back as far as I could. I thought he was going to grab me again, but he didn't. He just said, "I'm sorry, Mark. I just remember what it was like the first time the state police started their raids looking for people that they said were traitors to the state. I saw many of my friends go to jail and never return. There were homes burned to the ground. They would take all they could carry and head for the hills. The state government said that if they wanted to run and live in the woods, that was fine. The state said they were as good as dead because none of them would last the winter. Then they would come crawling back to the state begging for mercy. None of the people ever came back. That made the state look bad, and their raids got worse."

Mrs. Zabling tried to stop Mr. Zabling, "Dwayne, that is enough now."

"No! Mark needs to know the whole story, the real story. Not that garbage they teach you in school." Mr. Z continued to tell me the rest of the story. He told about his friends and family members that were raided by the state police until they either broke down or ran off. When he finished telling all he had to say, he leaned back on the dirt wall and closed his eyes. I was about to speak when Mrs. Z quickly put her finger across her lips to stop me. It had been quite some time since we had heard the last policeman around the property. I was getting hungry, and I motioned to Mrs. Z that it was time to eat. Mr. Z spoke. I thought he was sleeping. "Look around, Mark. There should be something."

I felt my way around the room, but all I was finding was dirt from the crumbling wall. "There is nothing but dirt here, Mr. Zabling."

"Look some more. Your grandfather was a very smart man. He always thought of others before himself. Sure, he's gone but he left some canned food in here also."

I crawled to the other side of the room to search when my hand came across something besides dirt. It was a wooden box. I was so excited I spoke out loud, "I found a box!" Mr. Z clamped a hand over my mouth. I pulled it away and said, "I'm sorry. I forgot." I whispered this time, "I found a wooden box. It has cans in it."

"Those, Mark, are old military food packs."

"How old?" I asked.

"Very old, but when you're hungry, you'll eat anything."

"I don't think I'm that hungry, Mr. Zabling."

I sat back and watched the Zablings look through the cans reading what was in each one, and then running it under their noses as if they could smell the food. One can read spaghetti and meatballs. They sounded like they were drooling. The two of them spoke to each other in strange voices. I think it was supposed to be Italian sounding. Sometimes they could be so silly.

Mr. Z pulled out his keys from his pocket and announced, "Lunch is served."

"How are you going to open the can? With your teeth? I don't see an electric can opener."

Mr. Z smiled and sorted through his large key ring until he stopped at this strange piece of metal. A sharp point unfolded, and he placed it on one side of the can. With several twists of his wrist, the lid fell to the dirt floor. Then I could smell the spaghetti and meatballs. Something wet landed on my arm. I couldn't believe I was drooling over a can of old food. It smelled so good, and I was so hungry. I didn't care how old it was anymore. Mr. Z opened up two more cans. I was so hungry I picked out a meatball with my fingers. Mrs. Z's hand stopped me from popping the meatball into my mouth.

I gazed at her and asked, "What?"

"We will say a prayer for our food before we eat."

I slowly lowered my hand away from my mouth and put the meatball back into the can. I didn't know anything about this prayer stuff, so I did as they did. We held hands in a small circle and then bowed our heads as if we were looking at the floor, except that they had their eyes shut. Mr. Z spoke softly to this Jesus and thanked him for the protection from the police. He thanked him for the food, and then he asked for wisdom for me because I would need wisdom for my upcoming journey. In my mind I was wondering what journey he was talking about. I wasn't going anyplace. I still needed more clues, because I didn't know where I was going. Mr. Z was still talking to this Jesus when he said the strangest thing. He prayed, "Give Mark the faith to believe and to trust in your leading. Let him know that he doesn't need to know where the journey will end before he starts. Give him the faith to start the journey now. In Jesus' Holy name, Amen."

Then the Zablings both squeezed my hands. I opened my eyes, and Mrs. Z said, "Okay, now you can eat, Mark." I had silverware in my backpack, but it was too hard to get to so we ate with our hands. There was no conversation during our short mealtime.

After we finished eating, I asked, "How long will we have to be in here?"

Mr. Z answered, "Until it is dark enough to travel across the field to our farm."

"Ahhh, but the police are gone now, and it is only a few yards to my back door."

"You don't get it yet, do you, Mark?" Mr. Z gave me a disgusted look.

Mrs. Z turned to me and replied, "Mark, I'm sorry to say that once the police have raided your house, they will be back again and again until they have found you. To the police, you are a threat to the state, just as your grandparents were so many years ago."

"Is that why they ran away?"

"Yes, Mark, that is why they went out to find a place where the state could not find them and where they could live in freedom. Why don't we all try to sleep a little before we travel across the field after sunset?"

No one said a word as we lay in the dirt trying to sleep. Finally I spoke, "Mr. Zabling, thank you for saving me from the state police. You're taking a big risk helping me. Thank you again."

Mr. Zabling reached over and touched my shoulder and answered, "It is okay, Mark. We chose to help you just as we helped many others find their way. Now close your eyes and get some rest." I was feeling tired. I closed my eyes, and before I knew it, I was asleep.

CHAPTER 13

The Journey Begins

I awoke from my sleep with a gentle shaking of my foot by Mr. Z. "Pack up your things and get ready to walk across the hay field to our farm. You will have to stay close so we don't get separated, okay, Mark?"

"Yes sir. What do we do with this food down here in the hole? Do we take it all with us?"

"No, Mark, only take enough for three days and leave the rest for the next people that may need help."

"Okay." I packed away nine packets of food in my backpack. I thought about grabbing a few more packages, but Mr. Z said only enough for three days. He had been right on everything else so far. I just had to trust him.

When we came out of the hole, it was already dark, and the air was cold and damp. The hole was warmer than the outside air. We walked toward the Zabling farm that was only two miles away. We came to a barbed wire fence that separated my backyard from the hay field. Mr. Z put his foot on the bottom strand of wire and grabbed the other two top strands. Then he spread the wire so Mrs. Z and I could crawl through.

"Mark, grab a hold of the wire," Mr. Z said.

I grabbed a hold of the wire and pulled them apart wide enough for Mr. Z to get through. I stood on the other side of the fence and stared back at my house. I thought that home was where a person should feel safe and free, not a place where every knock on the door could bring a police raid. You're not supposed to look out your window at the countryside and see people staring back, waiting to pounce on you for the slightest breaking of their oppressive rules.

Mrs. Z called me and snapped me out of my deep thought. "Mark, come on. You must stay close or you could get lost in the dark." I snatched my backpack and slung it over my shoulder. I had to run to catch up with them. We walked for what seemed to be hours until we came to the edge of the field.

We stopped for some reason. "Get down!" Mr. Z whispered loudly. The three of us lay flat in the hay field. I was afraid to move. Police searchlights streaked through the night sky. Mr. Z crawled over to me and told me of his plan. He was going to slip into the back door of the barn. Then he would come out the front door into the police searchlight. While they were talking to him, Mrs. Z and I would sneak over to the old chicken coop and stay there until they were gone. When the searchlight had moved away from our position, Mr. Z ran to the back of the barn. In just a few seconds he was standing in front of the barn. He had only walked a few feet away from the barn when a number of searchlights were shining in his face. You could hear the police come running.

With all the commotion, Mrs. Z and I ran toward the chicken coop. Once inside, we locked the door and looked out the dirty window to see how Mr. Z was handling the police. We were too far away to understand what was being said. It was obvious the police didn't like the answer that Mr. Z was giving them. The police kept yelling louder and louder until I could hear well enough to understand what they said: "Where is Mark Wilson?" Then we heard nothing until there was a loud crack and Mr. Z fell to the ground.

I glanced over at Mrs. Z and inquired, "Shouldn't we go stop them?"

"No!" she replied firmly. "We must stay put. Dwayne can handle it." The police kept hitting with clubs and fists, but Mr. Z would keep standing up after each time they knocked him down.

"Why doesn't he just stay down on the ground? Maybe they would quit hitting him."

With an unbelievable calm, Mrs. Z said, "Dwayne will not ever let them win. They would have to knock him out cold in order to keep him down."

The beating went on so long Mrs. Z could not watch anymore. She fell to her knees and began talking to God. She asked for the beating to stop before they killed Mr. Z. I turned back to peer out the window just in time to see Mr. Z hit the ground one more time. This time he was not getting up, and the police were walking away. I turned to Mrs. Zabling and said, "It is over. The police are leaving now."

All she could say was, "Thank you, God!"

We waited a few minutes to make sure the police had really left the farm before we went out to get Mr. Z. Then I opened the door slowly and checked. All was clear. I ran out the door and across the farmyard to where Mr. Z was lying with blood running down his face. The blood and dirt mingled on his aged face, and his eyes were almost swollen shut. I had never seen anyone beaten so badly. Just then, for a fleeting moment, a picture flashed in my mind. Then it was gone again as quickly as it came. I wiped the blood and dirt from Mr. Zabling's face. The picture flashed in my mind again. This time I recognized the picture. It was a stain glass window at the church. It was the picture of that Jesus nailed to the cross, and below that window it said, "His blood was shed for all." There was more, but the picture in my mind was gone once again.

By now Mrs. Z had cradled Mr. Z's head in her lap and was wiping the blood from around his swollen eyes. When Mrs. Z touched his head, he opened one eye just a sliver and said in a whisper, "It was just like the old days, Janice. They beat me back then and I said nothing. They beat me again, and I still said nothing. I will not let them win." Mrs. Z pressed two fingers across his lips and told him to rest. She told him that he had done well. Mr. Z's head slowly settled back into Mrs. Z's lap. We sat under the stars and a faint glow from a distant barnyard light. All of a sudden, Mr. Z awoke and cried out, "Janice! Janice!"

"I'm right here, Dwayne."

"I can't see, Janice!" he exclaimed as he reached out to find her.

Her gentle touch on his face seemed to magically calm him down. "You had quite a good beating. Are you strong enough to walk to the house?"

Mr. Z, being a proud farmer, answered, "Yes, I'm not going to let a little beating slow me down." He struggled to his feet only for a second and then he collapsed to the ground. We rushed to his side. Turning to me and squinting as he tried to see me, he spoke, "I do believe I could use a little help." We helped him to his feet again, and slowly we walked to the house, not saying a word. He must have known or sensed I was looking at him, because he said to me, "Mark, this beating I took tonight was because I love my family and friends like you; but it is only a drop of water in an ocean of love that God has for all his creation."

"How could God love the policemen that did this to you?"

"Our God is a loving God. He loves each of us but hates our sins. It says in the Bible, 'For God so loved the world that He gave His only begotten Son, that whosoever believeth in Him should not perish but have everlasting life.'"

I started to ask, "But what about . . . ?"

Mr. Z stopped walking and said, "God so loved the world, the whole world. Not just a few parts of it, the whole world. He doesn't love just some people, but all people like you, me and the policemen that beat me." Nothing more was said that night about what had happened.

Morning came quickly, too quickly. Mrs. Z was waking me up, handing me my clothes, and saying, "Get dressed. The police are knocking at the front door." She handed me my backpack and ran to the door, the closet door.

"I can't hide in the closet. That is the first place the police will look."

She reached down and opened up a trap door in the floor. I had learned not to stand around and ask questions but to just trust. I slipped into the hole in the floor. Then I turned to Mrs. Z and said, "Thank you and goodbye." She closed the trap door over me as I crawled on my hands and knees.

I could hear her crying. In between the tears she said, "Goodbye, Mark. God loves you, and so do we."

I crawled along under the house hearing what sounded like a battle and then silence. I was near the edge of the front porch. I peered out the lattice to see two policemen walking away from the house. Two more sets of footsteps walked across the front porch. They were dragging something. The police had been known to take what they wanted, and no one could stop them. Whatever they were dragging was big. Then one of the officers exclaimed, "Ooooops! I dropped her!"

Mrs. Zabling's beaten and bloodied body fell to the ground. Her face was just feet away from mine. Her eyes opened, she smiled, and then she whispered, "Find the tunnel in the big barn." Then her eyes closed, but the smile was still on her face.

The police officer said to his captain, "She said something."

The captain retorted, "What did she say?"

"I don't know, but it was as if she was telling somebody something."

The officer pushed his face up to the porch lattice. The captain barked out orders to pick up the two prisoners and put them in the car. I closed my eyes and curled up into a ball hoping he would not see me.

The captain yelled sarcastically over to the officer peering through the lattice, "Have you found your invisible friend?"

The officer jumped to his feet and replied, "No sir!"

"Well then, why don't you join the rest of us?"

"Yes sir!" The officer walked away, but he kept looking back.

Before the captain got into his squad car, he ordered, "Burn it! Burn it to the ground! That will take care of your invisible friends."

Within a moment, I could smell gasoline. Then I heard the roar of the flames engulfing the house. Thick, black smoke filled the air. I didn't know what to do or where to go. Just then I saw a mouse run by me. For some reason I followed it to the back of the house. When I looked back to the front, the porch floor had burned through already. By the time I looked in the back toward the barns, the mouse had slipped through the lattice. He was running to the barn. That's where I was heading, too. Mrs. Z had said that the tunnel was in the big barn. I looked around for police. I saw none so I kicked out the lattice, snatched my backpack and ran through the swirling smoke. I ran as fast as I could and didn't look back. When I reached the barn door, I slid it open and went inside. I crept over to a window to see the farmhouse that I had looked at from my house for almost 17 years crumbling into a pile of burning timbers. I could not look anymore, so I buried myself in the hay to hide and rest. I needed to find the tunnel before the police came back to the farm.

While I lay there in the hay, I could feel something crawling on my arm. I lifted a clump of hay to see what it was. "Hello, Mr. Mouse." I must have frightened it, because it took off like a rocket. I tried to reach through the hay and grab it, but as I did, my hand struck a cement wall. I felt around the cement structure. It was about four feet around and two feet high. I pushed back the hay to find a steel lid on what looked like a manhole. Could it be the tunnel Mrs. Z was talking about?

I tried to lift the lid, but it was too heavy. I needed to find something to help me pry it open. I ran in and out of the bales looking for something to pry the lid off. In the corner of a horse stall, draped with cobwebs was a shovel.

With shovel in hand, I ran back to the manhole. I wedged the tip of the shovel under the edge of the lid and tried to move it. I could barely get it to wiggle. Then I decided to put my full weight into it. I lay across the wooden handle, and the lid began to move. I bounced up and down on the handle even more. I went down to the floor. Still holding onto the shovel handle, I rolled over onto my back gasping for air. I had knocked the wind out of myself. I pulled myself up to my knees and crawled over to the manhole to see if the lid had opened some. Grabbing the shovel again, I put it into the opening. I began to work the lid over far enough so I could slip down inside when I was ready. I didn't want the lid to fall off because I wanted to close it up. That way if the police would happen to find the manhole, they would not be suspicious of the opening. Now that the lid was open, I took my flashlight from my backpack and flashed it in the hole. It looked like it was the tunnel entrance. I could see a ladder on the one side of the wall. I followed it down with my flashlight. It dropped about 12 feet onto the floor of the tunnel.

I could hear someone drive into the driveway outside. They were driving slowly, as if they were searching for something or someone. I carefully walked over to the window to see if it was friend or foe. After the past few days, I didn't think I had too many friends. I latched on to the frame around the window and pulled myself up to see who was outside. I was right. It was my worst foe, the state police. The squad car was driving right toward the barn. There were several people in the car. It stopped in front of the barn, and three men got out of the squad car. I ducked down so they wouldn't see me. I needed to know what they were doing without them seeing me, but what could I do?

Just then the window above me (the one I had just been looking out of) shattered and rained pieces of glass onto me. All I could do was close my eyes and hope I didn't get cut from the falling glass. With my eyes closed tight, I could hear a hissing sound. Then I could smell something terrible. I opened my eyes. A few feet in front of me was a canister with smoke pouring out. The smoke burned my eyes and throat. At that moment, I realized it was tear gas.

Then two more canisters came crashing in other windows. I needed to get out of there, but where? It appeared to me that the police had all four sides of the building covered. My eyes were burning to the point I could not keep them open, but I needed to so I could escape the police. One of the canisters had now started a fire in the hay by one of the stalls. I could feel my throat tightening up. It was getting harder and harder to breathe. I wasn't sure if it was the tear gas, the smoke or fear that was making it harder to breathe. Along with it getting harder to breathe, it was getting harder to think clearly also. All I wanted to do was to crawl into a hole and get away. Wait! That was it! The tunnel, I'd go into the tunnel and pull the lid back over. I would take my chances as to what I'd find. Out here I would either die in the fire or the police would get me. That wouldn't be the best for me as mad as they were at me.

I stumbled my way over to the tunnel and quickly

pushed my backpack in the opening. I listened for it to hit the tunnel floor. I could hear the police at the large door. My heart pounded inside my chest as the police pounded on the door. I pushed past the lid of the tunnel until my feet could find the ladder. Once on the ladder, I struggled to move the lid back in place. I couldn't move it with only one hand. I needed both hands free so I hooked my legs around the ladder. Then I placed both hands on the lid, and it began to move ever so slowly until it dropped into place. Moving the lid took a lot of strength out of me, so I just hung on the ladder for a moment. I made it into the tunnel in time, because the police had entered the barn. I could hear them running around. They would never find me down here. As I untangled my legs from the ladder, there was a loud bang on the lid to the tunnel. They had found me! Now I was trapped. I stared at the lid wondering when it would open. Then the police would drag me off to jail. There were five holes in the lid. I could see a black shape moving back and forth on top of the lid. I still could not see the person's face, even though the light of the barn fire was behind him.

The policeman yelled, "Hey Sergeant, what about this manhole? Can I get some help to remove the lid?"

The Sergeant yelled back, "If you need help to move the lid, do you think that skinny kid could move it?"

"No sir!"

Still staring at the lid, I could no longer see the shape of the policeman anymore. I climbed down the ladder one rung at a time, not knowing what I would find when I reached the bottom. It seemed that the ladder was never ending as I climbed down deeper into the earth. Then I placed one foot on what felt like solid ground. Testing it, I swirled my leg around in a small, half circle. Then I tried a bigger, half circle until I couldn't reach out any further. I took my other foot off the ladder and placed it on the ground. With some light shining in the holes of the lid, I could see my backpack.

I moved cautiously, not knowing my surroundings. I worked my way toward my backpack to find my flashlight. That is when I heard what must have been the roof of the barn collapsing. The light from the holes in the lid went black.

I blindly searched for the flashlight in my backpack, but I couldn't find it. I needed to have light before I could move on. From the sounds coming from above, there was no going back, only forward. I couldn't remember if I had put the flashlight in my backpack again after I opened the lid. I was starting to wonder if I had dropped it on the barn floor. I kicked something with my foot. I hoped it was my light and not a rat. I gave it another kick, and then reached out and picked up my light. When I turned the light on, I couldn't believe my eyes. The tunnel was about 7 feet high and about 6 feet wide. The room where the ladder was must have been almost 12 feet around.

I swung my backpack onto my back and walked to the beginning of the tunnel and shined my light down it. It seemed to go on forever. I turned around and shined the light down the other tunnel, and it also seemed to go on forever. Which way should I go? If I went to the right and it lead me to the part of the tunnel that had collapsed, I would waste a lot of time. I had only enough supplies for about three days. If I only ate two meals a day and only drank liquid when I had to, I could make it last four or five days.

I could still hear the barn burning. It sounded like another wall was collapsing. I looked in my backpack to find my candles and matches, so I could save on my flashlight batteries. With my candle lit, I put the flashlight back into my backpack and walked over to the tunnel on the right. I took another peek. I stared down the tunnel hoping to see something that would show me the way. I don't know what I was expecting, a sign that said: "Hey Mark, this is the way"?

I went over to the left tunnel making sure I didn't walk so fast my candle would go out. I only had so many matches. With my hand cupped around the flame, I stopped at the entrance of the tunnel. For some reason, the flame seemed to be almost dancing, trying to jump off the wick. I walked to the center of the room where the ladder was, and the flame calmed down. Then I walked back over to the left tunnel again, and the flame started to jump and dance in all directions. I moved further into the tunnel, and the flame leaned as if it was pointing down the tunnel. Was this the sign I had been looking for? I had to choose a tunnel because I couldn't stay down here forever.

With backpack on and candle in hand, I went down the tunnel. I moved only as fast as the candle would allow me so the flame wouldn't go out. The tunnel made long, sweeping curves first to the right and then back to the left. After many hours of walking, I stopped and sat down on the floor to rest my feet and my hand. I pushed some sand together in a pile and placed the candle in it. I slowly uncurled my fingers with my other hand. The pain was tremendous. As I sat with my back up against the wall, I leaned my head back. I looked down the tunnel to see if maybe the end was in sight. I shielded my eyes so the light didn't blind me. I couldn't believe my eyes, or was it my mind playing tricks. I could see the end of the tunnel just a short way from where I was sitting. Just then I was no longer tired. I remembered that the last clue said that there would be a box with the next clue in it. I was eager to see what the next clue had to say.

When I reached the end of the tunnel, I looked for the box with the next clue. I searched the floor of the tunnel for the box, but all I found was sand and more sand. I got down on my hands and knees. I crawled back and forth searching every inch of the floor thinking maybe the box was buried. After some time of searching, I had to stop because my hands were so cold from the cold, damp sand. I warmed them from the heat of the candle I was using for light.

Once my hands warmed up, I searched again. I moved

my candle over to the next section I was going to search. Once again I scraped some sand together to set my candle in. I dragged my hand across the floor and hit something other than sand. Could it be the box? I began to dig like a dog digging up an old bone. Sure enough, there was the box just as my grandfather had said. The box was about one foot by one foot by one foot, almost square you could say. It was made of wood with metal corners and a metal hook keeping it closed.

Now that I had finally dug the box out of the sand, I grabbed it and moved it closer to the light to see what was in it. I didn't get too far with it though, because there was a chain that kept it secured to a section of the tunnel wall. I brought the candle to the box. I slid the hook forward, and then opened the lid to see a folded piece of paper. I quickly grabbed the paper and unfolded it. I dropped to my knees to get closer to the light. The note read: "Well done, my son. Your journey to come back to your mother and me is at the halfway point. We pray you will continue your search for us, and we are praying for you daily to return to us. Pull on the chain that is attached to the wall, and it will swing open like a door. On the other side you will find another box with your next clue." It was signed, "Your Mother and Father, with much love and waiting with open arms. Pull hard, my son." I put the note in my shirt pocket, because I never knew if it would be part of the next clue.

I dug in the sand on the floor to find the chain. I grasped it with two hands and gave a pull, but the chain slipped through my fingers. The next time I wound the chain around both hands and pulled with all my might. The chain quickly tightened around my hands. The pain was so great that I was hoping I wouldn't pass out. I had to get the door open some-how. I had to think of a better way. Then I remembered the time when I was very small and father took me to the circus to see them put up the big tent. They used elephants to raise the tent up. They attached a chain to a harness around the elephant, and the elephant would slowly walk backwards and pull its load. If it worked at the circus, why wouldn't it work now?

I wrapped the chain around my waist and walked backwards until the chain got tight. Then I prepared myself to pull as the circus elephant did. I dug my feet into the sand and pulled thinking I was an elephant. I pulled and pulled until my legs started to have a numb sensation. I was about ready to give up when I heard the wall begin to move. That gave me the energy to pull even harder. My legs were burning, but I continued to pull. The wall was opening more with each step backward. I was in a hurry to get the wall open and get out of the tunnel, so I gave the chain one more large pull. That is when the chain broke, and it sent me tumbling to the floor. I lay on the floor of the tunnel for a while. The burning in my legs seemed to get better with each minute I lay there. I could smell fresh air rushing in the tunnel from the other side of the wall. I could not wait any longer. I got to my feet and walked over to the opening not knowing what I'd see. To my surprise, when I looked through the opening, I saw the inside of an old building. I gathered my equipment and squeezed through, leaving the tunnel behind. I didn't know where I was going. I wasn't afraid because of my grandfather's letter urging me to continue the search. The only part that bothered me was when my grandfather said I was only halfway there.

I put my supplies down eager to find the box my grandfather talked about in his letter. I carefully walked around the large room. It didn't take me long to figure out I was in the old mill just down the road from my house. I peeked out the window facing my house. I could see police cars parked all around the house. Who knew what the police would tell my mother and father? What lies would they put in my parents' heads? Would they say I was dead or alive? For just a moment I thought I should go back and let mother and father know I was alive. When a police car raced past the old mill, I knew that I couldn't go back. I slowly backed away from the window and continued to look for the box. After many hours of searching, I decided to take a break and eat something.

I dug in my backpack for some food. Each packet had crackers, the main meal, a dessert, toilet paper, matches, coffee and a can opener like the one Mr. Z had on his key chain. I looked through each packet to see what I wanted for supper. I found spaghetti and meatballs again. Just like before, I couldn't have a fire to heat it. The fire would be a beacon to the state police to know where I was. They didn't need any help, and I certainly didn't want the company. During my supper I found my thoughts drifting. Would my father be mad because I tarnished his image as a policeman? Would my mother cry her eyes out because her baby was gone or worse, dead? What would happen to the Zablings now that their farm was burned to the ground and they had been hauled off to jail?

Nighttime was coming soon and I needed to find a place to sleep. The closest thing to a bed was the firewood box over by the window. I unrolled my sleeping bag on top of the firewood box. With the moonlight shining in the window as my night light, I got ready for bed. I rolled up my shirt and coat to make a pillow. Once again I found myself staring out the window back at my house. After several minutes, I snapped out of my trance. I decided to continue my search for the box in the morning.

Once in my sleeping bag, I looked at the moon and I started talking. "Okay God, my grandfather believes in you. I will need your help if I'm going to make it through this alive. Since I'm talking to you, do you have a real name, or is God your real name? Oh, by the way, how will I know when you are talking to me? I would like to talk more because I have many more questions, but I am very sleepy. Maybe we can talk in the morning, okay?" I waited to hear maybe a voice or some sound, but I heard nothing. I looked at the moon and the stars in the sky. As I was closing my eyes, I saw a bright light coming in the window. It was the brightest shooting star I had ever seen. It sent shivers down my spine and all the way to my toes. Was that grandfather's God talking to me? I laid my head down on my make shift pillow and closed my eyes.

CHAPTER 14

The Tunnel

I awoke with the blare of police sirens in my ears. I sat up quickly. My brain was in a fog from sleep. I was all tangled in my sleeping bag, and I fell to the floor. Augh!! Well, that was one way to chase the fog from my brain. The sun was not fully up over the horizon yet, but the sunrise colors in the sky were amazingly bright. It looked like another nice day. The air was chilly, so I got dressed and put my coat on. As I waited for the sun to rise fully, I dug in my backpack for some breakfast. I should be able to find something to eat among the military food packets. I pulled many packets out. They all read dinner, so I continued to dig. The next packet I pulled out read scrambled eggs and ham. Ah, breakfast at last. While opening the can that held my breakfast, I looked out the window. The bright colors of the sunrise were fading and giving way to a bright blue sky. It would not be long before the sun was full up, and I would be able to look for the box my grandfather talked about.

I found the silverware in my backpack and picked out a chunk of cold scrambled eggs and ham. I was just about to put it in my mouth when I stopped. I put it back in the can. I remembered that Mr. and Mrs. Z talked to my grandfather's God and said thanks to him. I did say I would talk to him in the morning. I wish I could remember the words Mr. Z said. I would have to make up my own words. "Hello, God. This is Mark. I talked to you last night and, well, I'm back. I feel bad about what happened at the Zabling farm, but there was nothing I could do. They made me go and leave them behind. I learned a lot from the Zablings. Mr. Z said thank you to you for some food we ate one night and for protection, so I thought I would like to say thank you for this food. Can you help me in my search for the box? Oh yeah, then Mr. Z said in Jesus' Holy name, Amen. Or something like that."

I picked up the piece of scrambled eggs and ham and popped it in my mouth. It tasted so good that in just minutes, I finished the whole can. I needed to hide my trash so I would not leave a trail for the police to follow. I decided to put it in the firewood box. I lifted the lid and only saw a few pieces of wood in there, so I put my trash in the corner of the box. I began piling pieces of wood on the trash to hide it. I grabbed a piece of wood, but it felt soft and squishy and it squeaked. I dropped the wood and looked down in time to see a mouse running around the bottom of the box. I slowly moved some more pieces of wood to find a nest of little, pink, baby mice with their eyes still closed. I carefully began to cover them back up when I saw a piece of paper sticking out from under the nest. Yes, that was it! This was the box my grandfather was talking about. I cautiously removed the paper making sure I didn't hurt the baby mice. Then I covered them up again. I put the lid to the firewood box back on and sat on it.

As I unfolded the paper, I saw that the mother mouse had chewed on it to make her nest. I could only hope that the whole message was there. My eyes skimmed the paper and I noticed a few holes where there was some writing, but maybe I could figure it out without those words. I smoothed out the folds and wrinkles in the paper so I could read the message: "Dear Son, I know this seems to be a long, hard journey to find your way back to us. We must be careful not to leave a trail for the police to find. Here is your next clue. The wheels of progress turn slowly, but in time the door will open for you. Turn the s." Turn the what? The mouse had eaten the paper away. What did it say on the other side of the hole? The next word ended with the letter r, and then it read: "wheel to reveal the door that you must ent" (another hole but more words) "behind you." Maybe I could find the missing pieces if I looked in the nest. I took the lid off the firewood box again and uncovered the mice only to find tiny little pieces of paper. There was only one big piece under a baby mouse's little body. With my finger, I rolled him over and lifted the paper out. It read: "the wat." That was not much help, but it was better than nothing. I knelt next to the box and stared at the clue, hoping the missing words would come to me. I took the piece of paper and found that it somewhat fit in the first hole, but it could also fit in the other hole. Neither was a perfect fit.

I covered up the little mice once again and put the lid back on the firewood box. I got off my knees and sat on the box. I read the clue out loud many times. I was getting more frustrated each time I read it and could not see the missing words. I read it one more time. "The wheels of progress turn slowly, but in time the door will open for you. Turn the s....r wheel to reveal the door that you must ent..... behind you." I continued to stare at the paper at arm's length away. My eyes focused on the hole. Then it came to me. When I looked through the paper, I saw the old grinding stone. That was it! The s was for the word stone. I was supposed to turn the stone. If I put one of the pieces of paper in that hole, it could say, "the water wheel will reveal the door that you must ent. Enter, that you must enter!!" How was I going to get the stone to turn? Where was the door that was to be revealed?

There had to be a way to turn the stone, because otherwise grandfather would not have told me to do it. How did they do it in the olden days with the water and the water wheel?

I ran over to the window facing the creek to see if the water flume was able to send water to the water wheel. With just one look my question was answered. A large section of the wheel had been burned away. I had to figure out how to turn the wheel. Maybe just the water wheel needed to move to reveal the door and not both the stone wheel and the water wheel. My grandfather was always used to seeing both the stone and the water wheel turn together while grinding wheat.

I had it! If I got into the space where the water would go in the water wheel, maybe my weight would be enough to cause the wheel to turn to reveal the door grandfather was talking about. I opened the window and looked around to make sure no other eyes were watching me. I crawled out the window onto the flume. I walked to the edge with the boards creaking and popping with each step. I sat on the edge of the flume and placed my feet on the wheel to see if I could move it with just my feet. It only wiggled. I knew then that I had to get in and go for a ride. I got into the wheel and shifted my weight back and forth to get the wheel to move. Nothing was happening, so I moved farther out on the wheel. The wheel began to moan and creak as if it was talking to me. Then it spun and I hung onto the sides until the angle of the wheel was so great that I could not hang on anymore. I fell and landed on a wood beam just a few feet from the rocks and water below. I clung to the beam waiting for the pain to go away and for the water wheel to slow to a stop. During that time, I had to decide whether I would go up to the room and get my supplies now, or would I get them after I climbed down to find the door. I looked up the old, rock wall and saw how far I had to climb; then I looked down. It was only about three feet to a ledge where I could walk onto the water wheel. I decided to climb down and look for the door. If the door was not down there, then I could walk up the stone steps leading to the front of the mill.

Getting off the beam shouldn't be too hard. I jumped down and landed on the wide ledge. Landing on my feet was easy; dealing with the pain in my ribs from the fall off the wheel to the beam was a little more than what I had first anticipated. I squeezed between the stone wall and the wheel. That pushed against my ribs sending pain throughout my body. I may have broken some ribs in the fall.

There I was standing inside the water wheel. A large beam was shooting out from the large hub. As I walked, the water wheel would rock back and forth. I felt as if I was a hamster in an exercise wheel. I carefully searched for the door that my grandfather wrote about. I didn't know what I was looking for, because I didn't know what it looked like. I looked at the outside wheel and noticed that there were some boards missing. I was curious as to what was behind them, so I walked over and climbed up. While I looked, the wheel slowly turned. I peered through the spot where the boards were missing. To my delight, there was a small, square door. Carefully I reached out to see if the door would open. I gave it a push and it swung open easily. My heart started beating in my chest with excitement. I backed away trying not to have the wheel turn past the door so I couldn't get in. I squeezed between the wheel and the wall. The pain in my ribs was not as painful as before, or I was so excited that the pain didn't feel as great. I walked up the stone steps to the front of the mill keeping a watchful eye out to see if the police were anywhere nearby. I peered over the top step and watched for a moment. Then I hurried to the front door and found it was locked. I ran to the window and forced it open. I could see a car coming down the gravel road toward the mill. I had no time to worry about my ribs. I dove in headfirst and stayed low, clutching my ribs in pain until the car passed by. When all was quiet, I peeked out the window and saw that it was clear. I closed the window again. I grabbed my backpack and headed for the front door until I heard a car slowly driving up to the old mill. Was it the police? I had no time to look. I ran to the window overlooking the water wheel flume and climbed out with my backpack in hand. This time I climbed down between the water wheel and the stone wall. I tried not to move the wheel out of position of the door. Also, I didn't want whoever was driving up to the front of the mill to know I was here. I was halfway down the wall, and I heard the car stop. I, too, stopped climbing to listen. They were trying to get in the front door. Then I heard the police radio. A moment later I heard the car drive away. I finished climbing down the water wheel.

Once inside the wheel, I stopped to rest and catch my breath. I planned my next move up to the open door. The wheel was now easily moving after I freed it up with my first wild ride. The additional weight of the backpack could be enough to move the wheel out of position. I decided to tie a rope on my backpack and pull it up after I got through the hole and into the doorway.

With my rope now tied onto my wrist and the other end to my backpack, I moved toward the opening. I slowly stepped into the door opening. Then I turned to pull my backpack up to the hole and into the door where I was kneeling. Suddenly several cars drove up to the front door of the mill. I could hear police yelling. I started to panic because my backpack was not up to the door yet. I pulled faster, and then the backpack got caught on something. The police had broken in the door to the mill. I pulled on the rope trying to free up my backpack, but it was not moving.

The police were on the water flume above me. What was I to do? Should I leave my backpack and go? If I did that, they would find it, and then they'd find me. Someone was on the wheel, and it was starting to move. I pulled one more time, and the backpack came free. I pulled it through the hole just in time before the wheel spun past the door. Then I heard a large splash. The wheel slowed to a stop. The hole was in another position, so I found a board just inside the door where I was kneeling. I wedged it so the wheel would not move anymore. Then I closed the door behind me. I was plunged into darkness once again. I leaned up against the door and listened to the police laugh at the man who fell in the water.

I heard the captain say, "Patrolman Kyle Anderson, get out of the water and continue the search."

I laughed knowing that it was my dear, old classmate that had fallen into the water. After several hours of the police searching the mill, they gave up and drove away. Once again I could breathe a little easier.

As my eyes adjusted to what little light was coming in between the spaces around the door, I wound up the rope and put it back in my backpack for another time. I sat there in the dark listening to the sound of the water in the creek just outside the door. I smelled the damp, musty smell of wet dirt. Many questions ran through my mind. Was this the same tunnel I just came out of yesterday? Was this the right door, or was there another door in another part of the mill? What danger or trouble would I find in the dark? How long would I be in this tunnel?

I found my flashlight and looked around at the structure of the place I had now made my home for who knew how long. The block foundation of the mill was blended into the natural rock formation. That answered one question. This was not the same tunnel I came out of yesterday. As far as the rest of my questions, only time would tell. I'd better get moving through the cave. The sooner I got moving, the sooner I'd come out on the other side (providing there was another side). The ceiling height was not very high, so it was a good thing I wasn't very tall. I decided that before I got too far in, I would switch to a candle and save my flashlight batteries. I lit my candle and placed it in the camping candleholder. It would allow me to move freely without having the breeze affect the flame. I walked hunched over and it made travel slow and sometimes painful, but I kept pushing on. I felt as if I was going down deeper into the earth ever so slowly. I was only guessing; because it was getting colder the longer I walked. The floor of the cave was getting wet and slippery. It was getting harder and harder to walk. I had to run my hand along the wet walls to help keep my balance.

I felt like I had walked for a long time; but when I looked at my watch, I found it had only been 45 minutes. The muscles in my whole body were tense from trying to keep my balance as I walked down what seemed to be an endless ribbon of a cave. I found it strange that there had been no other tunnels branching off in other directions. I was still hearing the sound of water, but I was far from the mill entrance. The cave must be running under the creek. That would explain why the floor and walls of the cave were so wet. I kept slipping, sliding and falling down. If the floor of the cave weren't so wet, I would just crawl. It would be easier on my butt since I was falling down so much. Now listen to me; I had only been in the cave for maybe an hour and I was already talking to myself out loud, as if someone was out there to hear me. The worst thing was that I expected an answer back.

Ooooops! Here I go falling again! No wait, I wasn't stopping! I was sliding out of control. Oh no! My candle went out, and I couldn't see anything. I didn't know what to do, so I grabbed my ribs and hung on. I hoped to stop the sliding before I crashed my head into a rock or dropped down a shaft. Then I heard a big thud. I realized that thud was my head hitting the wall of the cave. I think I blacked out for a few minutes. I stopped sliding, but I had lost my backpack and candle lantern. Now I was worried. I lost my supplies and my light source. Now I was afraid to move.

What if I started to slide again? I just lay there until I thought of a plan. I needed to find my backpack, but where was I supposed to start looking? Did it keep on sliding, or was it hung up on a rock someplace where I started to slide? As I lay there thinking about all those questions, I also began thinking about my mother and father. What must they be thinking now? The police wanted their son, and he had run away. They didn't even know if I was all right.

The coldness of the cave floor was chilling me to the bone. I had to find my backpack and hopefully my candle or flashlight, too. I would work my way down the cave assuming my backpack kept moving downward. When I sat up, I could feel myself starting to slide. I reached out hoping to find something to grab onto so I wouldn't keep sliding into the unknown. My hand ran into something, but it wasn't a rock. It was my backpack! It was good to find my backpack, but I was hoping to stop this sliding. I didn't seem to be slowing down any. I was afraid where I might end up if I didn't stop sliding soon. No sooner did I say I needed to stop, and then I came to an abrupt halt when my back hit a large rock. Then my backpack slammed into me with all its weight. It knocked the wind out of me. There I sat gasping for air in the dark with no hope of any help. I grabbed my chest. Then I reached out to the darkness, for what reason I don't know. I felt light headed. That was when I felt myself slump over my backpack. I'm not sure if I passed out or if I rode the line between consciousness and unconsciousness. Time seemed to slow down, and before I knew it, I was breathing normally again. My lungs had stopped burning.

I blindly reached into my backpack and unzipped a side pocket. I pulled out the flashlight, because I was tired of being in the dark and not knowing what was around me. I slid the button forward on the flashlight and hoped that the bulb had not broken. I felt a great relief to see the light shining on the walls of the cave. I scanned the cave to see where

I had slid. I noticed that my backpack had taken a beating, as well as my body. As far as I could tell, I hadn't broken any bones.

The walls were still dripping with water. I knew I had to pick up my backpack and move along in the cave. I needed to find a dry spot to sleep. For some reason, I felt this was not going to be an easy journey. With the loss of my candle-holder, I needed to travel in the dark to save the batteries in my flashlight. I cautiously walked with one hand in front of me and one hand outstretched to feel the wall of the cave. I used the wall of the cave as a guide as I moved along in total darkness. The darkness had made me lose all concepts of time and how far I had walked. I could be walking in circles and wouldn't even know it. Then I noticed that my hand wasn't wet. The walls of the cave were dry and the floor had become sandy. I stopped and could hear nothing but my heart beating. I could no longer hear the water from the creek running as I did when I first entered the cave. I had been in the dark for so long. I wanted to know what time of the day it was. I turned my flashlight on to read my watch. To my horror, my watch crystal was broken out and only the hour hand was left. That was smashed down flat at the 3 o'clock position. Was it really sometime after 3 o'clock, or did the hand get pushed while I was sliding around in the cave? I had to eat something no matter what time it was. My stomach was growling so loud I thought I could hear it echoing in the cave. (At least I hoped that it was my stomach growling and not someone or something else.)

I lit a candle and stuck the one end into the sand. As the light filled the cave, my eyes became accustomed to it. I could see I was in a large room with a high ceiling. I prepared lunch or supper. It didn't really matter because I was so hungry. I was going to eat it cold. I didn't want to take the time to heat it up over the candle. I surveyed the room to see where I would go next after I was done eating. I couldn't see any tunnel but the one that I just came out of. I quickly ate my food and drank only a small amount of water. I had to conserve my water supply not knowing how long I would be in the cave and what it would be like when I got out.

I pulled the candle out of the pile of sand and walked around the large room to take a better look to find another tunnel out of the room. If I didn't find another tunnel, I would have to backtrack and start all over again. Getting past the portion of the cave where I was slipping and sliding my way along would make it very difficult to get back to my original starting point. I looked high and low to find even the smallest opening, but there was nothing to be found. I could feel my stomach churning into knots. I didn't know if it was what I ate or if it was the fear of having to start over.

I walked back across the room to my backpack. On my way over, I half tripped and half kicked a large rock. I heard it tumble along the floor. Then it stopped. Then it started again, but this time it sounded as if it was dropping down a shaft. I heard it stop with a crash. It frightened me. I froze in place and looked around. I held the candle out to get more light in front of me. I didn't want to fall in the shaft and end up like that rock broken into small pieces at the bottom.

There, just two feet away, was a dark spot on the floor of the cave. I picked up a small stone that was by my foot. I gave it a toss toward the dark spot on the floor. The stone disappeared into the blackness. Then I heard it hit the side walls of the shaft several times until it hit bottom like the first rock. I carefully walked over to the shaft opening and tried to shine some light from the candle down inside. The light couldn't pierce the blackness but for a few feet. I needed to get my flashlight. I backed away from the shaft opening and went to get my backpack.

When I got my flashlight in hand, I went back to the opening. I shined the light on it, and it was about three feet around. If I hadn't kicked that rock, I could have fallen into the hole. I didn't want to think about what could have happened. I got down on my hands and knees and crawled to the edge of the shaft. I shined the light down inside the hole. The light cut through the blackness of the shaft, and it revealed what was ahead of me. The shaft was not man-made; it was a natural formation. It looked like the only choice I had to go forward. If I didn't go down the shaft, I would have to backtrack the way I came. Neither way was going to be easy. I sat there in the candlelight pondering what to do. Do I go forward, or do I go backward? With my eyes closed, I pictured all the possibilities, both good and bad. I knew what I was in for if I went the way I came. But to go down the shaft was a total mystery and possibly a dead end. Would I be able to climb back up if it was? I decided then that it would be a good idea to make camp early and get as much rest as I could. I would travel hard tomorrow. The climb down the shaft would be hard.

I rolled out my sleeping bag away from the shaft so if I would toss and turn in the night, I would not fall down the shaft. I didn't know what time it was since I broke my watch in the sliding, but it was still ticking. Time inside the cave was not really that important because it was always dark. You could always sleep and not have to wait for sunrise to begin your next day's journey.

I lay there on my sleeping bag listening to the silence. From time to time the earth would break that silence by moaning. It would almost sound as if the earth was trying to talk. What it was saying, I do not know. Maybe that was for the best, because it may be calling out names of travelers that did not make it out. My eyes were getting heavy, and I felt sleep coming on. I'd try to sleep as long as I could and when I woke up, I would start my climb down the shaft.

CHAPTER 15

On My Way To A New Life

I'm not sure what woke me up, the moaning sound of the earth or the dream of the state police finding me in the cave. I felt rested and now I was hungry. I'd find something to eat; anything would do. The sooner I got started, the sooner I could find my grandparents. Another reason to get started was just in case the dream of mine was a way to say that I should get going because they were not far behind. I dug in my backpack and found a can of spaghetti and meatballs and another can that had crackers in it. That would have to do. I had to save some food not knowing how long it would be before I found the settlement. As I ate, I thought of what it might be like to see my grandparents for the first time. Would I know them? Would they know me? I had so many questions racing through my mind while I was eating. I didn't even remember eating the crackers. I had to bury the cans just in case the police made it this far. They didn't need any help in finding me. I walked over to the far edge of the room to bury the can. I put the flashlight under my armpit and began to dig in the sandy floor with my hands. After only a few scoops of sand, my fingers hit something. I stopped digging. I was afraid of what I might have found or whom I might have found. I pulled my flashlight out from under my armpit and shined it into the hole. To my relief, it was not a whom but it was more cans. I dug up the cans. They looked just like the ones I was eating from. That was a great sign that I was going the right way.

Then something funny struck me. I shined the flashlight on the floor of the cave. I didn't see any other footprints in the sand but mine. Had that much sand and dirt fallen from the ceiling of the cave to cover up their footprints, or did they drag something over them to smooth the sand out so you couldn't see their tracks? I quickly pushed the cans back in the hole along with my cans and covered them up with sand.

I packed up my stuff. I was thinking of what I could use to smooth out the floor of the cave to cover my tracks. Nothing was coming to mind, so I rolled up my sleeping bag. I was trying to find my straps for tying up my sleeping bag, and I noticed the smooth spot where I had slept. Then I noticed the drag marks in the sand that I made while I was rolling up the sleeping bag. That was it! I'd erase my foot-prints with my sleeping bag. I unrolled my sleeping bag and dragged it across the floor of the cave covering up any trace that I had been there just as the other visitors had done before me. Once again I rolled up my sleeping bag and tied it to my backpack.

I kept out some rope and my flashlight for the climb down the shaft. I slowly lowered the backpack down first until it hit the floor below. I tied the other end of the rope to my belt and positioned myself at the edge of the hole. With my hand, I smoothed out the last traces of my presence. I reached my hands out to take a hold of the rocky shaft wall. It was hard to climb with my flashlight in my hand. I needed the light, though, to see where to put my feet and hands as I descended down the shaft. The only place I could think of to put my flashlight was in my mouth. Then I remembered that the last place I had put the flashlight was under my armpit. I couldn't think about that now, because I had to make it down the shaft in one piece.

I carefully selected my foot and hand holds. It came very easy, as if I had always done climbing before. In just minutes, I had descended the shaft to the part where I had to drop to the floor. I shined the flashlight around to see that my backpack was in my landing spot, so I would have to move it. I found two good foot holds, one on each side of the shaft, and stood spread eagle. I took the end of the rope and tied it to my belt. Then I lifted my backpack and began swinging it back and forth enough to clear a landing zone so I could drop. With my backpack swinging just past the edge of the drop zone, I let go of the rope and the backpack landed and rolled out of sight of the flashlight beam.

I stood there trying to muster up enough guts to drop down. I went through my mind how I would land, taking up the shock of landing from my knees. I couldn't drop and roll because I didn't know what was on either side of the landing zone. I would count to 3 and then drop. 1 . . . 2 . . . 3 . . . I pulled my feet off the shaft wall simultaneously so I would land straight up and down. I hit with a thud, but I stayed on my feet. I stood up slowly to check out the height of the ceiling. I did not bang my head, so I reached up to touch the ceiling. I could reach up about a foot. That was a good thing to remember for when I had to climb back out.

I wiped the spit off the end of the flashlight and looked around to see which way to go. To my surprise, I saw a piece of cloth of some type not too far from my backpack. It was a sock! I scanned for more signs that would tell me which way to go since I saw three different tunnels to go down. I searched for a few minutes, but I found nothing so I decided on my own. I would go to the tunnel on the far left. I placed three rocks by the entrance just in case I had to come back and start over again. I would not choose that tunnel again.

I lit a candle to save on batteries. They were starting to get weak. I picked up my rope and backpack and started down the tunnel. The tunnel twisted and turned. Soon I had to crawl on my belly and drag my backpack behind me. How much longer would this go on? I liked it when I first started down this tunnel because I could stand up. I pushed and pulled my way along until I came to a room. I was so happy I could stand up again, but the happiness disappeared when the candlelight lit up the room enough for me to see three rocks piled up next to the entrance of another tunnel. I dropped to the floor in disbelief that I had traveled all that way in a circle. Now there was only one choice left, the tunnel on the far right. I gathered up three more rocks and piled them by the entrance I had just come out of to let me know that if I came out again and saw these rocks, I would have to go back to the shaft. The far right tunnel was very small, so small I would have to tie my backpack to my foot with some rope and drag it behind me. I squeezed through the small entrance and found the walls were very close, maybe less than four feet apart, which would make turning around very hard to do if I came to a dead end. Stop it! Stop it! Stop . . . it! Now just calm down and start thinking positive, Mark. I lay there trying to calm myself down before I continued on. I tried to think positive thoughts of getting out of the cave soon and seeing people, friendly people, most of all my grandmother and grandfather. Yes, that was the thought I must hold in my mind as I crawled along. I heard my voice echo out in front of me. What could that mean? Could it be that there was a large room up ahead? I knew it wasn't the room I just left. I had not crawled far enough yet that I would have circled back around. I crawled faster, dragging my backpack behind me. The walls of the cave were starting to move away, and the ceiling was not rubbing on my back. I could almost sit up, but there was no time to rest now. I must see what was up ahead. I crawled until I could stand up. I brushed the dirt off my clothes. Was this the place where my voice echoed? I said the word yes loudly, and again the echo was still ahead of me.

I was tired and hungry. I decided to rest, eat and drink something. Then I would continue on. I was so excited about the unknown ahead of me. I found myself eating like a wild man and dropping food in the dirt. I'd pick it up and push it in my mouth without wiping it off. When I drank water, it would run down my face and off my chin onto my shirt. I had to calm down again, so I stopped eating and counted to ten. While I was counting, I realized what I was eating was a can of scrambled eggs and chopped ham. Maybe it was good to eat that fast, so I didn't have time to think about eating cold eggs. I finished eating. I had to find a place to bury my can. The floor of the cave was not sand anymore. I would have to put the can in one of the large cracks in the wall and place rocks on top of it.

I slid my backpack on ahead. I was hoping I would get to the outside world soon. After being in the cave for as long as I had been, I was ready to see sunlight and breathe some fresh air. I looked at my watch to see what time it was, but I had forgotten that I had smashed it. The hour hand was halfway between 9 and 10, so I guessed that it would be 9:30. I didn't know if that was a.m. or p.m. I found myself walking faster and faster. I would have to slow down or I would wear myself out. After what seemed to be hours of walking, I looked at my watch again only to see the hour hand was just a small distance from the 10. I should not have looked at my watch. It only disappointed me, so I decided I wouldn't do that again until I saw daylight.

After taking a short rest, I felt ready to go until I couldn't walk anymore. I hoped I wouldn't have to spend another night in the cave. Walking was getting harder and harder, as if I was walking uphill. That could be good since most of the time I was going down. In my case, I always seemed to be falling down. My candle was almost gone, and I would have to get another one out of the side pocket of the backpack. Most of my candles were broken, but they were still useable. I would dribble a little wax where it was broken and let it cool. Then I'd light the candle with the old one. That way I could save on matches. The candle was fixed and lit; I was ready to go. I would save the stub of my old candle just in case I needed it for something. I rolled my wrist over to look at my watch out of habit. I stopped myself in time. I didn't need to know that it had only been a half hour since the last time I looked and get disappointed all over again. I rolled my wrist back over and kept walking. The steepness of the cave floor was so great that I needed to hang on to the rock on the walls to pull me along. I had to rest more often as I was doing more climbing than walking. When I rested, I listened to see if I could hear any sounds of the outside world. For the past two rest stops, I thought I heard running water. It was so faint I just let it pass and hoped to maybe hear it better the next time. I was getting tired, but I wanted to get up to the flat spot just ahead and rest there. It was only about another 25-30 feet.

As I neared the flat area, I pulled myself up and slid my backpack off. I just lay there with my eyes closed. I could hear the sound of running water. I wouldn't even open my eyes, because it was just my mind playing tricks on me. Then I heard a splash. Wait a minute! Would my mind go so far as to put a splash in it? I sat up and raised my candle high to see where the splash was coming from. It sounded so close. The candlelight was not bright so I couldn't see far. I grabbed my backpack and walked toward the splashing sound. As I rounded a bend in the cave, I heard the splash again. I walked faster as the sound of running water was getting louder and louder with each step. The cave took another turn and went up a steep slope. As I reached the crest, I couldn't believe my eyes. I just stared at it with my mouth open. It was a small pond of water, and water was also running down the cave wall. That was where the running water sound was coming from, but where was the splashing coming from?

I sat on the edge of the pond with the candlelight reflecting off the water and filling the cave with sparkling lights. It was a peaceful moment, something I had not had for a long time. Up and out of the water it came, breaking the moment with a splash. A fish!! I shouted and it echoed around the room. The fish jumping was the splash I was hearing. It was not just in my mind. It was in the pond; and if there were fish in the pond in the cave, there would have to be a way for the fish to get in. That meant that maybe there was a way for me to get out. I had to rest some because the climb up here had taken a lot out of me. I'd just rest a few minutes. I lay down and put my head on my backpack. I watched the candlelight's reflection dance across the ceiling of the cave. The light had a soothing affect on me. This would help me rest. When I woke up, my candle had burned out and there was only a small puddle of wax on the rocks. Even with the candle out, I could still see the pond of water glowing a bluish green. Toward the bottom, a brighter, white light glowed.

I looked around the cave. I could see shafts of light shining in. I ran to each shaft of light to see if I could get out that way. Many of the shafts of light were only the size of my hand. I tried to look out, but the light hurt my eyes. There were still many more shafts of light to check to see if there was a way out. I walked around the pond looking at the color of the water. I could see the fish swim in and out of the brighter, white light. Then they would disappear and then reappear again. Was that the only way out, or was there a drier way? I put my hand in the water. It was not that cold. I was a fairly good swimmer, so I could swim down to the light if it weren't too far. What if it was longer than it looked? I would run out of air and drown, I thought to myself. I continued looking for a drier way out. I'd swim with the fish, but that would be the last resort. Of course, I could use a bath. I smelled pretty bad.

First things first, I had to find a way out. I didn't want to spend another night in the dark, wet cave. I walked to the backside of the pond where there were some dim shafts of light coming from up on the ledge about 10 to 12 feet above the water. The climb was easy, almost like steps. I was getting higher and higher over the pond. I walked to the edge of the ledge and looked straight down where the pond was. I could still see the fish swimming in and out of the light. I watched the fish for just a moment. Before I turned away, the light in the pond dimmed so much that the cave became dark again except for a faint glow on the water. I didn't bring a candle or a flashlight with me. I was stuck up on the ledge. Should I go forward, or should I climb down to get a light? I decided to go forward. There was always time to go back. I carefully moved back away from the edge of the ledge, and reached out to find an outside wall. I felt my way along the ledge and moved forward. I had learned from the past to keep one hand outstretched in front of me so I didn't run into any walls or low hanging rocks from the ceiling. I could no longer see the faint glow from the pond, so I stopped and felt around. I could smell fresh air. I felt myself getting excited, and I started to walk faster. I told myself that I had to slow down and be careful.

Turning what felt like a corner, I could see light up ahead in a large opening. There was also the sound of rushing water. I stepped out to the edge and reached out to touch the water. My hand broke the curtain of water, and I could see the color green. I pulled my hand back and tasted the water as it ran off my hand. I reached for the water again, and a bright light shone through the water filling the room with light so bright my eyes hurt. I covered them with my hands, but the light was still too bright. I closed my eyes and stumbled back away from the opening, feeling my way back to the darkness of the tunnel. Never did I think that I would want the darkness of the cave, but the light was too bright. I walked back to the pond. I stood high above the pond, and I could see it was glowing bright again. The light danced on the ceiling. Then, in a flash, it was dim again. It must have been the sun hiding behind clouds for a time, and then breaking out from behind them to fill the pond with light. I would have to wait until the sun was not so bright, maybe around evening. My eyes had become very sensitive to the bright light of the sun.

I climbed down to the pond edge. I could hear my stomach rumbling, so it must be time to eat. I dug in my backpack looking for more food. I came across my father's Bible and a can of beef stew. I had plenty of fresh air, so I warmed up my stew with that old, stubby candle. A good, hot meal after all this time would taste really good. Maybe I could find a pound cake to celebrate what looked like the end of my time in the cave. Time!! That's right! I said I would not look at my watch until I saw sunlight. I rolled my wrist over to see my watch had lost the hour hand. The face was so scratched up; I could only read a few numbers. I unstrapped it from my wrist and put it in the side pocket with my candles. It was okay not knowing what time it was when I was in the cave, but I was hoping to guess when sunset would be. Was this early morning, or was it evening? Would I have a long wait or a short time before sunset?

I remembered I had a compass that could tell me east or west. If the light were coming from the west, it would be a short time. If the compass pointed east, it would be a very long time. I dug in my backpack for the compass, and I found my pound cake in a can. I set it aside and continued looking for the compass. I felt the cord it was tied to with my finger and pulled it to the top of the pack. I laid it on the floor of the cave and waited for the needle to come to a stop.

It seemed to take forever, but once it did, it said north was pointing to the tunnel that I came in from. That would mean the sunlight was coming in from the west. That could be good. Maybe the sun would not shine so bright into the water, and I could get past the falling water before it got too dark and my eyes could get used to the light again. I put the compass around my neck and lit the stubby candle to start what I would call my last supper in the cave. As I heated up my food, the words "last supper" kept coming back into my mind for some reason. I didn't know why.

My supper was warmed up and my pound cake was open. It was time to eat, but first I thought I'd do what Mr. and Mrs. Z did before they would eat. They talked to my grandfather's God. "God! It's me, Mark Wilson. I'm going to eat again. Mr. Zabling said it was a good idea to thank you for the food, so I'm thanking you. Oh, thank you for getting me this far. I probably shouldn't be asking you all this stuff since I'm not sure if you are out there, wherever out there is, but anyway . . . Can you help me find my grandmother and grandfather Wilson? Oh! Amen. I almost forgot that."

The warm food tasted so good, but I smelled something bad. I scanned the cave to see if there was a dead animal, but I didn't see anything. It was not until I reached across my body with my right arm to get something out of my back-pack that I figured out what the smell was. It was me!! Boy, did I stink! I had been wearing the same clothes from day one of the journey. I decided it was time I kick off my shoes. The smell of my feet was so bad I jumped into the pond clothes and all. I jumped in feet first and went down, down into the bright light. Even with my eyes closed, it still hurt them. I stopped descending and started my swim to the surface. With each stroke of my arms and the kicking of my feet, I moved closer to the surface. My lungs were starting to hurt, so I opened my eyes to see how far the surface was. I swam harder as my lungs felt like they were on fire. When

I broke the surface of the water, I gasped for air. My gasp was so loud it echoed. I swam to the edge of the pond and crawled up on the rocks. I lay there to catch my breath and to wait for my lungs to stop burning. I peeled off my wet socks. They smelled much better, and my shirt was much cleaner also. The water was a nice, refreshing temperature, so I went back in. This time I didn't jump in feet first. I just slipped gently off the rocks into the water and swam around. I floated on my back looking at the cave and the ceiling with each stroke I took. I was getting chilled. The water must have been cooler than I thought. I got out, dried off and put on some dry clothes. When I got dry clothes on, I felt like a new man. It wouldn't be long and I'd be 17. It would be a nice present celebrating my 17th birthday with my grandparents, since they missed all my other birthdays.

The cave was getting darker. I decided I'd move all my stuff up to the upper room. Why did I just call it "the upper room"? Where had I heard that before? I packed up my stuff and made sure I didn't leave anything behind. I was still always thinking that the state police might only be a few steps behind me. The light in the cave was fading fast, so it must be close to sunset. I quickly but carefully climbed to the upper room and made my way to what I thought I'd call "the window to the world." The light was still too bright, so I sat with my back to the window. I glanced around the upper room, and I could see that there were scratches on the rocks on the one wall. I walked over to take a look to see what they were or said, maybe another clue. There were drawings; one looked like a fish with x's and o's and some other symbol or letter. The next one looked like a plate of food and a cup. I didn't get it. If this was a clue, it was the strangest one yet. The next drawing was a t. Now I got it! It was that cross that I saw back at the church where I saw a picture of that Jesus guy. That's where I saw a picture of him at a big table. It was called "The Last Supper" in the upper room. That's where I got those strange thoughts. I knew I had heard of the last supper. That is why I called this place the upper room. I wondered if there were any more drawings and if they were a part of the clue. It was getting darker even up here in this room. I turned and looked out my window to the new world, and my eyes did not burn. The sun must be setting. I walked toward the window and reached out to break the curtain of water to see the new world. I could see green and yellow on the tops of the trees. I hadn't seen a view like that since I was in the church bell tower getting one of grandfather's clues. The sky was blue with white, puffy clouds. I pulled my hand back, and it was as if I had shut the curtains at home.

I peered to the right and then to the left to see which way I should go. Both looked like good possibilities for getting out. I got my backpack and chose to go right to find my new world and my grandparents. Hopefully it would be my last tunnel that I would have to go through. The tunnel was steep, so I had to hang on to the walls to slow myself down. The idea of going down again was scary, because I had to be in another dark tunnel. I didn't know how long I would be in the tunnel or if it would lead me to the outside world. I knew I had to descend to reach the ground, but where would I go once I was on the ground in my new world? That question would have to be answered now, because it was right there in front of me. I stood in the mouth of the cave looking out over the most beautiful spot in the whole world. There were the waterfalls that I saw out my window in the upper room. It dropped into a big pond. There were birds flying from tree to tree. There were many beautiful flowers. I stopped and looked around. Why didn't I move outside the cave? Was I afraid of what might be out there? Now that was a silly thought. What would be out there that I would be afraid of?

I took a few steps out of the mouth of the cave and turned to look at the size of the enormous rock wall. It must have towered hundreds of feet straight up as far as I could see. I only had a few hours of daylight left to find the settlement where my grandparents were, so I would have to search as much as I could before nightfall. If I found nothing, I would return to the cave and the upper room for safety from what animals may be out here.

I followed the creek, because all settlements would need water of some type. I walked along the creek bank and looked for signs of people, but most of the time I spent looking at the neat plants, flowers and trees. Some I had never seen before. When I thought about the city I came from and compared it to this place, there was no comparison. This place was so new and fresh. It was cold, dark and gray in the city. No wonder my grandfather came back only to leave clues for his son. I had walked for some time, but I had seen no sign of the settlement. It was getting dark, so I would have to head back to the upper room for the night. When I reached the mouth of the cave, I looked long and hard at my new world. Then I headed up to my room to have supper and a good night's rest. The watery curtain on my window was taking on the colors of the sunset, first the yellow and oranges, then the reds, purples and blues until it got black.

I lit a candle and walked around the room looking at the scratches on the wall. There, down in the corner, were some words: "Dear friends, let us love one another, for love comes from God. Everyone who loves has been born of God and knows God. Whoever does not love does not know God, because God is love. This is how God showed his love among us: He sent his one and only Son into the world that we might live through him. This is love: not that we loved God, but that he loved us and sent his Son as an atoning sacrifice for our sins. Dear friends, since God so loved us, we also ought to love one another. No one has ever seen God; but if we love one another, God lives in us and his love is made complete in us. I John 4:7-12" Wow! That was neat but strange at the same time. Who was I John anyway? Maybe this John guy was trying to say that everybody in the settlement loves each other, and there wouldn't be any police to beat on them and put them in prison for no reason. I rolled out my sleeping bag and settled in for a good night's rest. I was hoping tomorrow I would find the settlement and my grandparents.

Morning came quickly. It seemed as if I had only just closed my eyes a few minutes ago. The sun was shining in my window, and it would be a good day. I'd have the whole day to search for the settlement. It may take me far from here, so this may be my last time here. I thought I'd write something on the wall so that when the next traveler came by this way, they could read some words to help them along their journey as this John guy did over in the corner. I found a rock and began to scratch some words down as I ate some breakfast. When I finished, I looked at what I wrote: "This is my window. Come and see the wondrous new world. Just part the waters and see. I say this is my window, but it is not, for many have traveled by but claim it not. So I must give it up to the next traveler that stops and say to them, reach out and part the waters and see what I have seen. Reach for what you have dreamed. Mark W."

Now I was ready to begin my search. Part way down I looked back up to the upper room and said, "I will never forget this place." I walked to the mouth of the cave and carefully looked out to see if there was anyone out there. It was hard to forget old habits of always having to look for the state police or little, old ladies in windows who call the state police, because they see people in old churches. I took the creek trail where I had walked yesterday and continued from there. I was hoping the forest would open up to a meadow area where I could maybe see something, like a town or roads. As I walked along the creek, I could see that it was getting wider and deeper. The water was so calm I could see the fish swimming in it. The forest opened up to a rocky area where there were large rocks sticking out over the water. I found a large, flat rock where I could take a look ahead. As I stepped from the creek to the flat rock, I saw the rock was already wet with footprints. I scanned around me; I saw nothing. The forest was still very thick, and there could have been somebody out there. The footprints were small and were traveling the same direction as I was. The sun had not dried up the footprints, but there was no way of telling how long ago the person went by this way until I found him or her. It could have been five minutes, five hours or something in between.

Standing on the rock did not give me any clue as to which way I should go. All I saw was that the creek was growing into a small river. I would press on with my search, but I would have to see if I could find more footprints along the way. The footprints headed toward a path that lead up into the woods away from the creek. I wasn't sure which way to go. Do I follow the creek or the footprints? What would my grandfather do? I no sooner thought that, and then I heard a crash in the woods. Okay, I would take that as a sign that I should take the trail into the woods.

It must have rained a lot lately, because when I stepped off the big rock, I could see a couple different sets of footprints in the mud. They were all going into the woods following the trail. I walked slowly, carefully along the path. At times I got the feeling somebody was watching me as I walked. The path was very well traveled, so the people must go to the creek often. Did they know I was here? Were they hiding? Maybe they were setting a trap, because they thought I was the state police. Of course, they could be watching me hoping to find out if I was by myself or if there were others. The path came to a clearing further ahead. Maybe this was the settlement, but I would not get my hopes up. As I crested the hill, I looked out over a small meadow where the trail ran through the middle. Were my eyes playing tricks on me? It looked as if there was someone at the end of the trail waving at me. I blinked a few times. The person was still there. I waved back and yelled, "I'm looking for the Wilsons!" The person stopped waving.

I ran down the trail; I could see that it was a young girl. She was standing there at the edge of the meadow. I decided I would ask her where the settlement was, and would she show me the way. I tripped over a rock in the path and lost my balance. I landed face first in the dirt. I picked myself up and looked to see if the girl was laughing at me. She was gone. I ran faster thinking I would be able to catch up to her. I reached the end of the meadow before it went back into the forest again. I looked around and there, by a large stump, was the girl waving to me again. I waved back to let her know that I was friendly. As I waved, I walked faster. I kept on waving, and so far she had not run. There was a tree across the path, so I had to crawl under it. That was when she started running again. The tree was huge and newly fallen because the leaves had not yet wilted. I had to push through the branches. I was getting hung up on my backpack. With branches in my face most of the time, I lost sight of the young girl. I could only hope she would be there when I got out on the other side of the tree.

To my surprise, the young girl was still there. Now she was motioning me to come to her. I walked towards her. That is when two people dressed in what looked like leather and wearing some crude form of hat came out from behind the trees. "Hello, my name is Mark. I am looking for the Wilsons. I am also looking for the settlement they moved to many years ago. Can you help me?" I asked. They said nothing. "Please, can you help me? I need to find the Wilsons."

"I can help you," a voice behind me spoke. I turned quickly, just in time to see that it was a young lady. Her fist was heading straight for my face. Why was it always my face? Then the lights went out.

The next thing I remember was a mob of faces looking down at me and someone saying, "Don't move." I felt something warm and wet wipe across my face. "I'm trying to clean the blood off your face. You're a mess!" As the wet cloth went back and forth across my face, I tried to focus on the face above me. Finally the cloth was removed and there, sitting beside me, was this nice lady with a smile on her face. She said, "There you go. You look much better with all the blood and dirt washed off your face."

"Thank you for rescuing me from the band of robbers out in the forest," I said to the lady. "I suppose they took my backpack."

She just laughed along with a mob of faces standing around me. The lady said, "No, my son. They were not robbers. They were just some of the kids playing Maggie Hood. Your backpack is right here."

"Maggie Hood? What kind of game is that? I've never heard of it. Who is this Maggie Hood anyway?"

A voice from behind the crowd of people spoke and said, "I am Maggie Hood, keeper of the forest." That voice . . . I had heard that voice before, but where? The crowd of people split apart, and from the shadow into the light stepped a young lady wearing leather. She said, "And who are you, boy?" She drew a fist as if she was going to hit me. That was when I remembered the voice, the face, and most of all, the fist. She was the one who knocked me out. How embarrassing that would be if word got out that a girl punched out Mark Wilson. Maggie must have read the book, Robin Hood, a few too many times.

I could hear the crowd muttering to each other, so I figured something was about to happen. The crowd of people moved apart again, just as they did before Maggie Hood came up to my face. A large man with a beard came from behind and stopped next to Maggie. For just a moment, Maggie looked kind of cute. What was I thinking? She tried to rearrange my face with her fist. I must not have heard the man ask me a question. "Boy, did you hear me? What is your name?"

I was about to answer when Maggie Hood retorted, "I'll make him talk, father."

The man grabbed Maggie by the arm and said, "No Maggie, I'll do the questioning. You just go and stand over by your mother." I watched Maggie walk away, but she kept an eye on me. I was surprised when she stopped by the nice lady who cleaned me up.

"Boy, over here! I was asking you what your name was."

"I'm sorry, sir. My name is Mark. What is your name, sir?" I figured, why should he ask all the questions?

"Well Mark, my name is Pastor David Edwards. This is my wife, Rachel, and this is my daughter, Maggie."

"We've met!"

Pastor Edwards got a strange look on his face, and then his wife spoke up, "Maggie is the one who gave him the bloody face and dragged him into the settlement."

"Did she hurt you at all, Mark?" Pastor Edwards asked.

"No sir!"

"Could you tell me why you are here, and how you found the settlement?"

"I am looking for my grandparents."

"Mark, what are your grandparents' names, and why would they be here?"

"Well, sir, my grandparents' names are William and Frieda Wilson."

The crowd began to mutter back and forth among themselves. Pastor Edwards raised his hand and said, "Quiet down. Why do you think your grandparents are here, Mark?"

"I found a letter written by William and Frieda Wilson to my father."

"Just one minute, Mark." Pastor Edwards leaned over to

a man and said something, but I couldn't hear what he said. That man glared at me as Pastor Edwards whispered in his ear. When the pastor finished talking to the man, he left the room.

"Mark, tell me more about this letter. Did it tell you how to get here?"

"No sir. It gave me clues to follow."

"Did anyone help you along the way?"

"No sir. I don't have any real friends, but there was this nice, older man in the park. His name was Ernie." The crowd of people began to mutter again, and he motioned for another man to come to his side. He whispered in his ear, and then he left also, like the first man. "Oh, Pastor Edwards, there were two other people that knew I was looking for my grandparents. They were my neighbors, the Zablings. The last I saw them, the state police had them in their squad car; but they won't say anything. Mr. Zabling told me it was just like the old times when this first began. The police beat him and his wife, but they didn't talk. Now they were beat again, but they didn't talk. He said he wouldn't let the state police win. Then the police burned the farmhouse down and hauled them off to jail."

"Mark, where are your parents now?"

"I'm not sure. When I left with the Zablings, the state police were raiding my house. My parents were at the capital city at a meeting."

Pastor Edwards could somehow tell I was leaving something out, so he asked, "Mark, what kind of meeting?" I stalled as long as I could to think of an answer other than that they were at a meeting with the governor about the auxiliary state police work. "Mark, is there something you're not telling us? What type of meeting was it?"

"Okay, my mother and father are a part of the . . ."

Just as I was about to say what they were a part of, two older people, a man and a lady, stood next to Pastor

Edwards and said, "State Auxiliary Police." I couldn't
believe my ears. The crowd gasped in horror. Pastor
Edwards looked back and forth between the two older
people. The older man walked forward with his hand out. I
reached out my hand to his. We shook hands and he said to
me, "You must be Mark, Russell Wilson's boy."

"Yes sir, but how did you know that? I never said who
my father was."

"No need to tell me who your father is. Russell Wilson
is my son, and you are a spitting image of him. That makes
me your grandpa and this sweet lady is your grandma." The
crowd began to cheer and cry. Grandmother and grandfather
were crying; even I was crying. I had worked so hard to find
them. I looked over at Maggie Hood, keeper of the forest.
Even she was crying, but she tried to hide it.

Grandmother and grandfather said to Pastor Edwards,
"We will take responsibility for our grandson." That sure
had a nice sound to it, "grandson."

Maggie spoke up and said to her father, "I, too, will keep
an eye on this boy." Why did she say it as if I were only ten
years old?

I responded back to her, "Maggie, little girl of the forest,
I'm just a few days away from my 17th birthday. I'm not a
boy; I'm a man."

There were some snickers in the crowd, but when I
looked at my grandfather, he had on the biggest smile. He
gave me that nod of the head that said, "You tell her like it
is. You're a man."

That night I stayed in a small room in grandmother and
grandfather's house. I was still very tired, but I awoke hearing grandmother and grandfather talking. I got dressed and
came out to the room where they were sitting around a
homemade, kitchen table. There were three places set for
breakfast. Grandmother had made eggs and bacon with
some biscuits.

I said, "Good morning, Grandmother and Grandfather Wilson."

Grandmother waved her hands and replied, "Stop, stop that right now." I had only been here just a short time, and I had made her mad at me already. Grandmother reached across the table with her aging hands and held mine. She said with the softest voice, "You can call me Grandma Frieda and you can call him Grandpa Roy. He never did like being called William. People always called him by his middle name, Roy. No need for the Wilson. You are our grandson, Mark." Grandma Frieda had tears in the corners of her eyes, and Grandpa Roy was pretending he had something in his eye other than a tear. I pretended to do the same exact motion. Grandma Frieda looked at us both and exclaimed, "Oh you two, what am I going to do with you two big boys?"

It was as if I had known Grandpa Roy my whole life. We looked at Grandma Frieda and said at the same time, "We're not boys; we're men." It surprised us that we said the same thing at the same time. Grandma just shook her head and told me to eat up. She said I had a big day ahead of me. She was going to give me a tour of the settlement."

Grandpa Roy said, "Not today. We have a meeting this morning and another one in the afternoon."

"But who will watch over Mark if we are gone most of the day?" Grandma questioned with disappointment in her voice. I think she wanted to show me off at the same time as I got the tour of the settlement.

Just then I heard a voice say, "I'll give him the tour of the settlement now that the little man has finally woke up. Were you going to sleep the day away?"

That voice could only be Maggie. I turned around in my chair. She was standing in the doorway. Her hair was combed and her face was without all the mud I saw her wearing yesterday. "I see you got cleaned up."

"Yes, I did," she answered back to me. "I even got your blood off my knuckles." She smiled and gave Grandma Frieda a wink. Grandma winked back. I looked at Grandpa for some support, but he was too busy laughing. After I finished my last bite but hadn't even put my fork down on the table, Maggie grabbed me by the shirt, pulled me out of my chair and dragged me out the door. I waved to Grandma and Grandpa as we left.

"So Maggie . . . is it okay if I call you Maggie, or do I have to call you Maggie Hood, keeper of the forest?"

"Maggie will do just fine."

"Maggie, how long have you been at the settlement?"

She turned to me and said, "I was born in the settlement over 15 years ago, shortly after my mother stopped making rescue runs to the city to bring back more believers."

"What do you mean believers, Maggie?"

"Believers in Jesus! You are a believer, aren't you, Mark?"

"Well, I . . ."

"You're not, are you?"

"No, but I think I would like to hear more about him someday."

"We better start our tour at the church. It is in the center of the settlement."

As we walked by all the buildings, I asked Maggie, "What building is that?"

"I'll tell you later."

"There are people coming out with books, and . . ."

"Okay, it is the library. There are thousands of books in there. What is the big deal? I go there and read all the time."

"Back where I came from, there are no books except the two under glass at the information center. I have some discs in my backpack, and I can put them in your computer and show you our information."

Maggie just laughed, "We have no computers. We have

no electricity. We get our water by running down to the creek with a pail and running back."

We walked a ways without saying anything to each other. "Maggie, you said your mother made rescue runs back to the city. Was she the girl that brought Grandpa Roy and Grandma Frieda here to the settlement?"

"Yes, Mark, that was the run where she almost got caught. She only made one more run after that. That was to help your Grandpa Roy leave clues for his son and his family." We got to the church just as Maggie's father was leaving. "Father, I'm going to take Mark in the church and show him around. Is that okay?"

"That would be fine, Maggie." Maggie ran over to her father and pulled on his arm to get him to bend over so she could whisper in his ear. When Pastor Edwards stood up straight again, he looked at Maggie and said, "We'll have to work with him on that."

Once inside the church I asked Maggie, "What did you say to your father?"

"Oh nothing."

"You said something about me, didn't you?"

"Maybe, but don't you worry. It will be all right."

The church was very simple in comparison to the church back in the city. I could see that the church was a special place. Maggie's eyes and face shone as we walked around.

"Mark, you stay here. I have to do something over there." Maggie walked over to the other side of the church and sat down on a bench. I could see her lips moving, but I couldn't hear what she was saying. I could tell she was praying to Grandpa's God. When she finished, she came over and said we should go.

"Maggie, what is wrong with your eyes? They're all red."

"You know, Mark, you ask too many questions." She never did answer the question either. The rest of the tour went well. She introduced me to a lot of people, and they were all really nice.

Over the next few years, I had to learn a whole new way of life. That Jesus I saw on the windows of the old church in the city, I asked him into my life. I believe like Grandpa does now. Pastor David, as I call him now, has been teaching me about God and said I was a fine pastor. I married Maggie and we had two children, Carl and Kayla. The settlement is growing and we are safe from the state police.

I still hope and pray that my dad and mom will make the journey to the settlement before they get too old to make the trip. I pray for them each day. I also pray for Carl who I dedicated this book to. He has been gone for such a long time now. I lose track of how long he has been gone. His little sister, who is a young lady now, still cries for him each night.

I guess I preached one too many sermons on reaching the lost. Carl took my old backpack and loaded up with supplies one night. He headed back to the city to find his grandma and grandpa, just like I did so many years ago. He left us this note: "Dear Mom and Dad,

Don't be mad. I have gone to get Grandma Ramona and Grandpa Russell and bring them home to us where they belong. I will be careful, and I will trust in God to bring us all home safe and soon. Love, your son, Carl

P.S. Tell Kayla not to cry."

I guess Carl is just like his father, and I'm so proud of him. I hope he comes home soon. Little did I know he would trace my steps back to find Grandma Ramona and Grandpa Russell. I hope old Ernie is around to help him. "Carl, come home soon!!"

Pastor Mark Wilson

PAPERBACK BOOK PALACE
4106 18 AVE NW
ROCHESTER MN 55901
507-288-1218
www.ThePaperbackBookPalace.com

Printed in the United States
1250800003B/61-1008